STORM MOON

THE GODDESS CHRONICLES BOOK 6

KB ANNE

Published October 2020
Copyright © 2020 by K.B. ANNE
All rights reserved.

Published by Gripping Tales, LLC, Pennsylvania.

ISBN: 978-1-956915-05-1

Cover Design by Anika Willmans, Ravenborn Covers

Editorial Services by Laura Parnum, Laura Parnum Books

❀ Created with Vellum

To K's Koven,
Y'all know how to make a girl feel loved!

FIRE IS FRIEND

*F*ire is friend. Or at least it seems to be at the moment. And so far it keeps Breas and the Fomorian witch in the form of my high school nemesis, Kensey, along with the rest of the mindless swarms at bay while I figure out what we should do next. My fire shield encircles us along with the entire coven and what's left of Clarissa's cottage.

Alaric's green eyes find me. Thank the gods that the nightlock-imbued crystal necklace I threw around his neck as the Oak Moon reached its apex kept him from turning into a werewolf and tearing out my throat. As a werewolf, he isn't in control of his actions and would mourn killing me later. I'd mourn my death too, but still, stopping the change in the first place is much better. Why deal with the messy side effects? There's got to be a way to tame the wolf side of him, but today is not the day to enter him into wolf obedience school.

"As long as this fire continues to burn, we're trapped here," he shouts to me, scanning the fire shield to ensure it remains in place.

"I know, but I can't actually harm any living being, so until we figure out a Plan F.U., this is all I've got. Look on the bright side, at least I can create fire to keep our enemies out."

"Since returning from the seomra de rúin, I've had more than enough fire, thank you very much," he grumbles.

He's so cute when he's annoyed. Positively scrumptious.

Caer stands at attention on the other side of me. "There are many enemies here, but it is nothing compared to what Scott and I faced earlier."

She's not lying. The battle in the Shadow Realm reminded me of a *Clash of the Titans*–esque battle, with both Scott and Caer chopping off heads and *not* taking numbers. Medusa's fighting skills had nothing on Caer. (Although Medusa's stony expression packed a weighty punch reminiscent of Balor. The two should have a staring contest and save the rest of us a lot of trouble.)

"Any ideas what we should do next?" Scott asks on the far side of Caer.

Breas's eyes fall to the handle of Scott's sword. I got up close and personal with Scott's sword during our seomra de rúin visit to the Shadow Realm, but I hadn't noticed its ruby-encrusted handle. Where have I seen that before?

Caer grips her own sword's handle beside me, and I realize why Scott's looks familiar.

"Did you two purchase matching swords? It's kinda adorable."

She arcs her blade through the air. "There is nothing adorable about a weapon that can slice an enemy's head off."

Scott inches away from her, obviously familiar with her tendency to swing her sword around and probably not wanting to test their tenuous-at-best relationship—his words not mine.

"The swords were wedding presents given to our godly

forms," he says. "They return to us in every reincarnation and in time of need."

A werewolf lunges at the fire shield. As his body hits it, he yelps in pain and gets launched backward, his body aflame.

"We're in need of all the help we can get," Alaric says through clenched teeth, staring at the collapsed wolf.

Apparently, I can inadvertently hurt a living being if he or she were to propel themselves at one of my fire shields, although I don't feel as satisfied that I hurt someone as I thought I would be.

I step over to Alaric. "Can you retake command of your pack? Tell them to fight with us instead of against us? It would increase our odds."

More wolf eyes flash on the other side of the flames. "The whole pack's here," he whispers.

"And they've brought friends," Scott says. "Or your pack is much bigger than I thought it was."

Alaric crouches into a more combative lunge. "No. Declan's been recruiting."

My thoughts return to all the cells under the cavern. "Or Carman's made more."

He stiffens. "She knows how to make them?"

My gaze slides over to Maddie. He ever-so-slightly raises his shoulders in an I-guess-he-doesn't-know kind of way. From what Maddie told me, Alaric bit and created most of their pack, but apparently he was spelled by Carman to do it and possesses no memory of it—which fit his claims when he first showed up in my room at Granda's in the middle of the night all those weeks ago and acted like he didn't know how he got there. His attraction to me probably made it easier for Carman to spell him.

But Alaric was imprisoned in Brigit's shrine with his father for weeks. He couldn't have been spelled to create new ones.

However, there was another child of Clayone available, and "recruits" could have been sent into the shrine via the tunnel.

"Alaric, did anyone come to visit your dad while you were in the shrine?"

He blinks in surprise at my question. "Not that I remember. And I don't remember smelling anyone either."

"Was Lizzie there the entire time? Did she ever leave?"

"Guys," Scott says, "as much as I'd love to have a sit-down session to figure out how in purgatory's name there are so many werewolves, we need to figure out a plan of attack or an exit strategy because—wait . . . is that Kensey?" His jaw slackens as he stares at my nemesis and his occasional hookup.

"She's a vessel for a Fomorian witch. I warned you she was a back-stabbing, hex-throwing witch, only now you can see it for yourself."

He shivers at the potential ramifications. "Well, whatever she is, she's cooking up some type of curse that will be nasty."

All our attention shifts to Kensey. Her lips move as she palms dark smoke in her hands.

"Carman's not the only one familiar with Maleficium."

Witch Kensey smiles at me from across the flames. I can just imagine her saying, "I am going to enjoy this." There are an exceptionally scary number of similarities between her and Carman—that's probably what attracted Breas to Kensey in the first place. Evil attracts evil.

"What should we do?" Scott says, shifting from foot to foot. "I'm not too keen on discovering how well Moralltach blocks curses."

"You named your sword?" Boys with their toys.

"Swords of honor all have names. Mine is Freagarach," Caer growls, her Fae canines flashing. "I say let's fight."

The last time Scott and I fought a crazed Maleficium

witch, Dad and Calliope died in the crossfire. Tonight, we've already lost Gallean and Clarissa. I can't bear for anyone else to lose their life or risk injury. Caer might be ready to battle, but I'm not. Scott isn't either.

The shield bulges toward us as Witch Kensey starts pushing against it with her magical Maleficium smoke ball.

"The protections are breaking, Gigi," Scott says. "We have to get out of here. A portal would be great right about now."

Anna, Sam, Granda, and the rest of the coven nervously pace around the perimeter, chanting spells to keep the shields up.

I've only portal traveled with Scott.

"There are too many of us, and I won't leave them behind."

"No, there aren't. Join hands, everyone," Caer shouts.

The three of us take hands, further amplifying the power of the trí cumhacht. Alaric takes my other hand, Maddie takes his, and the rest of the coven members quickly form a large circle.

"Together," the three of us shout, and a giant portal pulls us through.

"No!" Witch Kensey and Breas roar, but the sound grows more and more distant as the portal removes us from the danger.

Portal hopping causes nasty side effects, especially when it's your first time, and when you're entirely human. The motion sickness can cause severe vomiting and dizziness—similar to riding a tilt-a-whirl by yourself five times in a row (and I speak from experience). Half the coven members collapse to their knees in exhaustion, clutching their stomachs. The other half crawl away on all fours, searching for some privacy so they can puke their brains out.

Anna recovers much faster than the others. She's portal jumped with Clarissa a few times. "Alysha? Bev? Are you okay?" she asks.

Alysha and Bev moan to indicate they're alive, but they still aren't sure how or why they feel so queasy.

"Milia, Chanti, where are you?" Sam, who also has some experience portal hopping with Granda and Clarissa, calls out.

"Over here," they sigh with considerable effort between dry heaves.

"Granda, Granda!" Scott shouts as he rushes over to his collapsed frame.

That's when everything goes to chaos in a handbasket.

Two werewolves launch themselves into the remains of our portal circle. Their teeth drip with saliva as loud growls fill the space. The smaller one is a cute-but-fearsome tan and white wolf. Lizzie. Her red eyes meet mine one second. The next, her muscles bunch and she launches herself at me. Her claws dig into my chest, sending me tumbling backward. Sharp canines snap at my exposed throat.

"No," Alaric roars.

Seconds before her teeth graze my skin, he rips her off of me and throws her across the circle. She spins around and growls, crouching down to relaunch herself at me.

"I said, no," Alaric's baritone voice rumbles, vibrating through the circle.

She hesitates.

"You will bow to me," he says. His tone leaves no room for argument. She crouches low as the alpha overpowers her.

Ferocious snarls tear my attention away from Lizzie. Granda's wrestling a large gray wolf with sadly familiar yellow eyes. Ryan. His teeth snap at Granda's chest. Scott raises his sword.

"No," I scream.

He pauses.

"Scott, don't kill him. It's Ryan."

Scott stumbles backward as if struck. "What?"

"It's Ryan and Lizzie." I point to Lizzie's now-folded frame bowing in front of Alaric. Her eyes flash red as she tries to fight his alpha command. She may also be the daughter of Clayone, but she ranks lower than her brother.

Granda screams and our attention immediately shifts back to where Ryan has him pinned against the ground. Caer catapults herself on top of Ryan and tears him off Granda. Scott drops his sword in surprise, dumbfounded at both Caer's raw power and the fact that the werewolf is his best friend who was supposed to be dead. Scott had pulled the trigger himself.

"Help her," I yell at him.

He snaps out of his daze and rushes to her aid. The two wrestle Ryan to the ground with brute force. His teeth snap at them as his four clawed paws try to push them off. He's a powerful werewolf, but they're far more powerful—especially together. They soon subdue him.

Lizzie emits a low growl as she continues to fight Alaric's dominance. Maddie stands beside her to ensure her obedience. He fingers the crystal around his neck, thankful that it keeps him from shifting into a wolf and turning on us. I've got a whole bowl of nightlock-imbued crystals inside. I'll force them on Lizzie and Ryan.

"Someone help us," Anna yells. She's trying to staunch the blood flowing from a wound on Granda's arm while Sam holds his blood-covered hands to Granda's carotid artery. "We're losing him!"

I can't lose him too. I can't. I head toward Granda's collapsed frame. There must be something I can do.

The Chalice of Healing, Brigit reminds me.

I can save them all. I lunge toward the front door.

"Gigi, we need your help now," Anna screams.

Her pleading freezes me in place. I war with myself. Take the time to get the chalice and the crystals, or try to heal him without it?

Alaric grunts as Lizzie launches herself at him, knocking him over. Her teeth snap at his chest. His crystal necklace—she's trying to tear it off of him and cause him to turn. How does she know the crystal is preventing him from turning?

"The crystals," Maddie yells, snapping me out of my daze. "Hurry."

Anna releases a string of curses, thinking I've abandoned them. I run into the house and grab the Chalice of Healing along with the bowl of crystals and sprint back outside.

"Here." I throw a crystal necklace at Maddie. He plucks it out of the air with his fast reflexes and prowls toward Lizzie, intent on circling it around her neck and turning her back into a girl.

"Scott, think fast," I shout and launch another one at him.

He releases Ryan with one hand and catches it on his middle finger. "Hold him," he yells to Caer—as if she needs a lesson on werewolf containment. From what I've seen, she's mastered that job.

Since I'm not as fast as Oegden, I slide across the ground to Granda on my knees. I've seen it done in movies a dozen times, so I figured if a plain old human can do it, why can't I? Granda's eyes widen as he sees what I'm cradling in my hands.

No, he wails in my mind, unable to speak aloud.

"Yes, and there's nothing you can do about it," I snap at him, leaving no room for discussion in my voice as I slice my palm and start to chant.

FAILURE IS AN OPTION

*G*randa smashes his lips together and refuses to drink from the Chalice of Healing. After a few attempts, I even try to compel him to no avail. Finally I manage to "persuade" him with the assistance of Anna. Sam is squeamish about forcing Granda to drink blood. Anna, who still isn't a Gigi fan, especially after she thought I'd abandoned them, has no qualms about wedging Granda's mouth open so I can pour my spelled blood down.

Granda coughs up some of the spelled blood but keeps most of it down. His stomach sputters and heaves, but the contents of the chalice stay with him. The healing effects of Brigit begin to take effect almost immediately. His fingers begin to twitch, soon followed by his arms and legs. Once again I am humbled by the awesome power of Brigit.

When he finally starts breathing normally on his own, he scowls at me.

I jump backward as if I'd been burned. "What?"

Anger and judgement swirl around him, reminding me of a hurricane. "You took a great risk using the chalice on me."

"There wasn't an option."

"There's always another choice."

I can't disagree more. "Well, Gramps, I wasn't about to let the last non–reincarnated-god member of my family die."

He clears his throat, still experiencing the healing effects of the chalice. "I wasn't going to die."

Ah yes, the stubborn streak in our family is strong in this one. "Your throat was almost ripped out at your carotid artery, and if that didn't kill you, you would have bled out from the chunk missing from your arm."

He groans, adjusting his elbow. "So that's what hurts."

"Listen, Granda, I appreciate the sacrifices you, Dad, Gram, and Mom have made for me—apparently my line is loyal to a fault—but no one else required the Chalice of Healing tonight, so win-win."

He glances at the supine human figures of Lizzie and Ryan, who are being closely monitored by Alaric, Caer, Scott, and Maddie. "And our werewolf guests. Are they under control?"

"It appears so, but how did they get out?"

He tries to push himself to a seated position. Sam rushes over to assist him.

"When Alaric killed you."

I frown at him. "Alaric didn't kill me."

"He didn't?"

"Well, he didn't mean to. He was under Clayone's power."

"I believe those few minutes when your lifeblood stopped, your more temporary spells were lifted. That would include the cells you created for Lizzie and Ryan."

Shock stills me. "And Clayone? Is Clayone still immured?"

Granda reaches for my hand. I willingly extend it to him, not wanting him to exert himself. "He is. The spell you placed on him is directly connected to Brigit. You are the only one who can lift it, and if you die—permanently, I mean —he'll be trapped in there forever."

He confirms what Maria already told me when she "gifted" me to Clayone. I release a long sigh of relief.

"Why didn't Ryan and Lizzie attack you when you left the cottage?"

"Think about it. Tonight is the full moon on the winter solstice. The Oak Moon. Why risk early detection when they could kill you using their wolf forms?"

"But why didn't they leave the property?"

He breathes in and out through his nose. "That is a question I will answer after you decide what you would like to do with them."

"Lock them in my room?"

His whole body shudders in a giant grimace. "In my house? Do you realize the racket they will make?"

He does make a good point. "Back in their cells in the crescent moon garden?"

He nods. "I think that would be best."

In hindsight, creating a portal and only skipping a few miles over to Granda's cottage might not have been the best plan for a "covert" location, but Lizzie and Ryan were still trapped in their invisible cells (or at least I thought they were), and I couldn't very well leave them there. They'd need to eat and drink soon, and it's not like I left them an all-access pass to a buffet (although given the fact that I brought an entire coven back here with me, I inadvertently almost did).

Though Lizzie might be lost to me, a small hope resides inside me that we can bring Ryan back—and by association, Lizzie. Besides, I brought Alaric back from wanting to kill me, so there's no reason why Lizzie, given time, understanding, and intensive persuasion, can't return to my side, and the first step to bringing her back to the light is to keep her from getting hangry.

Scott clutches my arm. "Why did you bring us here? It's too close to Clarissa's. The wolves will be able to smell us and will come running in no time."

Granda sits quietly, which is understandable since he almost died. That weighs heavily on a person. And Clarissa did die. They were close friends. Her death can't be easy for him. If I let myself linger too long on her passing, on all the death surrounding me, it wouldn't be easy for me either. And it gives me all the more reason to save the rest of them and shuttle them off to safety—wherever that may be. Lizzie and Ryan prove something of a challenge, but given more time, I'll figure it out.

"Granda," I grab his hand, pushing some of my energy into him to recharge his battery, "how long do we have before they find us? And where should we go?"

"Child," he says, removing his hand from mine, "save your strength. I'll be fine."

I reach for him again. "But, Granda . . ."

He blasts a little energy ball at me to keep me back. "You're not the only one with the ability to move energy," he says, waggling his eyebrows. "I've learned a few tricks along the way, including how to ensure that my property is protected. Breas, the Witch, and the wolf pack won't find us here."

"But if they got to us at Clarissa's, they'll get to us anywhere."

He shakes his head. "No, they will not be able to break through the boundaries and spells shielding this house. And even if they guess where we are, they'll never find us."

"Breas has been here. He knows where you live, and he's been invited in—though I don't know if gods follow the same rules that vampires do."

He shakes his head again. He's stubborn in his old age.

"There are a number of new spells around the perimeter that will deter anyone intending us harm."

Scott's forehead pinches. "Meaning . . ."

"Think of it like amnesia. They'll wind up forgetting where they're going in the first place and who they were after."

There are a number of uses for a spell like that.

"Will they remember later?"

"Eventually they will, but they won't be able to find my cottage even if they've already been here."

Something keeps needling at my brain. "Granda, why wasn't Clarissa's property protected? How did they set her house on fire?"

His eyes water. I'm not heartless. I do feel bad for him, but if Witch Kensey can break down the shields around Clarissa's house, we are in up to our kneecaps in crap.

"Many of the spells for her house were tied to her. Much like the protective spells around your grandmother's house. As Gallean's life-force diminished, so did hers. As a result, the spells weakened and the Witch could break through."

"Are your cottage spells tied to you?" I know it's insensitive, but there are too many lives at stake and only now am I realizing it, which isn't very goddess-minded of me.

Scott frowns. My gods, I missed him, but I forgot how judgy he can be and how freaking loud his thoughts are. "Gigi . . ."

Granda lifts his hand. "Scott, it's fine. Look at everyone here."

The three of us shift our attention from each other to Anna and Sam huddled together with a few other coven members mourning the death of Clarissa and recovering from the fire. Another cluster of coven members sit close-by. One woman crawls from person to person, attending to wounds by spell or by hand. Alaric, Caer, and Maddie stand together watching us. Tears prick at my eyes. Their lives are vital to my being.

Granda continues. "Gigi wants to ensure they are all protected. No, the spells are not tied to me. If I perish, the shields will stand."

Based on my readings of old spell books and what I've learned from all my mentors—Gram, Dad, Clarissa, Granda, Gallean . . . I've had so many—a cost is exacted for powerful spells, meaning something has to be attached to it in order to keep it powerful, to retain its life. My gut tells me there's something he's not telling me.

"Who are the spells tied to?"

His blue eyes lock with mine. *You know.*

I swallow the lump in my throat. There's so much pressure placed upon my shoulders already and now *this?*

"You will not fail," Granda says.

The winds pick up. Hair whips across my face, stinging my eyes. Leaves tumble and swirl around in mini tornadoes. A fine mist starts to fall, soon followed by fat raindrops. There is nothing natural about the storm. There is no way I can battle such a forbidding enemy and win.

"Failure is the only thing I excel at."

"Your failures have prepared you for the final test."

3

JUSTICE

*C*aer paced along the perimeter of the shield around the cottage. Adrenaline raced through her veins as she gripped her sword. She had expected to be engaged in a second battle upon her and Scott's arrival from the Land of Shadows, but with the full moon, there were too many wolves with too many teeth. There was also that witch. Caer didn't know her, but evil seeped from the Witch's pores and warped the air around her.

Who was she and what was she capable of? The Witch worried her more than even Balor, but that might have been because whenever she even thought of Balor she was blinded with pure rage.

She continued following the boundary to ensure there was no weakness in the shield. Soon Scott caught up to her.

Caer wasn't so nervous around him since they had spilt so much blood together. "Where are we?"

"Amorin is my grandfather. The cottage is his home. I guess it's Gigi's and my home now too since there's no one else still alive in our family back in the States."

Caer heard the sadness in his voice. She had felt loss before too. She never knew her mother, but losing her father had almost destroyed her. She never had the luxury of time to mourn his death, but she felt it keenly in her soul all the same.

"And these protective shields are enough to keep the enemy out?"

He lifted his shoulders. "That's what Granda says. They're tied to Gigi."

That piqued Caer's interest.

"Your grandfather entrusted your sister with his protection?"

Gigi did not strike her as especially powerful, but Gallean had often said Gigi was far more powerful than Scott and Caer put together.

"He did. She's worried it was a grave mistake, and that all of us, along with the coven, will be caught unaware. My sister believes she was born to fail. She's embraced that aspect of herself since she was a child."

"So why would your grandfather entrust her with it?" That seemed liked a fool's errand to her.

He stiffened. "Because Gigi isn't a failure. She always gets what she wants, and if she believes she can save the world, she will."

Skepticism filled her. "On her own?"

He grinned at her. "She will with our help."

A spike of warmth bloomed within. She fought it back by embracing annoyance. "I haven't committed to saving the world. Balor is still alive."

He stepped closer to her so that they stood toe to toe. Caer's heart raced.

"You will help save the world by killing Balor."

His proximity made it difficult to breathe. Powerful

energy charges pulsed through her. She felt as if she were standing on the edge of a cliff without her wings to catch her.

"Caer, you don't need to be nervous. You aren't in danger here."

She edged away from him. "Nervous? I am not nervous."

He pointed to her back. "Then why are your wings out?"

She eyed the strong swan wings protruding from her back, so different from Keturah's and the other faeries', yet the same in a way. It was the first time her wings had appeared without her actually transforming into a swan. It seemed with each passing moment since she'd met Scott, she was discovering new aspects of herself.

The wicked glint in his eyes returned. She licked her lips.

"I would very much like to kiss you," he whispered.

Without replying, she crushed her lips to his. She might be a skilled warrior and capable of taking care of herself, but as much as she tried to deny it, Scott held the keys to her heart.

Caer apparently liked to take charge in their relationship. Scott was okay with that. After all, he was the one who had wanted to kiss her and had asked her permission to do so. If by answer she took action, who was he to stop her? He intended to kiss her as long as she let him, because he also knew that, though he had considered using her in the Shadow Realm in order to get back to Gigi, he was now at her mercy. Caer was not a woman to be used or trifled with. She was to be cherished, and Scott hoped with all his might that one day he'd be able to care for her the way she deserved. But even with the threat of Balor and the rest of the Fomorians, along with Breas and Kensey (What in the hells had happened to her?), who were aligned with the werewolves, the coven needed to plan and prepare accordingly for the upcoming battle. But it wasn't within his power to end the kiss. And her lips, which tasted like strawberries, made it impossible to think of anything else.

"Is kissing necessary when there are wolves breathing down our necks?" Gigi snapped at them.

Scott broke away from Caer. "Don't you like wolves breathing down your neck? Or at least one wolf?"

Alaric blew on Gigi's neck as if to prove the point.

She swatted at his chest. "Well, duh. Of course I want Alaric to breathe on my neck, along with a whole lot more," she said, winking at Alaric before turning back to Scott and Caer, "but we narrowly avoided a potential shit show, and now we need to figure out a plan. Evidently the three of us have a trí cumhacht going on, which means that together we are especially powerful. Anything coming to either one of you with my presence?"

He and Caer glanced at each other. He could still taste the strawberries on his own lips as his eyes fell to hers. He had a lot of ideas, just nothing that would be especially helpful in fighting the enemy.

"My gods," Gigi exclaimed. "Alaric, get me away from them. Their thoughts have nothing to do with fighting the bad guys, unless fighting includes taking each other's clothes off."

A lovely blush crept up Caer's throat. She looked positively radiant. He wondered what other parts of her were radiant too. Someday he'd find out, but today he remained content on just kissing her. And now with his sister gone, they could return to doing just that.

Though admittedly their timing wasn't ideal. He sighed. "Shall we assist my sister in saving the world?"

Caer returned Freagarach to its scabbard. "If I get to use my sword, I would love to."

Caer was an intimidating woman, not only in her physical beauty but in her fierceness.

"Gigi's right. You are scary when you want to be."

She flashed her canines at him. "I know."

He'd like those canines to trail along his throat, but for now, he'd just fantasize about them. He reached for her hand, and she allowed him to take it. Together, they followed Gigi and Alaric over to Granda, who was sitting on a bench, staring off into space. The loss of Clarissa weighed heavily on him.

Scott rested his hand on his grandfather's shoulder. "Granda, I am sorry for Clarissa. We didn't know that Gallean's life was tied to hers. We would have never let him participate in the battle if we had known."

Granda frowned at him. "Do you really believe that Gallean would have listened to you? He was the world's most powerful wizard. You might be a reincarnated god, but Caer was his charge—he'd do anything to keep her safe."

Caer stepped forward. "What do you mean, 'charge'?"

Granda's eyes softened. "Your father and Gallean were very close. Both had made it their life's mission to eliminate Balor. Through the years, there were many casualties, including innocent ones. Neither foresaw the death of your mother."

"My mother died giving birth to me."

He breathed in and out before speaking. "She did, but the birthing process did not kill her. A curse was placed upon her when she was a child to ensure that she'd never birth any offspring."

"But she did."

"For some reason you are resistant to magic. When you were in your mother's womb, you kept the curse at bay.

19

When she gave birth to you, her protections disappeared and the curse took root."

It was clear by Caer's reaction that it was not the story she'd been told. Scott knew that her father had given his life to protect her. It would stand to reason that he would do whatever he could to keep her safe, even if it meant withholding the truth from her. Granda wasn't sharing everything he knew, and Scott planned to find out why.

"I don't understand. Why would someone curse her? Why would someone not want her to have offspring?"

Sam knelt down beside Granda. "Excuse me, Amorin, may I have a word?"

Granda nodded and left the four of them standing in a huddle with significant parts of the conversation lacking.

Caer looked to Scott and Gigi. "Who would curse my mother to prevent her from having offspring?"

He had no answer, and his sister didn't even provide a wise retort. Alaric, however, studied Caer for a long time. He'd done it several times already. In the beginning, Scott assumed it was because Caer was strikingly beautiful and lethal all at once, but now he suspected there might be another reason.

Gigi touched Alaric's arm and said, "I would tell them your theory."

He hesitated. Whatever he was about to suggest wasn't going to sit well with any of them.

Caer glared at him. "You test my patience."

Alaric's eyes shifted to Gigi's. She nodded in support.

Caer growled. Apparently she was even less patient than Gigi. Scott couldn't believe that was possible.

Alaric sighed before beginning. "If there was a prophecy predicting my death and it was attached to someone from my future generation, I'd make sure that there wasn't a future generation."

Scott stiffened. "But that would mean that Caer was destined to kill that person, and her only mission in life is to kill Balor."

Alaric raised an eyebrow.

Caer staggered backward. "No, it can't be."

4

CAN'T CHOOSE FAMILY

*A*fter Alaric dropped his bombshell, none of us spoke. The possible implications were way too freaking huge to even begin to talk about unless sufficient time had passed and several shots of whiskey could be distributed between us. Trouble was, no one handed out shots, so we stood around in shock with our thumbs up our bums, trying to wrap our heads around the notion that Caer could be related to Balor. I mean, she does cast one steely gaze, however none of us had turned to stone yet. (Though she did know how to ice Scott very well. And heat him up too, but that was for an entirely different reason.)

"It would explain why you're resistant to magic?" Scott offers.

Her forehead pinches into a V shape. "Balor as a relation to me? I don't understand."

"Well, it starts with the birds and the bees," I begin, but then Scott casts his own dreadful glare at me with the promise of violence if I keep at it, so rather than create a rift in our trí cumhacht, I drop the sidebar commentary and shut my mouth.

As I wait for Alaric's revelation to sink in, I glance around and realize we're standing in the garden in front of Lizzie and Ryan's cells, which are cloaked with invisibility and silence.

"Scott, you better sit down. I've got some more news."

"Don't tell me you're pregnant," he says, now casting his stony-eyed glare at Alaric. We're fortunate Scott's not the one related to Balor.

Alaric grins at me. "We haven't had any alone time yet."

Scott crosses his arms over his chest. "Nor will you with me around. Do we need to talk about practicing safe sex?"

"Brother, can we save the sex talk for later? I've got something much more important to share with you, but you better sit." Scott and Caer had been otherwise engaged when I put Lizzie and Ryan back into their cells and cloaked them. He'd have a heart attack if he wasn't sitting.

Scott squats down on the ground right in front of the invisible cells. He pulls Caer down with him. She doesn't sit on his lap like many of his old girlfriends would have, but she sits awfully close to him. And to Lizzie and Ryan.

"Y'all might want to back up a bit. It's about to get a little cramped in here."

They shuffle back a few feet.

"*Nocht*," I whisper to lift the cells' invisibility.

The two werewolves lunge at us but crash into the "walls" of their cells. Apparently, they'd ripped off their crystals after I locked them in and had turned back into wolves. At first glance, Lizzie's tan and white wolf looks like a dog you might want to cuddle up with on a sofa. That is until her eyes flash from yellow to red. The large gray wolf with giant canines warns us to stay away with a guttural growl.

The cells aren't a fifteen-bedroom mansion, but they're large enough for them to lie down and move around in. I'm not one of those heathens from Salem, Massachusetts who kept their "prisoners" in a cell that they couldn't even sit in.

"I still can't believe he's alive. How is he alive?" Scott looks to me for answers, feeling guilty that he got distracted with Caer rather than immediately worrying about his friend.

Wolf Ryan watches him. I want to believe there's recognition in his eyes, even in wolf form, but then, I've never been very optimistic. I never had reason to be until now.

"Breas, the stupid leech, switched out the silver bullets."

Scott stares at me. He's working through all the angles in his head. "But we saw him die. We saw his spirit leave his body with Lizzie's and depart Gram's house."

His confusion reflects my own when I first discovered Ryan was still alive, but then, it was easier for me to accept it because Ryan was in his human form, and especially because of the way he carried me like a pigskin.

"I don't know how it works. When Lizzie spoke to me in spirit form, she said she was in between living and dead. Maybe it's a werewolf thing. Maybe they go to an in-between place when they're 'killed' until they can rejuvenate."

Alaric studies Lizzie. He's searching for a family resemblance, though in wolf form it's probably a lot more complicated. "Why are her eyes red?"

"I don't know. I haven't been able to talk to her or work any of my magic."

We watch Ryan pace around the cell. Though twice the size, he's a lot less intimidating than Lizzie with her scary red eyes.

"I brought them with me after I escaped the cell at Breas's prison, and then the world went to shit."

Alaric grips my arm. "He imprisoned you? I'll rip his throat out."

I extract myself from his grasp. I don't like it when Alaric's alpha male testosterone takes over and tries to mark his territory. I am no man's territory.

"May I remind you that you tried to kill me?" I leave out the did-kill-me part so Scott doesn't lose his mind entirely. There's only so much a reincarnated god can take.

Alaric's face scrunches in pain. "I could never . . ."

Scott tenses, but I can't worry about soothing my brother's protective nature. I can, however, berate myself for lashing out at Alaric. My temper still sometimes gets the better of me.

"You didn't, and everything's fine now, but we've got to figure out what to do with them. We've still got a couple hours before dawn."

Maddie walks over to stand with us. He's overheard the entire conversation. "Why did they take off the crystals?"

"I don't know . . . Both you and Alaric wanted to wear them. Maybe it's because Ryan's brainwashed to work for Breas, and Lizzie is all Team Clayone."

Scott grabs me. "What do you mean Lizzie is Team Clayone? And why the hell did Alaric try to kill you? We still need to address that shit."

I push calming energy into him. "Scott, there's a lot you missed, and I'd like nothing more than to fill you in on what happened . . ." Alaric's eyes meet mine. He doesn't want Scott to know every detail about our time in Brigit's shrine. He needn't worry. I am not telling Scott everything—he'd never trust Alaric again. ". . . But, we don't have time for the 'What Happened While Scott Was Gone' quiz show. We've got to figure out what in the hells happened that allowed Balor to enter the Land of Shadows and kill Gallean, and how long before he can make his way to the mainland, along with what to do about Breas, Witch Kensey, Carman, and the infestation of werewolves—no offense, Alaric and Maddie."

"None taken," Alaric says.

Granda appears within our cluster. The way he manages to move so discreetly at his age is miraculous. "May I suggest we discuss everything over tea?"

"Tea?" Caer says. Her forehead furrows. "You want us to drink tea when there's an impending battle?"

I follow Granda toward his cottage. "I agree. Whiskey would be much more appropriate given all we've been through."

"Come on, Caer," Scott says. "Some tea is just what we need. Although if Gigi drops anymore mind-shattering doozies on us, I'm taking a shot."

I knock my hip into him. "That's the brother I know and love."

We shuffle past Anna, Sam, and the rest of the coven. Some stare at us with open-mouthed wonder. Others, including Anna and Sam, narrow their gaze when they see us. In their minds, we caused all the havoc they've been through so far, including the death of Clarissa. In a way, they're right. Gallean and Clarissa's deaths were our faults, but sometime this evening I finally realized that everyone I love and care about didn't die because of me. They risked their lives to protect me, but it was Carman who caused their deaths. She's the one who has made it her life's mission to kill me. She released Breas. She orchestrated the release of Clayone. She may even have been behind opening the door to the Otherworld for Balor, or at the very least has been in communication with him.

It's always been Carman, and that bitch needs to go.

Granda pulls out the teapot and begins filling a tea bag with a variety of herbs. There's chamomile and lavender for calming and sleeping, along with what appears to be salvia.

He wants to open our minds so we can find answers. He also adds some honesty-inducing herbs—the same ones he used on Maddie when Scott and I first brought him home. He didn't use it on us, but we witnessed the magic of those herbs.

As the tea steeps, Granda brings over six cups. A seventh one remains on the counter as a reminder of the person we lost this evening.

"Now," he says, placing the teapot in the middle of the table, "we need answers. The first being, how Balor and his army were able to penetrate Gallean's mist shields around the Land of Shadows."

Alaric isn't familiar with the Shadow Realm, but he's spent enough time with a powerful witch to keep his mouth shut and observe. Considering he stalked me for weeks before I realized it back in Vernal Falls, he's very good at it.

Caer's fingers curl around the teacup. Any one of her fingers is capable of crushing it if pushed to anger. "The night before the battle, I left Gallean's keep prepared to return to my realm at Lake of the Dragon Mouth."

Granda eyes her. "By yourself?"

Her eyes slide over to Scott before returning to her cup. "Yes."

As the lone mind reader in the room, I know exactly why, but I'm sure everyone else would like to hear it, and Scott should be smacked around for trying to use Caer to get to me—the big doof. "Why, Caer?"

Scott interrupts. He senses I'm pissed and that I'd like to make a spectacle of the situation. He's not wrong. "It's not important why, but I left to find her." He glances at me with a grin. "I shifted into a swan." *Take that, sis.*

Granda waves his hand back and forth, not impressed by Caer and Scott's transformation and disappearing act at all.

27

"What was Gallean's state of mind when you left? Did he appear weak?"

Caer frowned. "Actually, he wasn't as powerful before that."

"He wasn't as powerful? He kicked my ass," Scott says, rubbing his butt as if it still hurt. Given the beating I witnessed Gallean give Scott in the seomra de rúin, it actually might.

She whirls around to face him. "Did he? Soon after my arrival, you bested us both."

"You beat a girl?" I tease.

Caer's shoulders straighten. "I am a powerful woman."

"Oh, believe me, I know. But Scott never liked to play against girls during football games. He always took it easy on them and got yelled at by the coach."

He puffs out his chest. "I *am* a reincarnated god. It was an unfair advantage."

I roll my eyes. "You didn't know that at the time."

"Enough, you two." Granda sighs as he pours himself tea. "Banter time is over."

"We haven't even gotten started," Scott says.

"We've been away from each other for a while," I add.

Granda takes a long drink of tea without offering any to anyone else. "Apparently not long enough. Now, Gallean's power was weakened—is that correct?"

"Yes," Caer says.

"So, it would stand to reason that his mist shields weren't adequately strengthened. It also explains why Caer was able to open a portal within his keep."

As the mild hallucinogen begins to take effect, Granda's mind opens to me. I begin to understand what he's getting at.

"Just before the Oak Moon on winter's solstice, there was a solar eclipse. It could explain how Balor and his army were able to depart their Otherworld purgatory and penetrate the mist shields of the Land of Shadows. What happened after Gallean turned to stone?"

Scott and Caer exchange a long look before he answers. "Just before his death, Gallean cast a powerful shield encapsulating all of us, protecting us from Balor's death stare."

"Then I opened a portal for my people to return us to our realm. I do not know what happened to Balor after." Her voice was tinged with both remorse for Gallean and regret for not being able to eliminate Balor when she'd had the chance. This mind-reading stuff really comes in handy.

"You'll get your chance," Scott whispers. He squeezes her hand before turning back to the rest of us. "Caer passed out from the exertion. When she came to, her people had already raised a shield to protect her."

Granda isn't unsympathetic to Caer's state following her creation of the portal, but he needs the facts. "Did Balor return to your realm?"

Scott shakes his head. "No. Not while we were there. But there's something I don't understand. Why would Caer's people worry that he'd return there if we were in the Faerie Realm and Balor was stuck in some purgatory in the Otherworld?"

Granda sighs. "The Faerie Realm is part of the Otherworld. He can move easily between realms if he possesses the means."

"Like an evil Fomorian witch?" I offer.

"Like an evil Fomorian witch," he agrees. "She might be using a vessel here, but her body is fully intact in purgatory."

Scott glances at Caer in fear. "Will Balor be able to come here? I need to keep her safe."

She glowers at him. When will my dimwit brother ever learn? "I will keep myself safe. I have all my life."

Granda temples his fingers, lifting them to his chin. "If

my suspicions are correct, and I believe they are, Balor and his army were jettisoned back to their purgatory . . ."

All of us sigh in relief.

"But . . ." he says.

"I despise buts," Scott groans.

"But at the Storm Moon, there will be a total lunar eclipse."

I hold up my arms like an air traffic controller. "Whoa, whoa, whoa. We already had a total lunar eclipse during the Super Blue Blood Moon on Samhain. I didn't think there could be another one so soon. Aren't they every six months or so?"

Scott raises his eyebrow. "Geek much?"

"I had a lot of spare time when you were incarcerated. I did a lot of research."

He winces at the memory. It was a low jab, but he deserved it.

"You are correct, Gigi, but every two hundred years there are three total lunar eclipses in one year."

Three. Why is it always three?

The storm is coming, the Witch scraps across my mind.

5

NIGHTTIME NOOGIES

*D*aylight breaks on the horizon, casting brilliant shades of purple, blue, orange, and yellow across Granda's oak table. Soon sunbeams work their way into the front window of his cottage.

"We all need some sleep because we have much planning to do," he says, rising from the table with a quickness that surprises me, especially given the fact he almost died. Perhaps Granda will live forever. With only three of us left in the family, I'll do everything in my power to keep the other two safe.

Why *is* it always three? Stupid cosmic forces.

The rest of us rise from our seats. Alaric pulls me into an embrace when we stand. I nestle into his chest, feeling at home and at peace.

"Let's discuss sleeping arrangements," Scott says. He doesn't like our closeness at all—especially after he made the pregnancy joke a few hours ago and Alaric admitted we hadn't had the chance yet rather than acting bashful. I knew Alaric was just being sarcastic, but Scott didn't, and his protective brother mojo is working overtime.

I break away from Alaric. "Scott, honestly, we aren't going to do anything this morning."

"Speak for yourself," Alaric whispers into my ear.

I put my head back on his shoulder. "Not helping . . ."

Caer and Maddie stand awkwardly around the table. Caer and Scott have kissed at least twice that I've witnessed —both times were pretty hot—but they aren't as comfortable with each other as Alaric and I are, and Scott doesn't want to push Caer into anything that makes her uneasy.

I look up at the ceiling. "Fine. Caer and I can share a room, and the three of you can."

Maddie approaches the sofa. "No, I'll sleep here. It's totally fine. There are only two twins in Scott's room. Scott's been away, so he needs his bed, and Alaric hasn't slept on a bed for weeks."

I put my hands on my hips. "Are you sure, Maddie? It's been your room while Scott was gone."

Scott glances over at him. "You've been staying here? Why?"

Alaric stiffens, suddenly realizing the reason. "Because he left the pack and doesn't have a home now." He walks over to Maddie and bows before him. "Thank you for remaining loyal to me when I was gone. Thank you for your sacrifice."

Maddie shuffles his feet, completely uncomfortable with his former alpha's submissive pose. "It was nothing. You would have done it for me."

Alaric lifts his head to face him. Tears prick his eyes, making him vulnerable and even more drool-worthy. "Yes, I would have. You're my brother."

The two lock in a giant man hug. Those warm fuzzy feelings in my stomach that keep erupting every time something good happens escalate into hyperdrive. I'd like nothing more than to join in on the hug too, but I'll let them have this moment.

When they finally break apart, Scott pretends to wipe the tears from the corners of his eyes. "That was beautiful, but I'm about to collapse from exhaustion. Caer and I killed—" He stops, realizing how callous he sounds, how like a serial killer. "Caer and I haven't slept in days, and it sounds like the next few weeks are going to be a test of all our abilities. We need to be rested." He shyly walks over to Caer and takes her hand. "May I?"

She nods. Her chest rises in a sharp intake of breath. Scott's aware of the effect he has on her, and he plans to use it to woo her. He bends down to kiss her hand before letting it go. "I will bid you good night and see you soon."

Caer shifts her weight. She's so unsure around him, which an outsider would not expect given her leather pants, the giant sword and iron spear strapped to her back, and the numerous daggers in holsters around her waist and ankles. In short, armed to the teeth.

"You two are kind of adorable."

The heat springing between them ices over as they glare at me.

"But also very intimidating."

Caer smiles in agreement.

Scott suddenly remembers Lizzie and Ryan. He gestures in the direction of the garden. "Should we check on them?"

Alaric shakes his head. "After shifting on a full moon, they're exhausted. They'll be out for hours. But they will need to rebuild their reserves later."

I latch on to hope. "Maybe that will be the best time to try and bring them back to our side?"

He pulls in his lips and breathes deeply. "Maybe."

He's not sure we can bring them back to us. He thinks they're lost forever.

I sidle up to him. "I changed your mind."

He pulls me back in. "After I killed you and had to beg the Goddess to bring you back."

"No harm, no foul—or should I say wolf?"

Scott breaks us up again. "I'm not going to tear out your spine because I don't want to upset my sister, but if you mess with her, if you harm her in any way again, you are dead." His inner god flares with power.

Alaric backs away from him. Not because he's scared—he is the son of the Original Werewolf—but because he wants to earn Scott's trust. "I promise that I will protect her and guard her with my life."

Scott softens. "The only reason I'm letting you live is because Gigi says you've sacrificed your life for her before."

Alaric turns to me. "You told him."

"She tells me everything."

"Well, not *everything*." I air-smooch to Alaric. "I will see you later."

"If you need me, you know where to find me," he says, kissing my forehead.

"Now I do." I open my door and back into my room, because with Scott's inner god flashing, there won't be any intense romantic interludes tonight. Or heavy petting. Not even a tempting teeth grazing across the throat. "Good night."

Caer slips into the room, careful to avoid Scott. I don't care what they say. They are adorable.

Scott reaches for the door. "Sis, glad to be back."

"Bro, I'm glad to have you back."

We share a shiny brother-sister moment before his attention returns to Caer. "Good night," he whispers. "Sleep well."

She blushes and ducks her head. "You too."

He reluctantly closes the door, leaving the two of us staring awkwardly at each other, both wishing we were with someone else. I settle onto my bed in a cross-legged position then pat the other end with my hand. "Let's have a quick chat."

She hesitates, not knowing what I have in mind.

"Don't worry, I won't bite," I offer as a consolation. I almost add "unless you want me to," but that's not going to lessen her anxiety, and with her being from another realm, a faerie princess, and a reincarnated goddess, aside from being a ferocious, powerful warrior, my smart retort would be lost on her.

Her nostrils flare as she decides whether to join me or not. She knows I can read minds, but I try to act like I can't so she doesn't get any more nervous or annoyed and threaten to slice my throat. I pat the bed again, suddenly needing a friend since my former bestie is outside with a major werewolf hangover. Finally, she climbs up on the bed and crosses her legs to mirror mine.

I smile at her. "I haven't had a heart-to-heart like this for a long time."

Her forehead bunches. "Heart-to-heart? I don't understand."

I have to keep reminding myself she's not Lizzie. She doesn't just *know* things.

"We talk about what's on our minds and share our deepest thoughts."

"And why would we do that?"

"Because we're friends."

"Friends," she repeats. "I've never had one before."

"I haven't had many either. Believe it or not, I never really fit in at school."

Her eyes brighten. "School? I know what that is. Gallean would not have been a teacher at one of your schools."

I chuckle. "No, he wouldn't have. It feels weird not to have the old guy telling me what to do."

She nods her head enthusiastically because she grasped the meaning of a new word, but then she remembers Gallean's sacrifice. "It does feel weird, and sad."

I reach for her hand. She startles but then lets me take it. I never realized I had such a need to touch people, to give them energy to get through a difficult time. I took from so many people for so many years as I searched for what was within me all along. I'm thankful I can finally give back. My gods, if there was a license for black-twisted hearts, mine would be revoked.

"Caer, thank you for opening the portal for me."

"Your brother was not happy with me. He ignored me for many days and often lashed out."

"He's not mad at you anymore."

Her cheeks warm. "No, he's not."

"When did that change?"

Her eyes meet mine. *You know.*

"Is it that obvious?"

She smiles again. "Not right now. You're doing very well pretending you can't see inside my head."

"I can't read your entire mind. I can only read what you're thinking in the moment."

"Good to know."

"Were you surprised that he turned into a swan?"

"Yes and no. I'd heard the legend, but I assumed it was false. How can someone suddenly shift into another form just because they want to?"

I temple my fingers and rest my chin on them. "Caer, you make a very good point. Scott would be able to bypass rules of humanity because he's a reincarnated god, but how were Maddie and Alaric able to semi-shift when it wasn't a full moon? And how was Lizzie?"

She mirrors my position and breathes in and out. "Alaric's father is Clayone, the Original Werewolf."

The pieces begin to fall together. "I found out that Clayone is also Lizzie's father."

No reason to go into the bitter details about that discovery.

"Keturah mentioned Naisha, the faerie who disappeared from our realm a long time ago."

"And we realized Naisha could be Nancy, as in Lizzie's mom. So the combination of the Original Werewolf and Fae blood . . ."

Caer's eyes perk up. "Is she still alive? Can we question her?"

I breathe in and out, mulling over strategy. "There's a portal between Kildare and Vernal Falls for anyone from Brigit's line."

"Well, let's go," she says, climbing off the bed.

"Scott will kill us."

She folds her arms.

"I know you're not the least bit intimated by him, but aren't you worried you'll piss him off?"

She shrugs. "He forgave me for shoving you through the portal."

"You didn't shove me."

She raises an eyebrow. "Yes, I did."

"'Shove' sounds so . . . aggressive."

"Would you like 'assist' better?"

I pat her arm. "I'm really beginning to like you."

"I'm beginning to like you too." She pats the top of my head, which is below her chin. It reminds me of Scott giving me a noogie. Until now I hadn't realized how freakishly tall she is, or how freakishly short I am.

"All right, let's do it. I've been in need of some female companionship. Speaking of which, what should I do about Lizzie and Ryan?"

"Alaric said they'd be passed out for a while. We could

37

leave a note and ask them to give them some food in case we don't get back in time from questioning Naisha," she says, cracking her knuckles.

"How intense are you counting on this interrogation to be?"

She shrugs. "A sword to the throat is not out of the question."

Flashes of what Lizzie put Alaric through rush through me. Lizzie chaining him to a table. Each time he called my name, even in a whisper, she'd crank a handle and he'd scream in pain. After weeks of torture, it was his silence that scared me the most, and it was only when I "died" that he returned to me.

"No, I guess it's not."

"Well, let's go," she says, taking off toward the bedroom door.

I rush over before she opens it. "Wait."

"Wait?"

I bite my lower lip. "I don't know exactly where Brigit's portal is."

"Then we can open one."

"No, I don't think we should. We've both used a tremendous amount of energy already. We don't want any surprises when we find Naisha."

She rolls her eyes. I warm to her even more. She might have even less patience than I do. "Well, how do we find it?"

I stop and think. Clarissa's gone. I'm sure Granda knows, but I'm not going to wake him to ask him. He probably wouldn't tell me right now anyway and insist I get some sleep. Where could I find out . . . ?

Caer puffs out in annoyance next to me.

"You're not making this any easier," I whisper. "Just let me think."

"Is there a map, or did someone write it down?"

I punch her. "That's it!"

She crouches into a lunge, thinking I'm going to attack her.

"My dad's journal. He mentions it."

She throws out her arms. *Well, go get it.*

"Stay here," I whisper and quietly open the door.

I listen and feel for any noises or brain waves of anyone awake and find nothing. I creep down the hall to the table by the sofa. There, beneath a pile of books, is Dad's brown leather journal. Of course it's at the bottom.

I glance over at Maddie's figure. His chest rises and falls with sleep. I slowly move each book, with the realization that I am really pressing my luck. If Scott and Alaric had their own heart-to-heart session in Scott's room, they may have only just fallen asleep. Scott could be hit over the head with a log and still not wake up once he's out, but Alaric's enhanced wolf senses could be problematic.

As I reach for the book with the initials M.P.O, hands wrap around my waist.

Busted.

6

CAUGHT RED EYED

*a*laric lifts me up and carries me out the front door, moving with such stealth he'd make a burglar envious. Smaug would never catch him. I always prided myself on my ability to sneak around without making a sound, but compared to Alaric, I'm a clumsy beast. He gently sets me on a garden bench, then tucks himself in beside me.

"What are you doing awake?" he whispers, dipping his head to peek at the journal in my hand.

I slip it under my thigh. I don't want to lie to him, but there's no way I'm telling him what I was really doing. "I couldn't sleep. I figured I'd do some light reading."

He lifts his eyebrows as he reaches across me to grab the journal. "Light reading, hmmm?" His finger traces the initials. "M.P.O."

"My dad's journal."

Without opening it, he returns it to me. "What were you hoping to find?"

I roll my eyes, frustrated with what I'm about to admit to him. When did I become such a softie? I used to be able to lie, cheat, and steal without an ounce of regret, without a tinge of remorse. Hells bells, I thrived on it. Now, even the notion of lying to Alaric makes me nauseous. "Fine. I was searching for a map that would tell me where the portal is to get to Vernal Falls."

He sucks in a breath. "Gi, my nan opened the portal for me. I doubt she'd open it for you or even that she'd be able to open it while in Maria's form."

He confirms what I long suspected. Carman can create portals—at least sometimes.

"There's another one. One only accessible to those from Brigit's line."

"And why did you need to find it when the rest of us were sleeping?"

Time for the lie. Prepare for esophagus burn.

"To take a trip down memory lane."

He kneels in front of me, his gold-rimmed green eyes studying me. "Gi, what aren't you telling me?"

I look away from him. "Nothing."

He puts his hands around my face and turns me back to him. "Gi, tell me."

"Caer and I wanted to question Nancy."

He falls back onto his heels. "The woman who could be our mother?" His eyes fall on Lizzie sleeping in her cell.

"Yes," I say in a small voice.

"And you were going to go without me?"

"Yes," I whisper in an even smaller voice.

His eyes settle back on mine. "Gi, after all we've been through, after our time apart, you were going to leave me?"

"Not forever. For a quick trip."

He sighs. "We both know all too well that nothing is simple anymore."

"No, I guess it's not."

He sits back down on the bench next to me. "Well, let's see what you can find."

I let Dad's journal fall open. "Here goes," I whisper and start reading:

Total involvement in this world is the most powerful tool anybody will ever possess.

I smile to myself. Dad's statement proves he wanted me to be an active participant in this life. He didn't want me standing idly by, watching the world destroy itself. He'd want me to fix what's broken.

"What are you smiling about?" He peeks around my shoulder to see. "Your dad was a smart man."

"Yes, he was."

I notice a hastily written note in the margin. "Hmm, what's this?" I lift it closer. *Lycanthropes: Demons of Derg.*

I drop it like it burns my hands. I shudder.

"What's it say?"

"Nothing. Nothing."

I hurry to close it, but his werewolf reflexes are faster than mine.

His eyes find mine after he reads it. Tears fill the corners of them. "He's right. We are demons of Derg. I shouldn't be here. I shouldn't be with you."

He stands to leave, taking one last look at me.

"Alaric, wait," I beg, reaching for him.

He turns to go. My heart starts to break. I can't even . . .

"Please, please stay," I cry.

He hesitates.

"Please don't go. Don't leave me," I plead.

He's conflicted. He doesn't want to hurt me, but my dad's words cause him to question our relationship.

"Your dad wouldn't want us to be together."

I hurry over and wrap my arms around him. "He'd want

me to be happy. He knew that the universe works in mysterious ways."

He tries to break away, but he doesn't put much effort into it.

"The fact that we keep finding each other proves that we're destined to be together. The universe wants us together. You're everything to me."

He pulls me into his chest. "And you are everything to me, but what about your dad?"

"He didn't know you and—wait a second . . ." I glance back at the journal I left on the bench, but it's too far away and I'm not about to let go of Alaric. With one arm still wrapped around him, I shuffle back over to it with him in tow. I bend down and pick it up. I don't want to hurt the spine by holding it with one hand. I peek up at him. "A little help?"

He pulls in his lips but grabs the back cover. With the journal firmly in our hands, I squint at the writing.

"I don't think that's even my dad's writing."

He doesn't believe me. He thinks I'm making it up to make him feel better. "Then whose is it?"

I look even closer. "It's definitely not his. Hold on." I flip through a few pages and find one of Calliope's entries. "It's not Calliope's either." I turn back to the warning. I'd only seen a couple samples of Granda's writing, but it doesn't resemble his either. Then it hits me.

"There was one person who could have written it . . ."

One person who switched out the silver bullets. One person who had access to Granda's cottage when he came over for dinner. One person capable of pulling an equally sneaky move to cause me to doubt my love to Alaric.

"Breas," we say together.

"That bastard," he growls.

"I couldn't agree more. I love how your mind works, and it proves that my dad would approve of my choice in men. He's always liked my furry pets," I say with a smirk.

His eyes take on a dangerous glint. "I will be whatever you want me to be."

"Submissive. I like it." I pull him back onto the bench with me. "Now, let's find the map."

I close my eyes and ask the journal to reveal the portal location to me. I flip it open and peek down. "That was easy."

"You found it?"

"Ask and you shall receive, or at least I can ask and receive. Magic does have its perks."

I study the hand-drawn map. The portal isn't far. If the map is accurate, it's about halfway between here and Clarissa's. No real landmarks, but I have a feeling that I'll find it. Goddessy senses and all.

Alaric kisses my forehead, but before he goes any farther, he suddenly stills. His gaze falls on Ryan and Lizzie.

"Have you made any progress with her?"

"No, I haven't. I was so preoccupied with finding you, I haven't had time to try."

He scowls at me, pretending to be mad. "Yet, you were going to leave on a whim."

I purse my lips at him before returning my gaze to my sleeping werewolf besties. Lizzie wakes up. Her eyes flash red.

"Why are they still red?" he whispers. "She's through with her phasing."

"I don't know."

"Should I try talking to her?"

"If you want to."

Lizzie stands up and crouches before launching herself at the invisible cell wall. She crashes to the ground, stands up, and tries it again and again.

"The power of the moon is still with her," he whispers. He glances up at the sky. "More sunlight will help weaken her."

"It works like that?"

He reaches for my hand to pull me up from the bench. "It should. Let's go visit Mom first."

Lizzie crashes against the wall again, yelling "No!" Or at least that's what it looks like she says. We can't hear her, but her reaction is obvious.

"Can she hear us?" Alaric asks.

"No, but I think she read your lips. Apparently she really doesn't want us to go."

"Well then we must be on our way to uncovering the truth." He tugs me along, leaving Lizzie to battle her inner demons.

Alaric's absolute disregard of his sister's pleas are kind of endearing. He's the rebellious badass I've always been attracted to, but he's all good underneath. Birds of a feather stick together—wait that's Scott and Caer's line. Throw me to the son of the Original Werewolf, and I'll be happy as hell.

The perimeter boundary of Granda's cottage shimmers in front of us in a hazy wave. It's meant to keep everyone out, and since Lizzie and Ryan couldn't escape from the boundary, it seems that it also keeps everyone in. But the spells protecting the cottage are attached to me, so we shouldn't have a problem penetrating it either coming or going. I clutch his hand. "Hold on," I whisper as if the spells might overhear my intention.

"I'm not letting you go," he says, and we step through the boundary spell together.

A faint shock ripples through our bodies and then immediately vanishes.

"That was weird," he says. We're so much alike it's actually scary.

"It's about to get weirder."

We travel together in companionable silence across the countryside between Granda's and Clarissa's cottage. It almost seems strange not to talk incessantly to each other, especially after being separated for so long, except it isn't. It's like our souls are communicating even if our lips aren't flapping. We can just "be."

Finally I sense a pull, almost like a magnetic force. It's the sign I've been waiting for. "The portal's up ahead. Are you ready for this?"

He stops and tugs me to him. "With you, I'm ready for anything." Then he drags my lips to his.

Electricity shoots through me when our lips meet, but this time the shock doesn't disappear. It grows more intense. I tangle my hands in his hair to ensure he can't break the kiss until I'm ready to. In response, he slips his hands around my back and pulls me closer. As our bodies press against each other, an insatiable need surges through me. He lifts me to him. My legs dangle in the air until I wrap one around him.

My heart races with the thunder of a thousand stampeding hooves. He reaches under my shirt. I prepare for the explosion of his touch that I know will result as his fingers crawl across my skin at an impossibly slow speed toward my breasts. I push my body closer to him if that's even possible. He purrs deep within his chest as my fingers skim along the seam of his jeans. Why did we wait so long to do this?

"Now," a voice fills the air around us. A voice reeking of empty promises and betrayal.

We break apart in time to notice Breas's minions edging toward us.

But he's too late. They're too late. I step closer to the portal entrance.

The wavy edges of Brigit's portal appear next to us, and we leap together. A stronger shock pulses through us as we land softly on a bed of pine needles. I inhale the sweet smell of the pine forests of Western Pennsylvania, and my heart soars.

"Where are we?" Alaric asks.

I tug him to me. "Home."

"I like the sound of that," he says, his voice husky with need.

His lips find mine. With surprising efficiency, we disrobe as if we've waited a millennium to be together. And maybe we have. All I know is that a hunger has overtaken me that can only be quenched by Alaric filling it.

The voice of Lizzie, the one I once knew and loved and above all else trusted, whispers in my subconscious, *Do you have protection?*

It's almost enough to make me hesitate, but Alaric and I have waited too long, for too many lifetimes, and have overcome too much to stop now.

He trails kisses down my throat as his hands explore the rest of me. I'd savor his gentle caresses if my own hands weren't busy exploring the ridges of the powerful muscles that sculpt his body.

His heart pounds against my chest, matching the beat of my own. As my fingers skim along everything that makes him a man, he shudders. He reaches between my thighs, but he doesn't have to. They're already slick with need.

He enters me quickly. Sensation riffles through me. It's by no means my first time, but I've never felt like this. When he's fully engaged, he falls on his back, my legs still straddling him.

"Oh Gigi," he moans as I edge up and down his length.

When I return to his base, it is enough to undo us both, and we explode together.

We gasp for breath as I collapse against his chest. Lizzie's warnings come back to me, and so do Scott's, but I push them aside.

I wanted this. I wanted him, and whatever happens later, so be it.

7

TEN OF SWORDS

*W*hen Gigi didn't immediately return with the map, Caer took to pacing around the room. It was a habit she never noticed she had until she witnessed Scott's speed pacing. Hers was nothing compared to the acceleration he was capable of, but she still moved faster than the average, well, faerie princess.

She liked Gigi well enough, at least after their short time together. Neither one of them were patient, and both wanted answers. Caer had slept her whole life. A few days of wakefulness wasn't going to affect her. She had never had a friend before, and Gigi's presence gave her courage. She felt strong with Gigi around, especially since Scott sometimes made her feel weak. Mathair Mhór had warned her he would be a protector in this reincarnation, but she was a protector too. A protector of her people.

She didn't know why she was so intent on helping Gigi interrogate Lizzie's mother, but something within her felt like it was important. If her mother was Naisha, the lost faerie from the Faerie Realm, she might have answers about how she'd been able to leave the realm as she pleased. Keturah had mentioned that Naisha had traveled between realms when the veil was thin, but then wouldn't everyone travel between realms? Besides, she'd still require a means to travel, like a portal and someone to open it for her.

The Witch on the other side of Gigi's flame shield troubled her. Darkness emanated from every pore of the Witch's being, and that form was only her vessel. The true version of the Witch was still back in the Otherworld's purgatory, waiting for an opportunity for her Fomorian brethren, including Balor, to arrive in the Earthly Realm. Well, Caer would be ready for him. She gripped her iron spear as she paced around the room. She never let it far from her sight, but right now, with Gigi occupied, she needed to feel the promise of Balor's death in her hands.

What Alaric had said about eliminating future generations gave her pause. If she could find out the true reason why Balor had killed her father, it might help her discover a way to take his life without risking her people or her friends.

And what was Alaric? He was the son of Clayone, but Keturah and the other women believed he was Fae too. She hadn't caught his scent since her arrival in the Earthly Realm, but she had in the Faerie Realm, and though the scent was new to her, it was familiar. If his mother was Fae, that would explain why.

Alaric believed his mother had died in childbirth, yet Keturah was adamant that if his mother was Naisha, she would not have died during the birthing process. Fae were immortal. Caer as Faerie Queen was immortal. If she chose to remain in the Faerie Realm, she could live forever and never return to the Otherworld realm reserved for gods and goddesses and their kin. That concept both thrilled and scared her.

Caer remembered the desperation in Alaric's voice when he was asking Keturah and the others about his mother. She was desperate for answers too. Was Alaric's mother somehow connected? Was she the reason Balor had been able to penetrate the Faerie Realm? Were they working together? And if so, did that mean he wasn't able to immediately arrive into any realm Caer visited as she had once thought? Had Caer constantly lived in fear and on the move for no reason? She'd lived with Mathair Mhór for years until Balor found her. The Land of Shadows had provided her sanctuary until Balor finally penetrated its shields. But the question remained, why was Balor so desperate to obtain her? Did he want to kill her or imprison her? The answer would make all the difference.

The confines of Gigi's bedroom grew too small for Caer's roaming. She needed space, but more than that, she needed answers. She crept down the hall, knowing she could go invisible if she heard anyone stirring.

Maddie was sleeping on some type of cushioned bench beneath a beautifully knit blanket. Caer never had the luxury of possessing a blanket made of anything other than animal fur. She reached over to touch it and found the material soft and warm against her fingertips without the smothering heat of a fur. She watched Maddie sleep, curious about this friend that had become a part of the family as Scott had told her. She had once been told by her nursemaid that family meant blood, but she had come to learn from Mathair Mhór, and then Gallean, that family could mean anyone someone shared a special bond with.

Maddie's scent filled the air around him. She inhaled deeply. He was something other than a werewolf too. Perhaps he was Fae also?

He stirred in his sleep. Caer stilled and waited for him to return to his dreams. When he settled back in, she glanced around the room. The hanging baskets and dried herbs reminded her of Mathair Mhór's cottage. The stone fireplace and the piles of books were the same too. The Earthly Realm appeared to be similar to the realms Caer was familiar with.

Gigi was nowhere to be seen. Caer inhaled again to catch Gigi's scent and found it layered beneath Alaric's. She followed the trail out the front door and into the daylight.

Scott tossed and turned in bed. It felt strange to be back in his room in Kildare, acting as if nothing had changed when everything had changed. Gallean had sacrificed himself to save Caer and by auxiliary, Scott. Clarissa had died because her lifeline was connected to Gallean's. Scott had shapeshifted into a swan to catch Caer before she disappeared from his life forever, and they had battled Balor and his Fomorian army. The world had gone to shit, and he was still reeling from it. They all were.

He and Alaric had ignored each other when they first entered the bedroom, but eventually Scott broke down and tried to engage Alaric in conversation. He figured that since apparently Alaric and his sister kept finding each other in each reincarnation, he might as well get to know the guy. Although after discovering that Alaric had killed Gigi and begged Brigit to return her life to her, he really wanted to rail him instead. Moralltach had shifted back into a small knife, but it would return to a sword upon his need.

For instance, if he needed to swipe Alaric's head off. That gave Scott a substantial amount of consolation.

He seemed like an all right guy. Intense, sure. Preoccupied with Gigi, definitely. But his intentions, as far as Scott could tell, seemed genuine. His family ancestry definitely gave Scott pause. And the fact that Lizzie was Clayone's daughter? He hadn't seen that coming from several realms away. And Ryan was alive? The guilt that ate at Scott's soul for taking his best friend's life all but disappeared, but Breas was going to pay for messing with all of them. It didn't worry Scott in the least that Breas was an actual god. With Moralltach, a god would bleed all the same.

He adjusted the blankets on the bed. It was hard to sleep when it was light out. Plus his mind was still buzzing with activity. There was much that needed to be discovered before they battled Balor and his Fomorian army. Rest was the key to all of it.

A loud creak shot him out of bed and into a fighting pose with dagger in hand. He glanced over at Alaric's bed and found it empty.

"I'll kill him," Scott hissed as he prowled out of the room and stalked down the hall to Gigi's room. He found the door open and the room empty.

Panic kicked in.

"Where are they?" he growled, appearing in front of Maddie at god speed.

Maddie sprang off the sofa almost as fast as Scott had moved. "What? Who?"

"Gigi, Alaric, and Caer. They're gone."

"Gone?" Maddie echoed.

"Can you track them?"

Maddie inhaled. "Caer is the most recent. Alaric and Gigi's scents are more faint."

"Which way did they go?"

Without answering, Maddie followed the trail out the door with Scott close behind him.

There, standing in front of Lizzie and Ryan's cells, stood Caer. Scott didn't think he'd ever get used to her beauty. It literally took his breath away. As he neared her, he sensed tension exuding off of her.

"Do you know where my sister and the wolf are?"

She shook her head. "I was tracking them until their scent disappeared."

He clenched his fists together. Adrenaline surged through his body. Someone was getting an ass kicking. "Come on, Maddie. Let's see if you can pick it back up."

Caer reached for his arm. No ordinary human woman would ever be able to hold him back, but Caer was neither human nor ordinary. "It won't do any good. They're gone. But I think I know where they went."

Scott stared at Ryan still curled up in a ball. He sensed conflict in Caer. "Tell me."

"Well . . ." she said, sounding more and more like his sister, "Gigi and I were going to question Naisha."

"Naisha, as in Nancy? Lizzie's mom, and possibly Alaric's too?"

"The one and the same."

"How were you going to get there? Were you two going to use a portal and leave us?"

Her eyes skirted away from him. "Yes."

He stiffened.

"But we were going to return as soon as we were done."

He shook his head. Betrayal cut deep. "I thought both of you were going to recharge your energy stores like Granda asked you to."

"We were going to use a portal only accessible to someone of Brigit's line."

"Where is it?"

"I don't know where it is, but Gigi must have found it. I don't think you'll be able to access it."

Challenge accepted. Operation Ass Kick initiated.

"Won't I? I'm from Brigit's line as well, and I'll be godsdamned if my sister gets into trouble because you two were going to leave without telling anyone."

"We were going to leave a note."

"A note?" he said, storming off in Maddie's direction. "A note. Well that makes everything okay then."

She hurried to catch up to him. "You're mad."

"Godsdamned right I'm mad."

"What about Breas and the Witch? Won't they be able to find us once we leave the boundary?"

He stopped and scowled at her. "You and Gigi were going to leave the boundary. What's different now? Are you scared, or is it that you don't want me to go with you?"

She stepped away from him, her nostrils flaring. If he wasn't so mad, he'd ask if he could kiss her again, because she was sexy when she was angry. She held Freagarach in her hands.

"I am not scared."

"So, you don't want me to go with you?"

She growled. "That's not it either."

"Well then, what are we waiting for?"

Maddie stopped at an invisible boundary line. "I can't pass through."

Caer sheathed Freagarach and took both of their hands. "Come on," she said and stepped through the boundary shield.

Scott felt a passing fuzziness as they walked through, but with Caer's resistance to magic, it was tolerable. She released them both when they were well out of the perimeter.

Maddie hurried across the countryside, tracking Gigi's and Alaric's scents. Scott and Caer kept pace with him as he ventured farther and farther away from Granda's cottage and the perimeter boundary. He finally stopped at the top of a hill. Caer and Scott joined him. They stood halfway between Granda's cottage and the remains of Clarissa's. Smoke still spiraled in the air from the ruins.

"The trail ends here."

Scott could see the shimmery outline of the portal appear before them. He grabbed Caer and Maddie's hands.

"Not if I have anything to say about it. Hold on."

8

LUCK O' THE IRISH

"What the fuck are you doing?" my brother yells at us.

The irony of his statement is not lost on me. Alaric shields my naked body as he rolls us over onto our sides. I peek over his arm to see Caer studying Alaric's bare ass. I'm by no means jealous. It is quite divine. Maddie pretends to be fascinated by the pine bark of the tree beside us. Scott glares at us with folded arms.

Our clothes are in a chaotic pile next to his feet. There's no way I can reach my shirt without showing the melons.

"A little privacy would be nice."

Scott's eyes narrow. I'm thankful yet again that he can't shoot red lasers out of them.

"Do you mind?"

"Fine," he growls, reaching down and zinging the pile at me before turning away.

I slip my shirt on and climb partway into my pants before getting up from the ground. Before I can pull them up the rest of the way, Alaric gently cradles my butt as he stands inches from it with all his spent man glory hanging out. With my brother standing only a few feet away, it's not like I can scold him (or prepare for round two), so I give him an exasperated eye glare. He winks at me as he slides his fingers down my ass toward my va-jay-jay. I gasp in surprise.

"Gigi," Scott warns.

I pinch my lips and squint at Alaric as I pull my pants up the rest of the way and buckle them in a take-that move. He waggles his eyebrows as he slowly slips his jeans around his perfectly sculpted gluteus maximus, pausing halfway up. It is definitely one fine piece of man-flesh.

"You," I whisper, shaking my head.

"We're standing *right* here," Scott says.

"And it's very awkward," Maddie adds.

I feel a pang of sympathy for Maddie and Caer, but Scott can kiss my ass (which I definitely wouldn't mind Alaric doing, but that's a conversation for another time).

"You can turn around now."

He refolds his arms. "What the hell were you two doing?"

Hello, Mr. Obvious. "What did it look like?"

He scowls. Soon we will be able to journey into the Grand Canyon via his forehead. "We thought you were going to question Nancy."

"We took a little side trip."

"There's nothing little about me," Alaric murmurs, his eyes flashing in amusement.

I roll my eyes. "Not helping."

"Did you at least use protection?" Scott asks.

I pull in my lips and look away. "Let's take the trail to Lizzie's house. It shouldn't be far."

"Answer the question, Gigi."

I inhale deeply and exhale before turning to face my brother. "No, we didn't."

Scott lunges for Alaric. "Why you . . ."

Alaric knocks him away. "She's a reincarnated goddess. She can't even have kids."

Everything inside me stills. It feels like I've just been hammer kicked in the stomach by Caer during a training session and all the air's knocked out of me.

"I can't?"

He cradles my hands in his as he kisses them. He senses he delivered a tremendous blow and would do anything within his power to ease it. "Wouldn't there be multiple Brigit lines alive today if you could? When Brigit was human, she gave birth, but through the reincarnations, she hasn't because she can't. You and Scott are the last of the line."

It takes me a long time to answer. Everyone's staring at me, but it does nothing to relieve the sadness. "Brigit's line ends with us?"

He pulls me to his chest. "Yes, but you've got a lifetime to live before that happens."

I bury myself in his arms, and though he makes me feel full, an overwhelming emptiness hollows my chest. I am the last.

Scott is barely sympathetic as I cling to Alaric with the devastating news. To think that Brigit's line will no longer continue in the Earthly Realm is a sadness beyond measure.

Caer shifts around uncomfortably. She can't understand why I'm so upset that Brigit's line will end. Caer Ibormeith is a lesser-known god in Celtic mythology. Barely anyone has heard of her. Her story is overshadowed by the more testosterone-driven aspects of the pantheon. (I don't agree with the gender bias. It's symptomatic of many of today's current world issues.) But for some reason, people have worshipped Brigit since the beginning when they were just Druids, before her name was even adopted by the church.

When Christianity embraced her, Brigit found everlasting life, but her line didn't. It will end with me.

Caer casts an occasional glare in our direction too. She's mad at me for ditching her and bringing Alaric instead. She's also trying not to think about what Scott's butt might look like naked. I try not to think about what it looks like either, but for vastly different reasons.

Maddie clears his throat. All our attention focuses on him.

"What is it, Maddie?" Scott asks.

"Well, I'm no portal-jumping expert, but does time jump when you travel within a realm? When Gigi was in the Shadow Realm, she was gone for weeks, but to her it was only a few days. Is it the same when you jump within the realm? And if so, shouldn't we hurry and find this woman you want to question?"

Neither Scott nor I really have any experience portal hopping within the same realm except for the portal we took from Clarissa's to Granda's property last night, and time had stayed the same then.

Alaric's chest rumbles as he answers Maddie. It's not as sexy as the purr he gave when we were otherwise engaged, but it's still pretty darn sexy. "I traveled between Kildare and Vernal Falls via a different portal, and time remained the same."

Scott stands in front of us, reeking of judgement. "Right. I heard about that. And what exactly were you doing in Vernal Falls?"

Alaric tightens his arms around me as if he doesn't want to let me go. "My nan sent me to keep an eye on Gigi and Breas."

"So you were a peeping Tom, back-stabbing, pervert spy?"

Alaric ignores the jab. "It was during that time that I fell for Gigi and found it more and more difficult to keep my distance. Nan sensed that and called me home under the guise that Gigi would be in Ireland soon, and she was." He kisses the top of my head.

Sensing that Scott's interrogation could go on all day, because no matter how Alaric answered, it would never alleviate my brother's anger at catching us in the buff, I tear my head from Alaric's chest and the rest of me follows. Cold invades my limbs as my body immediately feel the absence of him, but soon we will solve the Naisha/Nancy riddle and in so doing maybe resolve the Alaric/Lizzie situation.

I take off walking. "So, who wants to lead the questioning?"

Scott and the rest of them follow along. "Well, you definitely shouldn't lead it. Remember the funeral fiasco?"

For the benefit of the group, because I know exactly what it feels like to be left out of something, I fill them in on Lizzie's funeral happenings. "Lizzie's mom scolded my dad and me for being there. She said it was all our fault that Lizzie had died—which at the time I believed it was. There was pushing, name-calling, and an overturned coffin that turned out to be empty except for the ripped fabric liner and the claw marks on the wood."

Alaric touches his nightlock-imbued crystal to reassure himself that it's there. "Claw marks? But it was between full moons."

Maddie and I exchange glances. He remembers when I forced him to semi-shift outside of the full moon. Alaric also did during my meditative visit to Brigit's shrine room, but with the rage that burned inside him, he doesn't remember.

"It seems that, with some persuasion, some werewolves can at least partially shift when it's not a full moon."

Alaric stops. "What? I never have. That's not possible."

Maddie takes the lead on this one. "Man, it is. Gigi took

the crystal from me without me knowing and forced me into a semi-shift."

Scott throws up his hands. "Gigi, are you crazy? You could have been killed."

I forgot how overly dramatic my brother is.

"I wasn't. Maddie wasn't going to hurt me. I was in control of his shift, and I gave him the crystal immediately after. Werewolves only assume they can't shift outside of the full moon because of the curses Brigit placed on them, but apparently some of them can, or at least they can semi-shift. I didn't want to push Maddie to fully change."

Maddie shivers. "And I didn't want to fully change either. I lose myself when I'm a wolf, and I don't like losing myself."

All during our conversation, Caer watches Maddie closely. "What else are you?"

Maddie starts moving along the trail to avoid her question. She unnerves him, and he's afraid to reveal to her the other things he can do.

"Show her, Maddie," I call out to him.

He stops on the trail, his shoulders stiff.

"It's okay. You can trust her."

Without more ado, he disappears.

Caer gasps. "He can go invisible? Is he resistant to magic too?"

Maddie appears beside me. He finds comfort in my presence. The feeling is mutual.

"I don't think so," he says. "Gigi's crystal works on me, and the wolfsbane ropes Breas used on me worked until I disappeared."

Alaric's temper flares. "He used wolfsbane rope on you? Breas will die a long, painful death for all he has done to the both of you."

"Chill, man," I tease. "Listen, this catch-up session has been riveting, and I mean that in the least sarcastic way possible, but it proves all the more reason to solve the Naisha/Nancy riddle."

"Agreed," Scott says. "Let's go. But since Caer is Fae and Maddie is clearly part Fae . . ."

"Fae? I'm part Fae," Maddie whispers as if he's been waiting his entire life for an explication—which he has.

I rest my arm on him and push some soothing comfort into him. "You've found some of the answers you've been waiting for. We'll find out more when we can."

"Thank you," he whispers.

A small part of him is still freaking out about being part Fae, but my little pep talk settles him. Plus, I pushed in some calming energy to speed up the process. He trusts me, and his trust means more to me than any kingdom. He's the first outside of my immediate circle to do so. I want more than anything to keep him safe.

Scott glances at Maddie and Caer. "They should go invisible. We don't know what Nancy might be capable of, especially if she's Fae. The element of surprise would be useful."

"Agreed," Alaric says, pulling me along. "I'll lead the way."

We continue down the trail bordering Vernal Falls. I love Ireland—the green, the intoxicating clean air, the feeling of oldness—but the crunch of dry leaves, the sweet smell of pine, the quiet creaks and moans of the forest remind me I am home.

Alaric strides beside me. To have him with me after longing for him for so long fills me with the possibility that we will figure this madness out. That we will get answers and that, somehow, we will stay together. But even if we don't, we shared something neither one of us will ever be able to take back. I will savor "us" forever.

"I like having you with me," he whispers as if reading my

63

thoughts. And maybe, after what we shared, he can. Maybe we connected in more ways than just physical.

"Only like?"

"Well, with the possibility that we're meeting someone who may be my mother but who abandoned me as a baby, I'm a bit on edge. I want to keep you safe, but I want to find answers. I'm not sure I'll be able to do both. I did find this though," he says, revealing a four-leaf clover.

"When did you find that?"

He bumps his hip into mine. "While I was hiding your gorgeous body from our unexpected guests."

If one of my past exploits had mentioned my nakedness, I would have been embarrassed. I always split after sex, never staying longer than the time it took to put my clothes on. But with Alaric, it doesn't bother me. Not in the least. We did what we were meant to do. What we've always been meant to do.

"May I?"

He hands it to me. "There's a legend about the four-leaf clover."

"That it brings good luck?"

He laughs. "You are a smartass. Yes, but do you know why?"

The four-leaf clover tingles in my hand. "Is it capable of magic?"

"The luck of it comes from warding off evil faeries."

"So I suppose it's a good sign that you found it. Must mean you aren't evil."

"I guess we'll find out soon enough." He stops, dipping his head toward the horizon.

There in the distance behind a grove of oak trees is a cluster of homes, including Lizzie's parents' house.

"Caer, Maddie, it's time."

I inhale deeply. "Let's do this."

9

KNIGHT OF SWORDS

Scott's fingers twitched with the desire to rip Moralltach from its bindings, have it transform into a sword, and slice Alaric's head off as he watched the bastard walk with his sister up in front of him. It wasn't that bloodshed excited him, but he couldn't forgive what Alaric had done with his sister without protection, even if she couldn't bear children. The bastard took his sister in the forest. He deserved to be punished.

Gigi and Alaric held hands and exchanged knowing glances at one another. Alaric had even given her a four-leaf clover moments ago. He wouldn't fancy himself so lucky when Scott was through with him.

Caer and Maddie walked in silence beside him. They had just gone invisible, so he wasn't entirely sure of their proximity. He sensed Caer's presence, but he couldn't offer her his hand or wrap an arm around her as Alaric did with Gigi. He and Caer were not "there" yet, and with her serious nature, he didn't know if they ever would be.

Gigi giggled at something Alaric said and swatted him on the arm. He'd never seen her so happy and carefree, even with the risk of danger ahead. Truth be told, he was jealous. Scott had dreamt about Caer for weeks, but he was no closer to her than he had been when they first met. A few kisses, some hand holding, but not the obvious bond that Alaric and Gigi shared.

"Hang back," he told his silent companions. "Keep your distance from us, just in case."

He sensed Caer's annoyance. She liked to be in the thick of the action, but in this case, the only action was the flirting of Gigi and Alaric as they entered the oak grove, and nobody else needed to participate in that. It was bad enough that the three of them were forced to witness it.

"Hey, wait up!" Scott called out to Alaric and Gigi. He stepped into the grove just after them, and that's when everything went to shit.

One second, sunlight was shining and the air was still. The next, leaves and pine needles lifted and swirled around them in a tornado of ferocious wind. He couldn't see anything. Not Alaric. Not Gigi. Not even right in front of him. Instinctively he reached for Moralltach, but his leg yanked out from under him as a snare caught his foot, knocking him backward and shooting him up into the air.

The chaos subsided as quickly as it appeared. Leaves and pine needles settled back to the ground, and the grove turned peaceful once more except, of course, for the three of them hanging upside down as caught prey.

"Stay back!" he screamed to Caer and Maddie, not wanting them to fall victim to the trap. He prayed they'd assess the situation first before acting.

An eerie, unnatural silence descended upon and around the grove, falling heavier than oxygen itself.

"I haven't feasted on human flesh for many years. Fifteen to be exact," a woman's voice drawled as she stepped into the now-calm clearing. "Of course, I shouldn't sample you beasties," she said, stroking Gigi's hanging hair, "but who can resist such a godly banquet?"

"Get your hands off of her," Alaric and Scott growled together.

Nancy's face shot to Scott's. "You were always too protective for your own good. I wanted to get rid of you long ago, but it was forbidden. Now, however," she said, appearing before him faster than humanly possible, "with your mum dead, you're fair game. Were you surprised to see her alive when she showed up at the juvenile detention center?"

Scott inhaled, trying to calm himself the way Gallean had shown him. Nancy sought to catch him unawares and use his bewilderment to her advantage. Even her cashmere cardigan, floral blouse, and tan slacks were meant to throw off her victims. All those years as a dedicated Jehovah's Witness follower were meant to hide her trail, but the truth was laid bare before his circle of friends now.

"Who do you think told her where you were? Did you think your mum was keeping an eye on you?" Her evil laughter spoiled even the afternoon sunlight. "No, she was too busy playing Carman's star apprentice to be concerned with your whereabouts."

She dragged a single claw across Scott's cheek. Burning wetness seeped from the wound and trailed down his face at an excruciatingly slow pace before dripping onto the ground.

"She's not her star apprentice now, is she."

"Get away from him," Gigi warned.

Nancy ripped off her cashmere cardigan and flew over to Gigi. Flew as in she sprouted freaking red and black fairy wings. "Or what? What are *you* going to do?"

Now, Gigi placed in his head.

Caer flashed outside the grove, hiding in the shadows. She stared at him with a promise for vengeance.

He shook his head no, mouthing, "Not yet."

With Nancy preoccupied, Scott contorted his body to reach Moralltach. With one powerful movement, he had the dagger in his hand. Now free from its constraints, it instantly shifted into the sword. He sliced the rope above his foot and swung his feet down to land easily. As his feet hit the ground, he lunged at Nancy, wrapping his free arm around her throat and yanking her to the ground. She punched and kicked her way free. Caught unawares, Moralltach dropped out of his hands to the forest floor. After years of being conditioned to her weak church-mom appearance, he'd underestimated her strength, even now equipped with the knowledge that every aspect of her was intended to ensnare.

He lunged at her before she could spring back up, and took her down using a chokehold he'd learned from his Vernal Falls High wrestling days. She swiped at him with her claws, but he dodged them. His cheek still burned from the single scratch of her nail. It was likely laced with something toxic. He pinned her in place, waiting for his circle to join him.

Caer and Maddie charged into the clearing and freed Alaric and Gigi from their constraints. Soon the four surrounded Scott at the four cardinal points with him and Nancy at the center.

"Talk," he growled.

"Never," she said.

"Actually, you just did," Gigi said from her position. "So tell us what we want to know."

"That your mom was a crack whore who deserved to die?"

Scott winced. Pre-goddess Gigi would swipe her sharpened fingernails across the face of anyone who dared to shame her or her birth status along with dropping a string of curse words that would make Satan blush. He had no idea how post-goddess Gigi would react. He watched as she knelt above Nancy's head. Gigi's expression was controlled, and her body movements were slow and methodical.

"You and Kensey use the same lines. Almost as if someone whispered in Kensey's little eight-year-old ear and taught her the nasty lies."

"They're no lies. She betrayed Calliope by birthing you. She deserved everything she got."

Scott applied more pressure to her throat. She spoke too loudly about too many nasty things for his liking.

Hunger for vengeance slammed into Scott's mind. An unquenchable thirst for blood hummed in his veins. He had never desired to harm someone so badly before, but Nancy's throat called for Moralltach's blade.

"My sword. I need my sword," he said to the circle.

No one answered. No one moved to retrieve it for him. Nancy stared at him. Impatience plagued him.

Finally Gigi spoke. "Scott, let Alaric take over."

"No. She deserves death for her crimes."

Nancy continued staring at him, but now with a maniacal grin. What was happening to him? Why did he speak with such loathing and hate? He'd never been filled with such a powerful thirst for vengeance or blood lust.

"She's poisoning your mind. Your thoughts are not you own," Gigi said.

"My sword. I need Moralltach. That will teach her to fear me."

"No, Scott," Gigi said. "Alaric, take over for him."

Alaric bent down and tried to remove Scott's hand from Nancy's wrist, but he refused to budge. Nancy was his.

Gigi chanted and his hand lifted. Alaric's replaced it. Soon Alaric was pinning Nancy down, and Scott was standing dazed between Caer and Gigi with Maddie supporting him from behind.

"Why do I feel hungover?" he moaned.

Without taking her eyes off Lizzie's mom, Gigi said, "Because she was poisoning your mind with a Maleficium spell, just like she did to Lizzie. She was trying to turn you into a murderous monster by corrupting your thoughts so you would turn on us."

Alaric began to wriggle atop Nancy. Claws protruded from his fingers. His back arched and curled as his body shifted into wolf form.

"What's happening to me?" Alaric cried. "I'm losing control."

Nancy targeted Alaric with her maniacal smile. "Hello, son."

Maddie quickly shifted Scott's arm to rest around Caer's shoulders and flew. Yes, flew, because wings sprouted from his back too. He landed where Alaric had been caught by Nancy's trap, retrieved the crystal necklace from the ground, and dashed back to Alaric. As Maddie replaced the necklace around Alaric's neck, he returned to human form and whispered, "Son?"

"So, it is true?" Caer said, returning to the task in front of them rather than processing what had just transpired.

"Carman told me he was stillborn, but I knew better. He was born to me, a full faerie. He'd be immortal too. Strong and powerful."

Alaric softened his hold on Nancy as she lulled him with her words. Then she swiped her nails across his chest. He screamed, falling backward, clutching the wound.

Nancy sprang up. Her wings erupted, flapping behind her, and she rose into the air. Caer charged at her and wrapped her arms around Nancy's legs.

"Caer, no," Scott cried as Nancy swiped her nails across Caer's back. Caer's white wings exploded out, protecting her from Nancy's assault before she could do any damage. Maddie flew up to help bring Nancy back to the ground.

Alaric writhed as toxins coursed through his body. Black ooze seeped out of the claw marks his mother had left on his chest. Gigi eyed him wildly, stunned into stillness.

"Gigi, do something," Scott yelled at her.

She snapped back to the present.

She chanted. Vines wrapped around Nancy. Gigi flung out her arms just as Nancy ripped herself out of Caer's and Maddie's arms. She slammed into a large oak tree at the edge of the grove. Gigi chanted again. Hundreds of vines erupted from the ground and wrapped around Nancy, pinning her against the tree. The evil faerie fought against the vines, but each time she moved, the bindings grew tighter. She screamed in rage.

Scott grabbed Moralltach from the ground and brought the blade to her throat.

"Scott, don't kill her," Alaric rasped, but he should have saved his breath. Scott wasn't going to kill her. He was back in control of himself now.

"The iron and silver will keep her still. Won't they, Nancy —or should I say *Naisha*?"

Red eyes flashed at him. "How dare you use my name."

"But if we know it, we should use it. Isn't that right, Caer?"

Caer appeared beside him, holding Freagarach. "Yes, use of the faerie name holds power over someone. Especially if a faerie *queen* uses it."

Naisha spat at her. "You are no queen of mine."

"That's where you're wrong," she said, lifting her own blade to Naisha's stomach. "We hold all the power over you. Now talk."

MOMMY DEAREST

I always thought Lizzie's mom was a bitch because she didn't approve of Lizzie hanging out with me. Now, calling her a bitch would be kind. She's full-on diabolical.

I chant spells over Alaric's chest, trying to undo whatever harm she did to him, but nothing is working. My hands hover inches above the gash marks, but the black ooze continues to seep from them. He bucks and writhes. His body is trying to rid itself of the toxins. He has no control over himself or the poison coursing through his veins.

"Do something, Gigi. Help me," he screams.

"I'm trying. I'm trying. Nothing is working."

Naisha cackles from her tree prison. I refuse to read her mind for fear she'll try to control me like she did with Scott, but if I can't get this poison out of Alaric, I might not have a choice.

"*Leigheas, leigheas,*" I murmur again and again, flicking my hand and trying to withdraw the poison.

"It's not working, Gigi," Maddie says. "Why isn't your magic working?"

"I don't know," I whisper, my voice hitching. "I don't know."

Alaric's eyes flash red.

"I am not losing you," I shout.

"Maleficium will soon corrupt his mind. He will turn on you or die," Naisha says, followed by another bout of evil laughter. Do villains get a how-to manual with instructions requiring evil laughter?

And then it hits me. "That's what you did to Lizzie. You poisoned her mind."

Panic blinds me. I try to push it away with deep breathing, but it wriggles its nasty head, mocking me. I frown at Naisha. What type of magic can I cast on her that will persuade her to talk?

She smiles. "Your magic won't work on me."

"Gi," Alaric rasps. He licks his lips, not from desire to kiss me but from the need to tell me something without having enough breath and life to do so.

I put my ear to his lips.

"The clover," he exhales, his life-force weakening with every passing second.

The clover? The clover! I dip into my pocket and withdraw the four-leaf clover he gave me. Naisha's eyes widen. Fear appears there.

Working purely on instinct, I run over and press the four-leaf clover into her cheek. "Tell me how to heal him."

She fights to pull away from it, but the bindings are too tight. The clover isn't burning her, but it does do something to her.

"Tell me."

"No," she hisses.

Alaric's back arches off the ground. We're running out of time.

"You will tell me, or I will shove this down your throat."

"No."

"Fine."

I call for vines to sprout around her lips and pry them open. Her eyes widen as I lift the clover above her mouth. She still doesn't answer me. I lower my hand. All I have to do is drop the clover in.

She gargles, trying to speak. Her eyes fall to Scott's blade still at her throat.

"The blade?"

She blinks.

"I'll take that as a yes. If you're wrong, this clover won't be good luck for you."

Caer flies over to Alaric with her sword. Her white swan wings fold into her back as I appear beside him seconds later. His skin and lips have turned gray. Black ooze fills his veins.

"What do you want me to do?" she asks, gripping the hilt with absolute determination.

Listen to your heart, Brigit whispers.

"His heart. Put it in his heart."

Alaric's chest bucks. Caer moves her blade up and down with it, being careful not to accidently stab him.

"His heart? Are you sure?"

No. No, I'm not sure.

"Yes, plunge it in his heart."

"Gi, there is silver and iron in the blades. Either one could kill him," Scott shouts.

I am not going to overthink the possible consequences.

"Do it. Plunge it into his heart."

Alaric's eyes fall to mine. They're no longer flashing red because they're all red. The poison has overtaken him. There's no time left.

"Now, Caer."

She presses her lips as she plunges the tip of her blade into him.

He screams as his body bucks and arches. He falls into a seizure. Black ooze shoots from his mouth in a constant flow of evil. When the Maleficium poison mixes with the clean Western Pennsylvania air, it turns to smoke and evaporates as the sun hits it.

Eventually, the spewing stops and Alaric collapses. I kneel beside him and begin the healing spell I tried earlier.

"*Leigheas, leigheas.*" Over and over I chant, but nothing happens. Not a breath. Not a sign of life. Red eyes or green ones.

"Is he gone?" Maddie whispers.

I pound on Alaric's chest to beat life back into him. I breathe into his mouth to push breath back into him. Nothing is working.

"I told you he'd either die or kill you," Naisha cackles.

"Please, Alaric," I beg him. "Please come back to me."

Inspiration strikes Scott. His thoughts penetrate my mind as he comes to an understanding of what he is capable of.

"Let me," Scott says. "Caer, take my place please."

Caer rests her hand on my back before returning to watch Naisha. That small gesture is enough to undo me. I cannot lose Alaric. Not like this.

Realization dawns on me as Scott arrives at my side.

"He's dead. Scott, I killed him," I whisper as tears stream down my cheeks and land on the cool earth. Clovers sprout from the soil to mock me. My chest heaves in and out as I fill my lungs before trying to breathe life into him again.

Scott kneels beside me. "Let me."

He bends down and breathes into Alaric's mouth. Nothing happens. He tries again. Still nothing happens, and any hope I had disappears. I place my hand on Alaric's chest, clinging to our last moments. On Scott's third try, Alaric's chest rises and falls.

Scott breathes into Alaric's mouth four more times. Each

time more air fills Alaric's chest. As Scott completes his seventh breath, Alaric coughs, his body shuddering with the effort.

Four white doves circle Scott's head as he stands to allow me full access to Alaric.

His rising and falling chest is the most beautiful sight I've ever seen. More tears fall down my cheeks, but these are tears of joy. I clutch Alaric's T-shirt and rest my head against his chest. "You're alive. You're alive."

Oegden can breathe life back into the dead when the love between two people is strong enough, Scott thinks.

It is a beautiful blessing, I drop in his mind.

He pats my back and returns to Naisha and Caer. He may be handy with a sword, but the ability to return life to those deserving it is his greatest gift.

My cheek rests on Alaric's heart. Each time his chest rises and falls, my heart races with excitement. As life returns to him, he places his hand on my back. I push energy into him to further aid his recovery, careful not to give him too much.

"Gigi," he whispers. "Gigi."

I lift my head so I can stare into his eyes—his all-green eyes with gold rims. "What is it?"

He tilts his chin to the side as if he wants to tell me something. I bring my ear to his lips so he doesn't have to work too hard to speak. His hands shoot up and grab the sides of my face. My head hovers just inches above him as I stare into his green eyes.

"What?" I mouth.

"Thank you," he murmurs before pulling my lips to his.

The moment our lips touch, electricity riffles through me. Heat and desire return to my extremities. Life explodes in me, blossoming just below my belly button. Alaric is alive, and he is mine, and I am his.

Overcome with joy, I climb onto him and shove my hands

into his hair to deepen the kiss. He died, and now, he's here with me.

Someone clears his throat, reminding me we aren't alone. That we have an audience of our circle, along with Mommy Dearest as our prisoner. I roll off of him, and he sits up. Thankfully the wounds are gone, either from Scott's breath of life or my healing spell. I help pull him into a standing position. He wraps his arm around me and stalks over to the oak tree where Scott has retaken his position next to Caer guarding Naisha, aka Psycho Mom.

"Scott, thank you," he says.

Scott nods in acknowledgment. "You're welcome, but had I known you two were going to go full-on 'get me some booty,' I would have reconsidered."

"Don't hate, man," Alaric says. "Don't hate."

Scott rolls his eyes. "Oh gods, you're just like Gigi. Lucky for all of us."

"Are we going to question Naisha, or are the three of you going to continue flapping your mouths?" Caer says.

Scott locks eyes on me. *She's a feisty one.*

Hope you can handle her.

So do I.

I rub my hands together, creating some heat. "Let's get started."

Without asking permission, without telling anyone what I had in mind, I grab hold of Naisha's temples and close my eyes.

"*Labhairt gach rud.*"

Normally, when I read someone's thoughts it's whatever they're thinking at that moment, and maybe with some probing or leading questions, I can read more of their mind. This time I figured I'd skip the questions, because she wasn't going to tell us anything anyway. I use my own magic touch along with a spell to reveal everything we need to know.

Naisha's life comes at me in hyper–warp-speed.

As a young faerie, she's fluttering around with friends in a large courtyard outside a castle. There's an instructor who's showing them how to manifest and control their own magic. Keturah and some of the others learn spells with ease, making a feather levitate, a plant grow with vigor, a potion change color. They also learn how to efficiently use their wings. Naisha, unable to master the new skills, falls behind. She grows desperate for a means in which to master her own magic. She studies the grimoires and discovers that when the veil between the realms is thin, she can use a forgotten portal she discovered along the boundary of the kingdom's land.

Another flash a few years later, *Keturah pulls a baby to her chest. "How is my little lovey?" she whispers.*

Naisha sits across from her. "What are you going to do? You won't be able to continue your studies with a child."

Keturah glares at her. "Why not? I am a capable woman who can both mother and learn. Besides, shouldn't you be the one worried about the King's wrath? Midsummer's Eve is fast approaching. You're not going to visit the other realm, are you?"

"He says I'm the one."

"The one?" Keturah frowns. "He just wants to get into your skirts or find a way into this realm."

"I've already told him I won't bring him here. He wants me all the same."

Keturah shakes her head back and forth as she places the baby in the cradle beside her rocking chair.

"It's true, and I'll prove it to you."

"No, you won't. You risk too much going there. You aren't powerful enough to resist the pull."

The baby whimpers.

"Oh, my sweet faerie boy," Keturah says, picking him up and walking inside.

Naisha stands at the open doorway. "Yes, I am, and I will prove it to you."

Another vision forms: *Naisha sneaks into the same cottage. She comes out seconds later with a bundle, her face alight in the Strawberry Moon. The brightness of her eyes from just days before is gone, replaced by fresh gashes across her cheek. The bundle starts screaming.*

"I am capable of stealing a baby right out from under your know-it-all nose," she hisses and disappears into the night.

I pull away gasping. My eyes jump to Maddie who's watching me with the utmost concern before I turn my gaze to Alaric, then Scott, and then Caer.

"What?" Scott says. "Gigi, what is it?"

I shake my head. "I need to keep going."

Naisha narrows her eyes at me. The faint scars of claw marks are nearly invisible on her cheek now unless a person knew they were there. The vines still hold her mouth open, preventing her from yelling or cursing, but she's furious with me for invading her mind. I delve back in.

Another flash, *Naisha's lying on a bed with a sheet covering her bent knees. Sweat pours from her brow. Someone wipes it with a cloth. The back of her head is to me, so I can't tell who it is.*

"Push," someone else instructs. I recognize the voice. I stare through Naisha's eyes, through her bent legs to see . . .

"Carman," I whisper but stay in the vision. There's still so much I need to know.

Naisha screams as she pushes.

"That's it. Good job." The woman who wiped her brow turns to smile at Naisha.

Calliope.

I gasp, wanting to pull out but force myself to remain in the vision.

"Push," Carman insists.

Naisha screams, pushing again. She falls back, panting as cries fill the room.

"A boy," Calliope whispers in reverence as Carman quickly wipes off the baby. Carman chants something and the baby's cries immediately stop.

Naisha stiffens. "What's wrong?"

Calliope wipes a wet towel across Naisha's eyes. She murmurs something, and everything goes black.

I dig farther into Naisha's mind and find a vision of her pregnant again. This time she's with Calliope and my mom. My eyes prick with happiness at the sight of my mother.

"Push, Nancy," my mom whispers. Calliope wipes Naisha's forehead again.

Naisha pushes with all her strength and soon cries fill the room.

"It's a girl," my mom says. She cleans off the baby, and quickly hands her to Naisha.

"Hello, Lizzie," Naisha whispers, kissing the baby's forehead. "I am never going to lose you."

While my mom's back is turned, Calliope hands Naisha a dagger. Naisha pricks the tip of her own finger, then Lizzie's. She presses them together and chants something. Magical energy swirls around them in a blood oath. Lizzie's eyes briefly flash red before returning to normal.

As the vision ends, I glare at Naisha. I clap my hands together for more heat. "Let's finish this."

Naisha kneels in front of a man with a crown sitting on a throne. Beside him sits a striking woman with strong features and eyes just like Caer's. Her belly is swollen with child. The King and Queen.

"Naisha, it has come to our attention that you are visiting other realms without our permission," the King says.

She bows in front of them. "I'm sorry, Your Majesty. I hoped to make new contacts with whom we can trade."

"Lies," the Queen replies with the same intensity of Caer. "You

were searching for Balor. You were seeking to overthrow the Kingdom."

Naisha places a scene in the Queen's mind just like her mentor, Carman, taught her to do.

"No, I would never . . ."

The Queen rests her hand on her stomach. "Lies."

"Enough!" the King roars. "You are upsetting my wife and our unborn child. Do not let me catch you visiting the other realms or you will find yourself without your head."

The visions become blurry and scattered as does my mind. Anger replaces the joy of witnessing Lizzie and Alaric's births. Rage fills me.

"Let go, Gigi," Alaric murmurs in my ear. "Let go. You're losing yourself. Come back to me."

I release the hate and bitterness and embrace the light surrounding Alaric's voice. My eyes blink open, and I find myself staring up at the blue sky. My head is cradled in Alaric's lap.

The world's soft around the edges. I smack my lips together. I am a desert.

"Water. I need water."

Maddie pours some water in my mouth.

The cool moisture sharpens my vision, and my eyes find Alaric's green ones with the golden halos hovering above me.

This is where I belong.

NINE OF WANDS

*C*aer watched Alaric cradle Gigi in his lap. Her eyes slid over to Scott's who stood just a few feet from her, still holding the sword to Naisha's throat. She wondered if one day he would show her the same pure love and tenderness that Gigi and Alaric freely expressed.

Scott grinned at her while four white doves circled his head. They arrived when he had breathed life back into Alaric and hadn't yet left him.

White-feathered birds suited him. She blushed at the thought, realizing the double meaning. Even though her belly felt like birds were flying around in it, she smiled back at him. She was going to try not to be so shy around him, but at times of intimate moments between Alaric and Gigi, it was difficult. And there were a lot of intimate moments. Neither Gigi nor Alaric had appeared embarrassed when she, Scott, and Maddie had caught them together after arriving from the portal. Caer was embarrassed enough for all of them because after staring at Alaric's well-muscled buttocks, she longed to see Scott's.

Get it together, Caer. Focus.

As if reading her mind, Scott nodded, and the white doves flew over to her. Each gently nudged her cheek before circling three times above her head and flying away.

"They like you," he mouthed to her. "I'm jealous."

She dropped her eyes and studied her feet but kept her sword in position.

Alaric and Maddie helped Gigi up. She brushed herself off and strode over to her and Scott. Naisha stiffened. Caer didn't know what Gigi had seen in the visions, but given the number of gasps and names she'd muttered, combined with Scott, Alaric, and Maddie's reactions to them, the visions had provided shocking news.

Gigi's nostrils flared as she breathed in and out. "You've been a very naughty faerie," she said to Naisha. "Some of which was warranted, and some of which was *definitely* not."

Naisha gurgled as if trying to speak.

"Hold on," Gigi said and flicked her wrist. The vines around Naisha's mouth broke apart and fell to the ground.

"I will tear out your throat," she growled.

Gigi rolled her eyes. "One would think, after everything you've been through, you would have learned to choose your words wisely. But then, you weren't a very good student, were you."

Naisha began chanting something.

Gigi threw her hand at Naisha's mouth. "*Ciúnas.*"

Naisha's lips clamped shut.

"You really shouldn't have done that," Gigi chided her. "I wanted you to be able to respond to some of your actions, but you blew it."

"What did you see, Gigi?" Maddie asked.

Gigi's chest rose and fell as if deciding what to share with the circle. "Let's sit, because what I'm about to share affects all of us. Caer, Scott, you can drop your swords. She's not going anywhere."

"Are you sure?" Caer asked.

"I am," Gigi said.

The five of them positioned themselves in a perfectly aligned circle.

"I'm not going to share all the visions. Most of them, especially when she was young, are unimportant. It's her more recent history that bears relevance to us and our situation."

"Just tell us, sis. Enough of the drama," Scott said.

She gave him a mischievous grin. "You do know how I love drama."

He groaned.

"Okay, fine. Who to begin with . . ." she said, tapping her lip with a finger as she glanced around at each of them. "I'm going to start with the Northern point and work my way around the circle."

Her eyes stopped on Maddie. "Maddie, you know how your parents accused you of being a fairy changeling when you went invisible for the first time?"

He leaned forward. "Yes."

"You are. And she," Gigi pointed at Naisha, her voice filled with bitterness, "stole you from your mother who is Fae."

Maddie's mouth dropped open. "And who is my mother?"

"Keturah."

Caer gasped, as did Scott and Alaric. They all knew her. She was Caer's second in command. The fact that her child was stolen from her was a cruel twist of fate.

"Keturah," he repeated.

"And soon, we will introduce you to her."

Tears filled his eyes. "You know her?"

Gigi smiled at him. "We all do."

Alaric and Scott both reached out to grasp Maddie's shoulders in congratulations.

Gigi's eyes shifted to Scott's. "To the East, I share with you that Naisha, Nancy as we knew her, has been spying on us for Carman and Calliope since we were born."

"How?" Scott asked. "We never saw her."

"We did. She watched us from the window next door. She was Gram's judgmental next-door neighbor who we never saw."

Scott's forehead bunched. "But how?"

"She hid behind the curtain or used the window as a scrying glass."

"Gram didn't know?"

"Apparently not, but I guess your mom was keeping tabs on you. She wanted to make sure you were okay."

Scott's jaw feathered with tension. Caer and Maddie reached over to comfort him. Caer sensed confusion in Scott. She'd do anything to ease it.

"Now, to the South," Gigi said.

Caer stiffened. She wasn't sure she wanted to hear how Naisha was involved in her life.

"Naisha was born in your parents' kingdom. She tried to excel in all aspects of her life, from her studies, to magic, to love, but always failed. One day she stumbled upon a forgotten portal—I know where it is. I'll show you sometime and we can block it."

Caer nodded.

"Naisha traveled to different realms. She was secretly meeting with Carman and Clayone, although she planted a false account in your mother's mind that she was searching for Balor."

Caer took a sharp intake of breath. "Did she?"

"Not at the time she was accused by your parents."

Caer sensed there was more. "When?"

Gigi blinked away tears that had pricked her eyes. "She was the one who opened the portal for Balor the day he attacked the Shadow Realm. She's been in constant communication with him. Caer, he knows where you are."

Caer swallowed. She wasn't going to run anymore. There was no point anyway. Balor would find her. She was going to face her demon and kill him. Besides, Gigi hadn't told her anything she didn't already know. It just gave her a deadline, and the person behind the betrayal.

Alaric and Scott squeezed Caer's shoulders. Scott pushed energy into her. It felt like a warm embrace. For now, it would do.

"And finally, Alaric."

He dipped his head to look at her. "Do I want to know?"

Gigi breathed in and out. "I would."

"Fine," he sighed, locking eyes with her. "Tell me."

"Naisha is your mother. She clearly didn't die in childbirth."

Alaric's jaw clenched. "So she abandoned me?"

"No. Carman and Calliope lied to her. She thought you were stillborn."

He frowned. "But faeries are immortal."

"Given that Clayone was the father, she believed the Fae-werewolf combination bore too much power for a baby. She trusted Carman and Calliope. At the time, she had no reason to believe otherwise."

Alaric's gaze fell on Naisha. She watched him from across the grove. "She tried to kill me," he said bitterly.

Gigi leaned forward and rested her hands on his folded knees. "No, she tried to turn you."

He shrugged her away. "Into a monster who would have wanted to kill you."

"Yes, but also into someone who would be on her side. She knows you'd never align with her as long as I'm alive."

His lips turned down. "I'd never align with her even if you weren't."

Naisha winced at the finality of his declaration.

"What about Lizzie?" Scott asked. "Did you find out about her?"

"I did," Gigi sighed. "Naisha is Lizzie's mother too. To avoid losing her daughter, she conducted the same Maleficium blood-binding spell that she just tried on Alaric, but she did it on the day of her birth."

"At birth?" Scott whispered.

"Can my sister be saved?" Alaric asked.

It amazed Caer that he so readily adopted Lizzie into his family.

Tears pricked Gigi's eyes. She shook her head. "I don't think so. Even a sword to her heart won't stop the evil coursing through her."

Alaric stormed over to Naisha. Angry. Hurt. Broken.

"How could you ruin your daughter? What did you wish to gain?"

Gigi stood beside Alaric. She hadn't flown, and she hadn't moved at the speed of Scott. She'd just appeared there. She rested her hand on his back to calm him. "She can't hear you now, and she can't respond."

He turned to her, grasping her hands. "Please, Gigi, let me speak with her."

Gigi glanced at the remaining circle for advice. She was unsure what Alaric's intentions were or what would be gained by allowing him to speak to his mother.

"Please, Gi," he whispered.

"*Nocht.*"

Alaric glared at his mother.

"Hello, son," she drawled. "You're quite the disappointment."

Scott's chest flared beside Caer. "That is unnecessary. You gain nothing by your cruelty."

Her eyes landed on Scott's. "No? I disagree."

Alaric's hands curled at his sides. "Why did you bind evil to your daughter?"

"I didn't want to lose her the way I lost you."

"But you just nearly killed me."

"What is it that teenagers say? 'My bad.'"

Gigi groaned. "You did not just say that. And by the way, I find it ironic that you forbade Lizzie from saying that or even from chewing gum for that matter. Why the Jehovah's Witness front all those years?"

Naisha's eyes pierced Gigi's. "Ever hear of forbidden fruit? It was the best way to ensure that the two of you would become inseparable."

Gigi's jaw twitched as she worked through what Naisha revealed to her. "But something happened, didn't it? Something you didn't intend." She paced back and forth.

"Everything happened according to plan."

Gigi's head whipped toward her. "Did it? You anticipated that Lizzie would buy that eyeball necklace and become possessed by Carman?"

At the mention of the Maleficium witch's name, Naisha fought against the bindings.

Gigi studied her. "So, you didn't know. Did you know that I found a spell book and that she stole it from me?"

Naisha twitched.

"I guess not. Did you know Lizzie intended to release Clayone?"

If looks could kill, Gigi would be dead.

"No? You didn't know anything, did you."

Naisha threw back her head and cackled. Caer

remembered stories from her childhood about evil witches tossing frog legs and diseased fruit into a cauldron. She believed they were cautionary tales, warning children not to venture into dark magic, but now, with Naisha, she could see the truth in those tales.

"Carman is an all-powerful Maleficium witch, but she is only human."

"Meaning you orchestrated everything."

Naisha lifted her eyebrows. Her eyes flashed red. "Maybe."

"No," Gigi shook her head. "I don't believe you."

"You should."

Caer approached the traitor faerie. She sensed that Naisha was working her word magic to cause doubt in Gigi. She pressed her sword into Naisha's throat. Not drawing blood, but close. "Tell her the truth."

"Fine," she choked. "Carman found out about Lizzie. In order to keep her, I promised to be her eyes and ears."

"But she didn't trust you completely?"

Her throat veins danced around the blade point. "No. She possessed my little Lizzie with the eyeball necklace. The spell book was unforeseen."

"Did you know she sent Alaric too?"

Her eyes fell on Alaric. Above all else Naisha wanted him to understand. Caer didn't know why. She had just tried to poison him.

"She kept him veiled from me. I found out afterward, when Calliope came to retrieve Scott. She was so happy to be reunited with him that she confessed everything. That my son was alive, and that she had helped Carman raise him."

Alaric's shoulders stiffened. Caer could picture his inner hackles raising. Hers were.

"How can we reverse Lizzie's spell?" Alaric asked her.

Naisha's eyes flashed red again. "She's mine forever. You can't have her."

Without warning, he ripped Scott's sword away from him and sprinted at Naisha, aiming the blade at her heart.

"Wait!" she screamed.

He slid to a stop in front of her, the point hovering inches above her heart.

"You have ten seconds before I run you through."

Caer's eyes met Scott's. He didn't seem uncomfortable without his weapon. He winked at her. She blushed, her grip loosening on her own sword.

"Tell me," Alaric roared, breaking Caer's attention away from whatever was happening between her and Scott. She shook her head to clear it and repositioned her sword.

"There's a coven of powerful witches in Kilkenny. They may be able to help. They don't follow our ways."

"So, in other words, they aren't Maleficium witches? That's refreshing," Gigi said. "Why should we trust you? How do we know it's not a trap?"

Alaric pushed the point in harder.

"Because they veil themselves to us. I only know about them from Lizzie's spell book."

Gigi's eyes lifted. "Do you have the spell book?"

"I know where it is. I'll give it to you."

"In exchange for what?"

"My freedom."

"And why should we let you go?"

"Because I won't tell anyone what you know. I'll keep my mouth shut."

Gigi looked at Scott and waved him forward. He stopped next to Caer. She could feel his heat radiating off him and longed for his warmth.

"Let's see what this trí cumhacht is capable of."

Scott's arm brushed against Caer's. Tingles skimmed

across her skin. Whatever was happening between them was growing stronger.

"What do you have in mind?" he asked.

I'm thinking some compellation.

Caer's eyes widened. She still hadn't grown used to Gigi's thoughts in her head.

Scott rubbed his hands together. "Well, let's get started."

EXIT STAGE LEFT

*N*aisha had been telling us the truth when she said there was a hidden coven of witches in Kilkenny, or at least she believed there was based on her understanding of the spell book. Not that I've had a lot of experience with compelling people, but with the power of the three of us, I'm ninety-nine percent positive she didn't guide us astray, which means there might be hope for us with Lizzie.

Alaric paces around the grove, his shoulders stiff, his movements tense and jerky. "What should we do with her?"

Mommy Dearest is not the cardigan-wearing strict mother that she appears to be, but a fallen dark faerie capable of committing malicious deeds against her own flesh and blood. The gods only know what she's capable of doing to the rest of humanity.

"I think we should send her back to my kingdom," Caer says. "Let Keturah and the rest of my people decide what to do with her."

Naisha's eyes jump to Caer in alarm. "No. I won't go back. You can't make me."

Caer strolls up to her. "Actually, we can. We can do whatever we want to you."

I smile to myself. If I wasn't in love with Alaric and if she wasn't my brother's chosen, I would have a total crush on Caer.

"Alaric, I'm your mother. I carried you in my womb for all those months. We're family."

Alaric stops, his mouth open in shock. "Family? You don't know what family means. Nan, as cruel and evil as she was to Gigi and Scott, was kind and more motherly to me than you ever could be. She didn't try to kill me."

Maddie and I share a long look. Alaric doesn't know how often Carman spelled him to carry out her revenge. If she acted motherly to Alaric it was only because she wanted to use him. She needed his obedience, and "kindness" was the easiest way to get it.

"She may have used me, but she never tried to kill me."

So maybe he does know what she made him do. He had told me he'd always suspected that he'd done awful things he couldn't remember.

"And Calliope," he glances at Scott, "she may have forsaken her own son for reasons I don't entirely understand, but she cared for me. She made sure all the needs of a growing child were met. A rebellious, difficult one at that. But you . . ." he snarls, "you are pure evil. You deserve punishment. Send her to the Faerie Realm. Let them decide what to do with her."

"No," Naisha shrieks. "No!"

"So, it's decided?" Scott looks at each of us. We nod unanimously.

"Caer, can you open a portal here?"

She whips out her sword. "I don't see why not."

Maddie steps forward, careful to keep a distance from Caer and her swinging blade. "I'd like to go and meet my mother. Keturah was her name?" His eyes slide to mine for reassurance.

"Yes, Maddie."

He lifts his chin confidently. "Do we have time?"

"We do. Alaric and I will go to Kilkenny and find the coven. We'll see if they can undo Naisha's spell on Lizzie."

Scott rubs his hands together. "Let's do this."

Caer lifts her sword, preparing to rip open the portal.

"Wait," Naisha screams. "Wait!"

Caer pauses.

Scott rolls his eyes. "What is it this time?"

"I need to see Lizzie one last time. Think of it as a mother's final wish. Calliope was able to see you one final time before she died."

Scott stomps over to her. "Don't bring my mother into this."

"Please," she cries. "One last time."

All of our eyes meet except for Alaric's. He stares outside the grove, his jaw working overtime. Everyone had received some type of shocking news, but his burdens were the greatest.

Maddie raises his shoulders. "What harm can she do, with all of us around her?"

"Alaric?" I call out to him. When his green eyes meet mine, I whisper, because I know he can hear me with his wolf hearing. "What do you think?"

"I will not be a part of this decision. She means nothing to me," he says with enough venom to take down a pack of wolves. Pun intended.

You don't mean that.

"I do," he growls.

The five of us agree to take her to Lizzie before the other three take her to Caer's realm. I add new bindings and a few spells to dampen her magic and keep her wings to herself.

Caer's blade shoved between her shoulders should also make her behave. Caer does not approve of anyone who betrayed her people. For all my faults, neither do I.

As we head back to the portal, a wave of unease, like I'm forgetting something, falls over me.

Alaric stops beside me. "What is it, Gigi?"

I don't want to voice my concern aloud. Words give power, and Naisha doesn't need any more of it.

There's something I need to get, I drop in all their heads. I've never done that before, but all their heads snap up, indicating they heard me.

"You all go ahead. I'll meet you back in Kildare."

"No, not a chance," Alaric says, gripping my arm so as not to lose me. "I'm going with you."

"No way," Scott shouts.

"Scott, we're not going to have another wham-bam-thank-you-godsdamn. I need to grab something."

My brother's jaw feathers across his cheek. "What is it you need to get?"

Naisha's ears prick with curiosity.

I can't say. Trust me.

Fine. "But no touching my sister, and clothes remain on."

Even with the fate of the world in our hands, my brother is still worried about my virtue. It takes everything in my power not to roll my eyes and zing an energy ball in his chest to knock him flat on his ass.

"Meet you back at Granda's," he says.

"You got it."

I mean it, he think-shouts at my disappearing back.

"I know," I say aloud as I also drop it in his head.

"So, what is it you need to get, or did you really want a wham-bam?" he says, trying to flirt, but there's no life in his voice. Naisha's attack on him along with my revelations about what I saw weigh heavily on him. He carries a giant yoke that even the Hulk would have trouble with.

Something tells me not to say my intentions aloud. That even in the sweet-smelling pine forest surrounding Vernal Falls, we're not without enemies.

"Just trust me."

He stiffens. "You don't trust me enough to tell me because of my heritage?"

Oh, here we go. He's going to try and pull that card from the tarot pack.

"I trust you with my life, and clearly Scott does too or he would not have let you stay with me."

"Then what?"

The trees have ears.

His ears twitch as he glances around. *They do?*

Something is amiss. Stay on alert.

Should we go back with the others?

No, there are actually two things I need.

I have your back. "And your front. And, well, anything else you have in mind."

"Maybe Scott shouldn't have let you stay."

He laughs, and after the anguish he's been through, the sound is like bells—which makes sense since he is part Fae.

"Hey, did your back ever twitch and you found wings sprouted there?"

"Not that I remember, but there are black holes throughout my childhood."

Maybe you're glamoured.

"Maybe."

Now that I've mentioned it to him, he is curious, but he knows he has to wait for the right time to discover his Fae attributes, if he even has any.

We stop at the perimeter of Gram's property. Her sweet

little house sits all by itself surrounded by overgrown gardens that need attention. My fingers twitch, wanting to work in the earth, but there's no time for weeding.

My eyes pool with tears. It's the first time I've been back since Gram passed. She won't be working in her pottery studio or making me my tea blend. She won't be doing anything because she's dead. Sadness gathers in my chest. I was never able to properly mourn her passing, and all the emotions come rushing into me like a tsunami.

Don't you realize that I'm with you always? Gram's voice says.

I jump and look around.

"What is it, Gigi?" Alaric asks, searching for a possible threat.

He's a good one.

I smile at Alaric. "He is."

"Who are you talking to?"

"Gram. She's here with us."

His eyes widen. He swallows hard. "You're talking to a . . . to a ghost?"

Gram laughs in my head as I laugh aloud. "You're the son of the Original Werewolf and an evil faerie, and you're concerned about a harmless ghost?"

"Yes. I can't fight what I can't see."

A sense of knowing falls over me. "You already have. You chose me even when you were tortured and conditioned not to."

"I'd choose you every time. I will always choose us."

Aw, Gram whispers.

"She thinks your adorable." I step up to him and wrap his shirt around my fingers. "And so do I."

My lips find his. Electrical charges surge through me. Kissing him feels so right. I could do it forever.

Except you do have to collect the spell book and the eyeball necklace. By the way, why didn't you tell me about either one?

I break away from Alaric. "Gram, way to spoil the mood."

My eyes fall on the nosy, judgmental neighbor's house. It should be empty now with Naisha in our captivity. If she had the spell book, it could be there.

Is it? I ask.

You know I can't tell you those things.

"Of course not." My eyes shift from the neighbor's house to the woods behind Gram's. "Alaric, it's time to go digging."

"I dig you," he says, trying to pull me back to him.

I laugh and tug him with me. "While I do appreciate cheesy innuendos, we've got to hurry."

A pain pinches the center of my forehead. I rub my hand over it to try and calm it.

"What is it, Gi?"

Your third eye. It senses trouble.

"Something's happening. We need to hurry."

I sprint to the spot beneath the giant oak tree where I hid the eyeball necklace. I try not to think too hard about the fact that if I had embraced my inner goddess months ago, I would have destroyed the eyeball necklace rather than bury it. Something tells me it's somehow linked to Lizzie, and I need to remove all the Maleficium curses connected to her.

I use a stick to dig. The thought of touching the eyeball even by accident makes me nauseous.

Alaric hovers beside me. "I'll dig."

A small pile of dirt gathers on the side of the hole. "No, I don't want you to touch it. I don't want anyone to touch it. Once it's exposed to the air, I'm going to destroy it."

The stick hits something hard. I slowly push the dirt aside to completely expose it. The eyeball winks at me.

I throw up my arm and knock Alaric away. "Get back," I hiss.

We crabwalk away from the hole. When we're far enough away that the necklace shouldn't be able to hear us, I'm still not willing to take any chances.

She saw us, or at least she saw me.

Who did?

Carman. She knows I'm in Vernal Falls.

What does that matter?

I don't know, but it's not going to be good. We need to destroy it.

Alaric searches around him and lifts a giant rock.

I shake my head. *We need something magical.*

He raises his eyebrows.

Yep, I'm going to curse it. Stay here.

No way. I'm coming with you.

I don't want her to know you're here.

He groans inwardly. It reminds me of a purr.

You're sexy when you do that.

He rolls his eyes. *I don't like this.*

You're close. What could possibly go wrong?

Let's not find out.

*S*cott wasn't happy about leaving Gigi alone with Alaric again. Though he trusted Alaric with Gigi's life, he didn't trust him not to sleep with her again. Sure, they were destined for each other in some cyclic reincarnation sort of thing, but that didn't mean that in this life they had to be all over each other like a pair of bunnies in heat. Of course, he wanted Gigi to be happy, he just didn't want her to have sex. And he especially didn't want to *see* her having sex.

His eyes slid over to Caer's as they continued toward Brigit's portal. He wondered if he'd ever get the opportunity to be with her the same way Alaric and Gigi were with each other. Yes, he was a hypocrite. Sue him. He was protective of his sister. In his mind, that made it okay.

Caer saw him looking over at her and blushed. The heat rising up in her cheeks did something to him, and he found it almost impossible to focus on where he was going.

Maddie broke the awkward silence between them. "Uh, Scott, I might be wrong, but shouldn't we have turned right at that pine tree we just passed?"

Scott shook his head. Evidently he did get distracted with

Caer nearby. Caer pursed her lips, trying not to smile. She knew he was thinking about her. Good. She needed to be reminded that, even though he wasn't constantly flirting with her, it didn't mean she wasn't always on his mind. He'd had a lot of girls back at Vernal Falls High who had needed repeated assurances that he cared about them, but the truth was, he never cared about any of them. Not really. It didn't matter how smart, or beautiful, or athletic the girl was, Scott didn't want to date anyone for more than two, three weeks max. After hearing the tale about the swans from Granda, he finally understood why.

"Yeah, let's take a side route."

Caer laughed.

"What?"

"Gigi said men don't like to ask for directions. Now I understand what she's talking about."

He grinned at her. "So, you and Gigi are friends now?"

Her eyes shone brightly in excitement. "Yes, I guess we are. Though I'm not happy that she left to find Naisha without me."

Naisha slowed, her eyes flashing red. She was trying to use their conversation against them. It wouldn't work. Especially since Caer, Scott, and Maddie knew what she was trying to do.

"Hey, Caer, what will happen to her when she gets to the Faerie Realm?" Maddie asked.

"I'm not really sure. In my youth, there were sometimes strange noises coming from the dungeons. Maybe my father imprisoned other fallen faeries?"

"Are they still alive?" Maddie asked. Scott heard both the curiosity and the concern in his voice.

"I don't know. Keturah says Fae are immortal, but I didn't hear any noises from the dungeons when I snuck back into my father's castle."

Scott wanted nothing more than to reach out and touch the long, powerful muscles of her arm, but he couldn't get distracted. Besides, Caer had a tendency to whip out her sword and slice the air around her with very little provocation. If not for her sword pressed between Naisha's shoulder blades, he could be her next innocent victim.

"Caer," he said in a husky voice he didn't recognize, "you need to start thinking of it as *your* castle. You are the Queen."

"You are?" Maddie asked with admiration. "Congratulations."

"Thank you," she said, then laughed at his enthusiasm.

Maddie was very easy to like and trust. Scott was thankful that he had joined their side, especially now that he was the long-lost baby of Keturah, Caer's most trusted guard. He still had a hard time believing that werewolves actually existed, let alone that there were at least three part-Fae werewolves who he knew personally. Gigi was probably still holding out for glitter-farting unicorns to reveal themselves, but every other supernatural being appeared to be based on fact.

"Do you want me to check the dungeons when we get there? So you don't have to?" Maddie asked. Scott could tell Maddie was terrified of the idea of finding dead evil faeries in long-lost dungeons, but he would do it for Caer.

"We don't have to make a decision about the dungeons until all of this is over," she said, indicating Naisha. He knew Caer didn't want to or couldn't imagine a future in which she wasn't fighting Balor, but if Scott had any say in the matter, she'd have a long, successful reign as Queen.

Brigit's portal shimmered as they approached. The goddess sensed her bloodline and presented her portal to them.

Gigi had mentioned that Breas, the Fomorian witch, and some of their minions had tried to lay a trap for Gigi and

Alaric before they leapt through the portal. "Be ready," he warned the others. "We don't want any surprises when we return to Ireland."

Maddie curled his fists together.

Scott glanced at him. "Do you have a blade?"

"I don't need one," he murmured, sounding very threatening.

"No, I guess you don't. All together now."

Naisha darted to the left in a last-ditch effort to get away from them.

"Not so fast," Scott called to her as Maddie quickly had her under his control. "Caer, ready your sword."

She brandished it in front of his eyes as if to prove that no man would tell her what to do.

No, he expected no man would dare to do so.

He readied Moralltach. The blade hummed with the potential promise of blood. His sword had grown hungry for action. It wasn't that Scott relished killing—he definitely didn't—but now he wasn't afraid to take a life if warranted.

"Join together," he called out.

The four of them stepped into the portal and left Vernal Falls a distant memory.

Upon landing back on the grass knoll, Caer swung her sword to warn anyone who was idiotic enough to approach her that they'd be run through.

Caer and Scott had killed many foes in the Land of Shadows, but since their arrival in the Earthly Realm, not even an ounce of enemy blood had soaked their blades. Gigi's protective fire shield around the home of Clarissa, Gallean's counterpart, had kept the god Breas (gods how she hated him) and the Fomorian witch (gods how she wanted to slice off her head and send it to Balor to serve as a warning of what would happen to him) out of Freagarach's reach.

Neither Breas nor the Fomorian witch appeared when they returned from Scott's homeland, and neither did any of their counterparts.

Amorin had warned her that Balor and his Fomorian allies most likely wouldn't be able to penetrate the Earthly Realm again until the lunar eclipse on the Storm Moon, but it didn't hurt to be ready ahead of time. It would be a storm indeed if Caer had anything to say about it.

Could she be Balor's relation? Was that why she could never tell if he wanted to imprison her or kill her? Was she as much an anomaly to him as he was most certainly to her?

A light mist cooled her hot skin. She was naturally always warm, and with Scott so close, she felt herself radiating heat most of the time, especially when she caught him looking at her, which he always seemed to do.

Amorin stood at the perimeter to greet them when they made it back to his dwelling. His eyes widened when they landed upon Naisha. Her clothes didn't bear the mark of a warrior, but Caer never underestimated the enemy. She would be very lucky indeed, however, if they underestimated her.

"Who is this?"

Maddie kept his hands firmly locked on Naisha's arms, which were still bound behind her back. She had already tried to escape once. Caer, Scott, and Maddie weren't taking any chances a second time.

"This is Naisha, aka Nancy, aka Lizzie's mom, aka Alaric's mom, aka Clayone's sometimes concubine," Scott said, prodding Naisha forward with his tip of his blade. "She's an evil fallen faerie from Caer's kingdom, and she's committed unforgivable crimes."

Amorin studied her. The wizard was wise and knew that

no one should pass judgement of someone's appearance. Caer couldn't believe the verbal lashing Amorin had given Gigi when she'd used her blood in the Chalice of Healing to save his life. Gigi, of course, stood her ground. She was formidable. Perhaps not on the battlefield, but with her spell making and the manner in which she used her words, she was terrifying.

"Why did you bring her here?" he asked, halting the four of them from passing over into the boundary of his cottage.

"She wanted to see Lizzie one last time before we exiled her to Caer's kingdom. We thought we'd honor her last request," Scott said, beginning to sound as if he was questioning his own decision making. But they'd all agreed to bring her here, had they not? Caer couldn't really remember. Everything was a bit hazy.

Amorin's jaw set. "No. I cannot allow you to pass."

"Granda, why not?" Scott asked.

"You've all been tricked into bringing her here."

Scott griped Naisha's arm. "What do you mean tricked? We made sure she couldn't spell us the way she had before."

"Are you so sure?"

Clouds blew in front of the sun, blocking it from view. Birdsong grew quiet. The wind picked up leaves and debris and spun them around in tighter and tighter circles.

"What's happening?" Caer asked. She heard fear in her voice that she didn't realize she was harboring.

Naisha cackled.

"What's happening?" Maddie asked, backing away from Amorin's perimeter, his hands still gripping Naisha.

It's a trap! It's a trap! Gigi screamed in Caer's head—or at least she thought it was in her head. It sounded like Gigi's voice carried on the wind echoing all around them. *It's a trap!* Gigi said a third time.

"*Veet!*" Naisha shouted, fighting to break free from

Maddie. *"Veet!"* She pushed away from him, her wings bursting from her back. He tried to maintain his grip, but her flapping wings were too powerful. *"Veet!"* she shouted a third time, lifting into the air.

Two wolves sprinted over. Amorin turned in alarm at the pounding claws.

"No," Scott screamed, leaping forward and flinging his sword toward the larger wolf. He miscalculated the aim, either intentionally or by accident, and the wolf missed a stride as the blade sliced through his shoulder causing him to overshoot Amorin by several feet.

The smaller wolf barreled straight toward Amorin. Her red eyes targeted the wizard's back. She bared her canine teeth and lunged. Caer knew that the wolf was the best friend of Gigi, who was currently doing everything in her power to reverse the evil haunting her friend, so instead of killing the wolf, Caer lunged at her and the two collided in the air and fell to the ground, snarling and clawing at each other.

The small wolf was a worthy opponent. Caer couldn't dispatch her immediately. When she finally subdued her, Caer cast her eyes around for further threats.

"Maddie!" she yelled as she spotted him struggling to hold on to Naisha's legs in midair.

Caer was unsure what to do. She could easily catch Naisha and return her back to the ground, but the wolf was under her submission right now. Unless she knocked her unconscious, she would go after Amorin.

"Go, Caer! Go!" Amorin said, eyeing the wolf. "Return that evil faerie from whence she came."

With that command, she released the wolf and shot into the sky, determined to bring the fallen faerie to justice.

14

A CATASTROPHE

I crabwalk back toward the hole. It normally wouldn't be scary to find a necklace at the bottom of a hole. In fact, under different circumstances I might even be excited to find a piece of jewelry at the bottom of a hole, or in the middle of the street for that matter—if it wasn't watching me. And when the eye blinked, it was definitely watching me. Carman now embodies Maria, but that doesn't mean she hasn't retained control of her magic. She still harnesses the same dark Maleficium power that she's always had access to.

An energy ball should do the trick. I summon one between my hands, then glance over at Alaric.

He nods. *Go ahead.*

I gather it into one hand, then slam it into the hole and crouch away. Light shoots out of the hole, hovering above as if mocking me, before dissipating in an unenthusiastic poof.

I grit my teeth. Fine. Two can play that game.

Be careful, Alaric says.

I pool the energy around me, careful not to utilize too much of my own stores. Gallean taught me that while my energy is powerful, if I use too much of it, I will be depleted in the event that another enemy attacks immediately after, and then I'm a goddess out of luck. When I've gathered a potent fireball, I utter a spell as I slam it into the hole.

Fire explodes out of the hole toward the high oak branches hanging overhead. I watch as my powerful spell rebounds off the evil object, scourging the steadfast oak leaves and the underside of the branches. I murmur a quieting spell as heat from the fire burns my stomach. I suddenly realize in horror that the edge of my shirt's on fire. Swatting at it will cause me to burn my tender belly skin. In a panic I rack my brain for a water spell. The fire keeps growing stronger. Alaric leaps over, fists my shirt into a ball so the fire won't touch me, and cradles me to his chest. We roll several times before he stops to check that the flames are out. Bits of singed clothing fall away from me as the stench of burnt fabric works its way into my nose. I gag on the smell.

"Are you okay?" Alaric whispers, examining the skin beneath the gaping hole in my shirt. He gently prods the area to ensure there aren't any burns.

"I am now. Thanks for saving me. I don't know what happened."

He purses his lips. "I do. That eyeball necklace was created in the fiery cauldrons of Maleficium magic."

"How do we destroy it?"

"I need to get into Nan's cottage. One of her spell books might have an antidote or at least a counter curse."

"No way. It's too dangerous."

He rolls his eyes. "You're talking to me about dangerous actions?"

I start crawling back to the hole as smoke spirals out of it. "Let me see if we did any damage."

His hand wraps around my ankle and he pulls me back. "No. You don't know what that smoke is capable of."

I frown at him. "Did you practice with Nan and Calliope?"

"No, they kept it hidden from me, but I am very observant. I used to sneak out and watch, so when I tell you that smoke can be malevolent, you better believe me."

A vision of a young Alaric with shiny green eyes sneaking out in the middle of the night to watch his nan and Calliope perform evil magic makes me both sad and proud that he was as curious as I was and managed for the most part to stay out of trouble.

"I told you that they protected me and kept me safe."

"You did. It's just hard to imagine them as caring, loving mother figures given how determined they were to rid the world of me."

"I *am* very adorable," he says, pushing his head into my chest playfully.

I rub the top of his head. "Yes, you are."

He lifts his head and pulls me onto his lap as we watch the last remnants of smoke disappear. "Now, how do we carry it without letting it invade our minds?"

"Let me just check it. Maybe I managed to destroy it."

I try to break away from him, but he keeps a firm grip on me. "No, let me."

"Alaric, I don't want her to see you."

"What difference does it make? If my dad, sister, and mom couldn't turn me against you, Carman certainly can't. Besides, what if I can bring her to our side? She'd make an impressive ally, especially against that Fomorian witch."

He makes a valid point. Trouble is, Carman's had a vendetta against me for fifteen hundred years and is the cause of every single problem we're experiencing now. Case in point, she almost burned me to a crisp with a freaking eyeball necklace.

"You never know," he says.

"No, I guess you don't, but let me peek over the edge. I *am* a reincarnated goddess—I've got to have a bit more magic than the sexy son of the Original Werewolf and an evil faerie."

"I'm staying close."

"Fine."

We both crawl on our bellies to the edge of the hole. If anyone happened upon us, they'd scratch their heads and think we'd lost our minds. And maybe we have, or at least I have.

I slowly peek over the edge, and there, blinking back at me, is that freaking eyeball necklace.

"Dún," I whisper, and the eyelid slides over the eyeball and remains closed.

"*Ardaíonn.*" The necklace lifts into the air.

"*Cásáil.*" Fresh green oak leaves shoot from every direction and encase the eyeball necklace. When it's completely covered with layers of leaves, I reach out and grab it.

"Be careful," Alaric murmurs.

"I always am," I reply.

"Remember, I watched you for weeks without your knowledge. You are anything but careful."

"Well, I do like some excitement, but the necklace is completely encased with green magic. Think of it like magical armor. No eyeball-peeking witches are going to spy on us."

I slip the bundle into my pocket and turn to him. "Now, we've got one more thing to get."

"Can you say?"

"I'd rather not."

I do like listening to your voice inside my head.
I like yours inside of mine too.

All those months ago when I showed Lizzie the spell book in my room, I unknowingly must have triggered her part-werewolf, part-Fae nature, or at least awakened it. I don't care what Lizzie or Naisha says, or anyone else for that matter. All the years of friendship Lizzie and I shared were not a lie. I was the one who lied, cheated, and stole. Not Lizzie. My jaw tightens. Not Lizzie.

The spell book disappeared the day Lizzie was up in the school attic when I caught her trying to . . . exorcise, possess, curse—I'm not really sure what—Kensey. The candles blew out and then Kensey was gone along with the spell book. Kensey was obviously taken by Breas, so I had assumed he took the spell book too, but Naisha said she knew where it was, so it stands to reason that Lizzie had still been in possession of it.

"Where are we headed?" Alaric asks.

Next door.

As we approach the boundary of Gram's property, tears prick my eyes. I'd love more than anything to watch her finish a new creation, carefully remove it from the wheel, cradle it with the utmost care as she carried it over to the drying rack. She'd wipe her hands with a wet clay-stained rag and toss it over the back of the chair, where it would land perfectly in half. Then she'd turn to me and say, "Would you like a spot of tea?" and we'd sit in her bright yellow kitchen at the oak table, the one I knew every knot and age line of, and we'd drink tea and talk about the day. She'd listen to me complain about Kensey and whatever method of torture she'd exacted on me that day, and when I finished my tale and my cup, she'd pour me more tea, and she'd right every wrong in my world.

I stop and stare at the place I called home for sixteen years.

"Do you want to go inside?"

Yes. More than anything.

"We don't have time. I'll be too distracted."

"I'll keep you focused," he murmurs low and needy.

"I'll bet."

We wander along the boundary. I'm careful to maintain a distance from Gram's property. If Boo Bear or any of the other pets get wind of me, they'll come running, and then I definitely won't want to leave. I pause. Unless Darius brought them over to his place. It would make sense. Granda and Dad probably made it clear to him that we were leaving for good. Maybe even along the lines of, "The Goddess is returning home."

But as I stare at the red back door and the brightly colored railings and even the gardens that seem to bend in my direction, I realize I am home.

"Well, hello there," Alaric says.

I whirl around, wondering who snuck up on us without my knowing or without Alaric warning me. There in his arms is a big, fat calico.

"Sphinx!" I cry out and reach for my cat. My *blind* cat, who's *studying* me as if he's assessing my appearance.

He pushes his head into Alaric's hand and blinks at me, seeming to say, "I'm mad at you."

Or maybe he did say it because the words ring out in my head.

Finally.

"You can talk? And see?"

He turns his head to Alaric. *Can you believe this girl?*

"Apparently, yes," Alaric says.

"Why couldn't I hear you before?"

Sphinx's eyes blink at me. *You were spelled to hide your magic.*

"Right."

A lot of good it did. Look at the mess you're in.

"How much do you know?"

Enough.

"Are you my familiar?"

We prefer the term "partner in catastrophe."

"Of course, you do."

Glad you finally met Alaric. Took you long enough.

"You know him?"

Alaric hands Sphinx to me. Sphinx licks his cheek, then leaps into my arms. *Someone's been hitting the treat box.*

Don't judge. I was stress eating.

"Your cat and I met the night I brought you home from Radley Pond, after that godly prick almost killed you on his bike and then left you for dead when you pulled your pepper spray on him."

Anger sweeps through me at the memory. "I wish I'd sprayed him."

"I wish I'd killed him, but I'll soon get the chance." He exposes his canines as he snarls.

"You're scary when you're angry. Is that your inner wolf appearing or the faerie?"

The canines disappear as he returns to himself. "Does it matter?"

"Well, one did kill me."

"You do have a point. I don't know."

We both turn our attention back to my partner in catastrophe. "Sphinx?"

He yawns, stating loud and clear, *I'm bored with this conversation.*

"But I don't understand. How did you meet?"

"Did you ever wonder how you wound up in your own bed in a house protected against werewolves and other evildoers?"

"I do now."

He scratches Sphinx's head. "Our friend invited me in."

"So, werewolves are like vampires? Once they're invited in, they can come and go?"

Alaric and Sphinx exchange glances then laugh. I never realized Sphinx had such a sense of humor.

I dropped the shield to allow him to deposit you in your bed.

"You can do that?"

He puffs his chest. *I am very powerful.*

"Apparently. Is Boo Bear also a partner in catastrophe?"

Don't be dull. He is a flea-bitten blind dog always searching for the next meal.

"That's harsh," I scold him.

Harsh but true.

"Where is he?" I monitor the yard for my favorite dog.

At Darius's house.

"Why didn't you go?"

I do not need human interaction.

"Oh yeah?" I challenge him as Alaric scratches his back while I rub his arms. A loud purr fills the air.

Well, perhaps the two of you would be acceptable.

"Do you know where we're headed?"

He growls. *You reek of intention.*

"Are you going to lead the way, or shall I carry you in the manner fit for one of your status?"

Your sarcasm is noted, but since you asked, I'll allow you to continue holding me.

"How kind of you."

And with that, Alaric and I, along with Sphinx, continue walking to the judgy next-door neighbor's house to see if the spell book is there.

15

A CASE OF MISDIRECTION

e now had a partner in catastrophe. The difficult, selfish cat who'd always acted like he couldn't see or hear me, is all of a sudden the not-so-awkward, in fact, way-too-comfortable third wheel in our relationship.

"Sphinx, before we enter the house, do I need to perform a searching spell to make sure no one's inside and check for booby traps?"

Sphinx yawns again and blinks up at me like, "Why are you bothering me with this question? I'm just getting comfortable."

"Fine. Alaric, would you mind holding Sphinx while I ensure we don't get maimed or injured when we go in?"

He reaches out and cradles Sphinx to his chest. "Sure."

Sphinx purrs into Alaric's chest. I am not the least bit jealous. Honestly, I'm not.

"I thought dogs didn't like cats and vice versa."

"You are a piece of work."

"Thank you. Now, give me a few seconds."

I conjure a searching spell and cast it toward the house.

The spell erupts in flames the second it hits an invisible boundary. That didn't work.

This time I gather energy from the surrounding area before pushing it out. The boundary shield grows hazy when my energy encompasses it. Then suddenly—*poof!* The shield shatters to the ground.

"That was easy."

I send out another searching spell, and this time it passes through the boundary, enters the house, and after a minute or two, returns to me.

"All clear."

Alaric watches the house, deeply inhaling as if he's doing his own intensive search through smell. Maleficium is a much different type of magic. It stands to reason it smells different. "Is what you're looking for inside?"

"We will soon find out."

Sphinx leaps down from Alaric's arms and curls up in a ball on the ground. *I'll wait here.*

"Don't overexert yourself."

I won't, he purrs and immediately falls asleep.

"Guess we're on our own."

Alaric rests his hand on my lower back. His fingers find a bare patch of skin. "I'm fine with that."

I still can't get over that Alaric is actually here with me. Half the time I want to throw myself at him and smother him with kisses. Half the time I want to gawk at him and his powerful body and treasure the fact that he's mine—and then jump his bones. Then there's that tiny sliver of reality that keeps reminding me there's a task at hand that must be completed.

I sigh as I lead him through the back gate and into the fenced backyard. Every few boards there's an inch-wide gap —just enough space for a person to peek through it. I creep over and look into my own backyard.

The bonfire area is well hidden on the other side of the garden shed. Even prying eyes wouldn't have been able to witness any magic that was conducted there through the years. But Gram's bench is clearly visible. The spot where she and I sat for hours talking about . . . well, everything. No wonder I always had the strangest feeling I was being watched—I was.

"Gi," Alaric says, "we need to get moving. We promised Scott and the rest of them we'd be back as soon as possible."

I swallow. "I know. Let's go."

The back door's unlocked. We enter into a kitchen filled with endless cabinets.

"Should we split up to search?"

He pulls my hand into his. "Not a chance. We'll move slowly and methodically. Now, what should I smell for?"

I grapple with whether I should tell him or not. It's not that I don't trust him. I don't want *anyone* to know. But his nose might be able to find it faster than my magic, which seems to be blocked inside the house.

A really old spell book. It'll probably be protected with Maleficium.

He squeezes three quick times. "Got it. I need to go to the center of the house."

He guides me through the kitchen doorway and into the living room. Sheer curtains hang from a rod covering the giant picture window. I creep over to the side of the window and hide behind the heavy decorative curtains. I peek outside to see the front yard where my mother gave birth to me one snowy winter night. How did Naisha feel when my mother fell to the ground in the midst of a contraction? Did she want to run out and help her the same way my mother had assisted her during her delivery of Lizzie, or did she watch from her post and immediately report the news of my birth to Carman? Naisha tried to claim she was in charge, but I

117

know better. Carman doesn't share. Even Naisha's relationship with Clayone was probably orchestrated by her.

From my position, I study the picket fence surrounding the front of Gram's property. I can clearly see the sidewalk, the front porch, and the yard. When Naisha was here, she was always watching me.

"Okay," Alaric says, lifting his nose. His nostrils flare in and out as he inhales deeply, sniffing for an object we're not even sure is here.

After what seems like an eternity, I break the silence. "Well?"

He shakes his head. "I don't smell anything."

"Are you sure?"

"Even if there was a trace of Maleficium on it, I would smell it."

"Your nose is that good? Or maybe we need to go upstairs?"

No, trust me. It's not here.

"Okay," I whisper as he pulls me back toward the kitchen door. I take one last look at the picture window in the living room before he closes the door behind us. I can't believe all this time Naisha was watching us. I shiver, feeling so invaded.

"I've got you, Gi," he says, rubbing his hands up and down my arms. "I got you."

Sphinx lifts his head. *I told you not to bother.*

"Actually, you didn't."

That's why I took a nap.

"Where to next?" Alaric asks.

"Follow me."

"With pleasure. I love a take-charge kind of woman."

I lead him along the greenway to Lizzie's development.

. . .

Apparently, Lizzie and Naisha shared many secrets. It would stand to reason that they hid their secrets where they felt safest, where they spent the most time, where they could cast Maleficium spells to keep away even the most persistent of friends. All those times I tried to speak with Lizzie's parents after she "died," they never came to the door, even when their car was in the driveway and the front window had a candle lit as a welcome sign for unexpected guests. But I was never welcome there. And now I know the reason.

"Her dad might be there," I whisper, as if even the air around their backyard could be spelled.

They have the same style fence as the house next to Gram's, but instead of a peephole between every few boards, it's sealed shut. Familiar with the protective spells Naisha added to the other house, I conjure one powerful spell to knock out the barriers. I fling it at the house with sick fascination, hoping that maybe the boring cream vinyl siding will melt away and reveal the twisted frame that once housed incredible malicious intent.

My spell encompasses the entire shield again and crushes it. I smile at the power of it. Maleficium might be capable of unfathomable levels of evil, but green magic will destroy its counter-magic with vigor.

I flick a searchlight ball at the house to make sure Lizzie's dad isn't home. I wonder if he knew who his wife really was, or who his daughter's real father was. He always seemed dull, but maybe that's why Naisha chose him. He made an excellent cover parent, especially since Lizzie's birth father was locked away for all time (or at least until I screwed it up).

"All clear," I whisper and reach for the latch on the gate.

"Wait," he says, throwing out his arm to block me. He sniffs the air. *Someone is there.*

But my spell didn't find anything.

Are you going to believe me or your spell?

What should we do?

Sphinx's ears perk up. He crouches down in front of the gate. *I am a majestic beast.*

"Oh brother," I groan aloud as Sphinx launches himself through the air.

Cat screams erupt from the other side. Absolute chaos breaks out. Sphinx may be my partner in catastrophe, but he sounds like he needs my help. I quickly reach for the latch.

Alaric stops me. *Wait.*

Sphinx needs us.

He shakes his head, his ear tilted toward the fence. "Okay, now."

I leap into the yard with my palms ready to throw a quick protective shield up or shoot vines out of the ground, but my magic isn't needed. Sphinx has a black cat pinned to the ground. The other cat tries to move but the effort isn't very convincing. Sphinx hisses, baring his teeth, and the black cat gives up.

"What's going on here?"

Restrain him please.

"Sure."

Vines quickly spiral up and wrap themselves around the black cat's body. The cat screams like it's being mauled to death, but Sphinx has already climbed off of him and is busy licking his paws.

"Why did you attack this cat? It seems pretty harmless."

He's harmless now, but he's no ordinary cat. He's the evil faerie's familiar.

"I thought the politically correct term was 'partner in catastrophe.'"

That is reserved for those who align themselves with good. Those who choose to align with evil are familiars.

"And who is this?"

This, Sphinx says and flicks his paws at the black cat, *is Greg, Lizzie's dad, or at least he pretended to be.*

"Greg?"

I can't believe my eyes as the black cat morphs into Lizzie's dad. Naked. There are sights for sore eyes, and there are sights that make eyes sore. I don't know if mine will ever recover.

Did you ever wonder why you never really saw her dad anywhere? It was always her mom.

Lizzie's funeral flashes before my eyes. Me, an inconsolable mess when I finally gathered the nerve to enter the funeral home and say goodbye to my best friend one last time. I remember latching on to the anger because my classmates were acting like they were the ones who had lost their best friend. But they hadn't. I had. I blamed myself for killing Lizzie, no matter what Dad, or Gram, or Scott said. If it wasn't for Dad manhandling me, I would have slashed out at my classmates, slicing faces and poking out eyes to try and relieve some of the emotion swirling around inside me. I remember seeing Nancy watching me. Her eyes flashed red when she whispered to Greg before she stormed over to us. What did she say?

I'd been far too self-absorbed to notice her red eyes or what she'd said to who I thought was Lizzie's dad. All I wanted to do was tell them how much their daughter meant to me. How much she meant to me still. The girl who'd given me the gift of friendship when no one else had. She was my person. When she died, the best parts of me died too.

My eyes kept skimming over the casket. I was relieved it was closed, but then I also wanted to see her one last time. Nancy had marched up to my dad and asked him what I was doing there. My dad defended me, telling her I had nothing to do with her death.

She accused him of being a devil worshipper—oh, the

irony. She said when they had left the coven all those years ago, they should have moved far away. Also lies.

When she said, *"That thing* killed her," I thought someone was finally talking sense, but when she started pushing my dad, he had to release me in order to stop her. She'd screamed, "You and this heathen had everything to do with it!"

Every eye had been on me standing there awkward and sad, not really sure what to do. They missed it when she turned and glared at my dad with red eyes. They missed her lifting her hands and running at him. They missed her hitting his chest so hard that he stumbled back into the casket. And then the casket had smashed to the tile floor. A thunderclap shattered the shocked silence as the cover fell open. She'd wanted us to see that the casket was empty.

Then she put on a show by crashing to her knees and wailing, "Noooo," over and over again.

The only thing Lizzie's dad did was walk over and ask Dad to leave.

My dad offered Greg his hand, horrified by what had occurred. He was trying to salvage some semblance of dignity. Her dad stared at my dad's open hand. I assumed that he was ignoring him, but now, I wonder if he couldn't. My dad was a powerful witch. He would have noticed that something was off with Greg if they'd touched.

"Gi," Alaric says, "what does this mean?"

"It means that lies have abounded in every aspect of my life. But at the funeral, I'm almost positive Naisha had wanted me to know that Lizzie wasn't in the casket. Why would she risk it?"

"Why did she do any of the things she did? She's pure evil."

"But then why did she offer to give me the thing we're

looking for? She had to know we'd go searching for it and discover that her husband, 'Greg,' was a black cat."

Sphinx grimaces at the human's naked frame. He raises his paw, and Greg morphs back into a cat.

"What are we missing?"

"Let's go see," Alaric says and pulls me to the door. "Wait right here. Don't move."

For once, I do what he asks me. He lifts his nose and smells the air. Finally, his green eyes find mine. "There's not a trace of Maleficium here either, now that the shields are gone and Greg's been exposed."

"In more ways than one."

He winces, reminding me of Sphinx's reaction to Greg's body.

"There's one more place we could look."

"Third time's the charm."

"I certainly hope so."

The day I realized that Lizzie had stolen the spell book was after I went to school with a neck full of hickeys from the biggest mistake of my existence, both godly and otherwise. The rumors about my hickeys and where I had gotten them almost put me over the edge I already skirted on, but my protective nature flared, and all I wanted to do was find Lizzie. I remember cutting through the greenway to get to her development after leaving Gram's, but instead of turning toward her house, I followed the path to the abandoned Smith farm. The very one where Scott had once fallen down the well and little old me had found him without ever having been to the property before. I refused to accept that I was a reincarnated goddess, even after Gram and Dad made it exceptionally clear I was magical. I was and am a stubborn asshole.

Alaric follows along beside me with Sphinx in his arms. He's even more sexy cradling my cat. I lick my lips as I meet Alaric's gold-rimmed green eyes. He gives me a seductive smile as if he can read my mind. Maybe he can.

"Sometimes your thoughts are very loud."

"You heard me call you sexy?"

"I did. And I think you're sexy in your black leather jacket, tight black jeans, and beat-up Docs, searching for what will remain unnamed."

I snort. "Finally, someone gets me."

"Oh, I got you, and I will get you again many times."

I laugh at his innuendo. He makes this effed-up situation tolerable.

As we approach the barn, I remember hearing Lizzie crying inside. She had hidden herself in a corner. And she was scared. Definitely scared. If she had been already evil, she wouldn't have been scared. She had no idea what was happening to her, and she wanted me—no, she needed me to help her. I remember reaching out to touch her hand, thinking, *she falls. I fall.*

But she hasn't fallen out of reach yet, has she? There's still hope we can retrieve her and turn her back to our side. I just need to find the spell book and destroy that along with the eyeball necklace. The sooner the better. I break away from Alaric and hurry into the barn.

"Gigi, wait! We need to check—"

But it's too late. As soon as he steps in after me, the ground rumbles and breaks apart.

"Gi," he shouts, leaping over to me. He clutches me to his chest along with Sphinx. Sphinx's eyes widen in alarm, which scares me. Sphinx seems to know everything that's going on, but he certainly didn't foresee this.

The floor falls away around us. Boards crash toward us and the roof goes up in flames. We are going to die in here.

We are going to burn to death. All because of my impulsiveness. I should have known better. I *do* know better. The spell book is not here. It was never here.

"It's a trap! It's a trap!" I scream, but it's not for Alaric to hear. Of course, he knows it's a trap. It's for Scott and the others. "It's a trap!" I shout a third time, knowing there is awesome power in threes.

"Hold on!" I shout as I envision a portal. The Maleficium magic combats it, pushing the edges back down. I concentrate on Granda's cottage. My portal keeps fighting the Maleficium. Maleficium magic is strong, but my magic is stronger. Finally a bright, shimmery light emerges.

"Jump!"

And we do.

She falls. I fall.

16

SEVEN OF SWORDS

*C*aer flew toward Naisha and Maddie. Maddie clutched Naisha's legs. No matter how hard she kicked at his face or how powerfully she jerked her body, he held on. Naisha flew higher and higher, as if trying to reach what lay beyond the clouds. The air grew noticeably thinner. Their breathing became labored. Caer assumed that was exactly what Naisha was trying to achieve. The only way Maddie would let go was if he passed out.

Caer glanced down at the earth. Scott and Amorin's figures grew smaller and smaller the higher they flew. Caer had to make a decision. She could save loyal Maddie and most likely lose Naisha, overpower Naisha and risk losing Maddie, or wrap them both in her wings, tear open a portal to the Faerie Realm, and force Naisha to face judgement from those she had betrayed. It would mean leaving Scott, but it wouldn't be forever. She'd be back before the Storm Moon. She'd be back to fulfill her destiny. In the end, it was her only choice.

"Maddie, don't let go," she yelled to her new friend.

"I . . . I . . . won't but it's getting c-c-cold. I c-c-can't breathe."

He was fading fast. She had to hurry.

"Hold on," she said as her wings burst from her back. She didn't need them to fly, but she'd cocoon them all within them.

Once she had a hold of them, she focused her emotion on opening a portal. Her sword usually aided her in portal making, but now her hands were otherwise occupied. Intense emotion was an old friend, however, and had aided her portal making in the past. It would guide her now.

The air around them shimmered. The portal was locking into position below them.

"No," Naisha screamed, her body stiffening. "No!"

Naisha should be terrified, especially after what she had done. Keturah was a force to be reckoned with.

"Oh, yes," Caer said, adopting one of Gigi's lines, and they plummeted back toward the earth before disappearing into the portal.

They continued spiraling and spiraling toward the ground. Something wasn't right. They shouldn't still be falling.

"What's hap . . . pening? We . . . aren't . . . slowing down," Maddie yelled, most of his words getting lost.

Caer realized the problem as the wind tore at her hair and eyes. They'd entered the portal in a freefall. It felt like her skin was getting ripped off. She'd have to use her wings to slow them down, but to do that she'd have to release Naisha and Maddie because if she continued to hold them, the abrupt change in direction with their added weight could damage her wings.

"Maddie, don't let her go," Caer instructed him.

"I won't," he said through gritted teeth.

She released Naisha and Maddie and flapped her powerful white wings. The air whooshed beneath her wings, and she soon gained control of her flight. She hovered in the sky to get her bearings before folding her wings behind her and diving toward Naisha and Maddie. Naisha was trying to use her own wings, but they were plummeting too fast. Her wings were neither as large nor anywhere near as powerful as Caer's. Caer easily caught up to them and wrapped her arms around them. She held Naisha with everything she had, preparing for the jolt that came as she expanded her wings and caught the air once more. Maddie wouldn't let go. He was the son of Keturah. Powerful. Strong minded. His own force to be reckoned with.

When she mastered control of their fall, she flapped her wings and carried her cargo to her father's castle. *Her* castle, as Scott had reminded her.

Scott. He'd worry about her. He'd been so engaged in fighting the two werewolves that he hadn't see them disappear into the portal. She'd return to the Earthly Realm soon. After all, she had a monster to kill.

The last thing Scott remembered was Naisha saying *"Veet!"* three times, and then the hellhounds had broken loose. Well, the werewolves. Now he was so caught up with restraining Ryan without killing him that he'd lost track of Caer, Maddie, and Naisha.

"Where are they?" he called over to Granda as he maintained a choke hold on Ryan, who had just now reverted back to his human form. It wasn't a full moon. There was no reason of this world that would have caused him to shift. It must have been the word Naisha had said. She'd triggered the werewolf curse and somehow released them from their cells.

When Granda didn't answer, Scott spun himself over

Ryan to make sure his last living, breathing human relative was still living and breathing. Granda was chanting over Lizzie, who had also turned back into a person. Her eyelids were pulsing as if she were entering into REM sleep, but Scott knew that whatever spell Granda was casting on her was the cause. Granda couldn't break his train of thought or chaos would ensue.

Scott was torn between placing all his attention on Ryan or searching the skies for Caer, but one needed him and the other could take care of herself. She was a warrior. A sexy, powerful warrior who would sooner split open someone's skull than shake their hand.

"Ryan," he whispered, careful to keep his voice slow and lulling. Scott possessed magic too, but it was not a skill he'd spent much time with. He could masterfully break a table in half or chop an opponent's head off—he and Caer were alike in that way—but he'd had little experience with the kind of magic Gigi wielded. He was, however, a master of compellation.

Ryan's eyes flashed open. His pupils were the size of saucers.

"Come back to me, Ryan. Come back to your best friend."

The black began to shrink, exposing his green eyes, which were all the more striking against his dark skin. They captured the attention of every girl who laid eyes on him, including the one currently being spelled by his grandfather. Scott knew there were many guys who would have happily fallen under Ryan's eye spell too, if he hadn't been in love with Lizzie, and if he was so inclined.

"There you are," he whispered. "I've missed you."

Ryan's eyes widened in recognition.

Scott didn't want Breas or Clayone or even Lizzie to try possessing his best friend again. Scott would keep talking to keep any evildoers out of Ryan's head. "When Gigi mentioned—"

Ryan jerked at the name, and Scott changed direction.

"When I heard you were alive, I couldn't believe it. I was so happy. We've been through so much together. All the classes, the football practices, the games . . . all the touchdowns. All the girls."

Ryan's eyes lasered in on him.

"There were a lot of them, weren't there. But neither one of us ever fell for one for a long time."

Ryan's gaze fell on Lizzie lying on the ground not far from him.

"Lizzie fit, didn't she. She crushed on you from the moment you set foot in school. You befriended someone, and she introduced you to Lizzie. Do you remember?"

Ryan blinked.

"It was Gigi. She accepted you into her inner circle the moment she met you. She's the one who introduced you to me and Lizzie. Gigi's my sister. I love her very much and will do everything in my power to protect her. You can understand that, can't you? Loving someone so much you will do anything for them?"

Ryan's eyes fell back on Lizzie.

"We're trying to help her too. To bring her back to the light. You like it in the light, don't you?"

Ryan blinked in agreement.

"You were always a good person. You always protected people. You always defended Gigi."

Ryan stiffened again at the name but soon released the tension.

"I'll help you. We don't need to put you back in the cell if you don't fight. You're not going to fight, are you?"

Suddenly Gigi appeared before them. He didn't know where she'd come from, and though he was relieved to see her, he was terrified that she would unknowingly undo all the work he'd just done with Ryan—the trust he was beginning to elicit and his good nature.

Gigi got down on the ground beside them. She touched Ryan's forehead and lightly ran her hand down the side of his cheek. "He's not going to fight against us, are you, Ryan."

His eyes twitched, and the remaining film of darkness disappeared.

"Hi," she said, bending her head in front of his face.

"Hi," he whispered, tears now in his eyes. "I'm so sorry."

"You don't have anything to be sorry for."

His lips pursed as he tried to argue, but he was powerless against Gigi.

"Have you forgotten that I'm the boss? I'm pretty sure I pointed that out with a black dagger-like fingernail to your elbow in Principal Donahue's office on your first day of school."

Ryan's eyes twinkled with amusement. "Yes, you did."

She stood up from the ground and brushed her knees off. "We can let him up. He's not going anywhere, are you, Ryan?"

"No, I promise."

Scott glanced at her. *Are you sure?*

A hundred and fifty million percent.

He trusted his sister but . . .

Now would be nice.

He climbed off of Ryan and stood up. Alaric appeared beside Gigi. His brow was spotted with sweat, and his clothing was ripped and dirty. Scott took in Gigi's appearance. Her clothes were shredded and charred, and the parts that weren't, were covered with dirt, straw, and building debris, almost if a building had collapsed on them.

A building did collapse on us.

"What?" he said, and Ryan jumped back from him.

Idiot, chill. We'll talk later. Focus on Ryan.

"Sorry, man," Scott said, putting out his hand for Ryan to shake.

Back at home, the two shook hands whenever they met. It was a very high-school-almost-man greeting. Ryan stared at Scott's open palm, swallowing.

"Come on, man. Don't leave me hanging."

Ryan's eyes brightened and he grasped Scott's hand firmly. Scott gently pushed some calming energy into him.

Already done.

"It's good to be back," Ryan whispered.

Gigi tugged him into a hug. "It's good to have you."

Scott and Alaric hovered close in case anything went sour.

"You want to get in on the action too? I got you," Ryan said and flung his arms around Scott and Alaric.

"Group hug!" Gigi cheered, her face happier than Scott had seen in a long time.

I told you both. Trust me.

Ryan was back, and that was all that mattered for the moment. Caer could take care of herself.

17

TIME'S A WASTIN'

J put my hands on my hips, assessing our surroundings with Ryan at my side. "So, apparently Alaric and I missed some excitement."

"Though we did have some excitement of our own," Alaric adds.

Scott reaches for the hilt of his sword, the red ruby glinting at us. "Don't even go there, man, just don't."

"I was referring to the trap waiting for us at some barn in the middle of nowhere. Apparently, my mother did not want us returning with the rest of you. She misdirected us instead."

I could tell that Mommy Dearest's constant betrayal and attempts at killing him were really getting on his nerves. Mine too.

"Well, that was obvious the moment we approached Granda's property line. She mumbled a single word three times." Scott glances at Ryan. He purposely doesn't say it aloud, just in case, but he doesn't need to worry.

Trust me. Ryan is fine, I tell him.

"And Lizzie and Ryan broke out of their cells as werewolves."

I interrupt. "Werewolves? But the full moon is past." I turn to Ryan. "And why the heck did you guys take off the crystal necklaces?"

Ryan frowns. "Gi, did you think we were going to keep wearing them? We knew what they did. They also reeked of you."

"Reeked?" I turn to Alaric and search his eyes.

He sidles up to me, pulling me into his chest. "'Reek' sounds like it's a terrible smell. I find it intoxicating, alluring, absolutely captivating."

"Okay, okay," Scott says, stepping between us. "That's close enough. We get the point. Alaric loves it, Lizzie and Ryan, not so much, and since Maddie never complained about it, he clearly finds it palatable. So, werewolves who want to resist the change like it, those who want to change or who blame Gigi for the whole full-moon curse thing can't stomach it. Sound about right?"

We all nod our heads in agreement.

Scott then turns to Ryan and studies him.

Ryan backs away. "What?"

"I wonder what you'd think of the smell now. Alaric, may I?" Scott asks, pointing at the crystal hanging from Alaric's neck.

Alaric hesitates. He doesn't want to risk anything happening to him or me without the crystal on.

I rest my hand on him. "It'll be okay. It's only for a second."

He breathes in and out, then pulls the necklace over his head and hands it to Scott.

Scott puts it below Ryan's nose. "Smell."

We watch with bated breath as Ryan inhales and exhales.

"I no longer find Gigi's smell repulsive."

I burst out laughing. "Well, that is a relief. Now, can anyone tell me what happened to Maddie, Caer, and Mommy Dearest?"

Scott drops his head. "I don't know. I was fighting Ryan, and when I had him under control they were gone."

Granda grips Lizzie's arm on the ground beside us. She's apparently unconscious and under his command, at least for the time being. "The fallen faerie tried to fly away. Maddie wrapped his arms around her legs, but he was not successful in returning her to the ground. I asked Caer to send her back to where she belonged."

Scott staggers backward, clutching his heart and staring wildly at the sky. "They're back in the Faerie Realm? I need to go. I need to help her. Keep her safe."

I place my hand on his shoulder and send calming energy into him. His green eyes fall to mine.

"Scott, Caer can take care of herself."

Then my sight grows blurry, dizziness consumes my body, and it feels like Brigit steps inside of me. I see Maddie, Caer, and her people fighting. Balor is in the distance. Caer lifts an iron spear and launches it.

Scott grips my arms, pulling me out of the vision. "What did you see? Tell me."

"She has her own destiny to fulfill."

"What do you mean, her own destiny? Her destiny is to kill Balor at the Storm Moon. What do you know? What did you see?"

"Maddie is there to aid her, and so are her people. They will give her strength and the means by which to take destiny into her own hands."

His fingers dig into me. "But what does that mean?"

"It means that she is following her own path, and so should we."

He backs away from me. "She left without me."

"Your paths will meet again. She's got a thing for a hot reincarnated god. I can only assume that it's you."

His eyes light up as he smiles. "She thinks I'm hot?"

Ryan raises the back of his hand to Scott's forehead. "I'm sure she means your temperature. Can't possibly have anything to do with your appearance. I mean, she saw me, didn't she?"

Granda groans. "Here we go. Is it purely an American thing to stand around and jest for hours?"

I glance at Ryan, then Scott. The three of us smile together. "No, I'd say it's merely *our* thing."

Scott pulls Ryan into a hug. "I'm so happy to have you back."

They hold each other for several minutes. The two had a rough go of it. It's heartwarming to see them back together.

I don't want to rush them, but we don't have a lot of time. When they finally break apart, I gesture for them all to follow me to Lizzie.

"If the man-hug fest is over, we need to discuss Lizzie. Scott, will you carry her over to the fire circle?"

Ryan studies Lizzie's unconscious frame in his best friend's arms. "Do you think you can help her?"

"We'll see."

I head over to the fire. The flames will further ground me to this plane. Scott places her down on the ground, then he and Alaric flank me, soon followed by Ryan.

"Three overprotective bodyguards is not what I had in mind when we brought Ryan back to our side."

Ryan musses the top of my head. "I like to think of it as rejoining the rebel alliance. Me, taken in by the dark side. You, bringing me back to the light."

Scott smiles. "My brother, how I've missed your socially relevant pop culture references."

"Should we man-hug again?"

"Let's wait on that until Gigi tries to return Lizzie to the light."

Ryan tenses. "Right. Do you think it'll work?"

Granda purses his lips as he closes his eyes to search inward. He inhales deeply, then as he exhales his gaze returns to us. "The Maleficium curse binding her is very powerful. A blood bond at a very young age."

Now that Granda's strength has returned after drinking from the Chalice of Healing, his mind is closed off to me. I've grown so used to reading everyone's mind at will, I find it annoying.

"Birth actually."

His gaze snaps to mine. "A blood bond at birth?"

"Is that bad?" Scott asks.

"It's not good. It will prove a tremendous challenge. Every Maleficium touchpoint she's connected to must be destroyed."

I withdraw an object from my pocket. "Would an eyeball necklace count as a touchpoint?"

His eyes widen. "Yes. It's good that you've wrapped it. Did you come in contact with it?"

I glance at Alaric. "No. I tried to destroy it with fire and other spells, but nothing worked."

"No, it wouldn't. A green magical object needs to destroy it."

"Like a sword?" Scott says, withdrawing Moralltach.

"Possibly. I need to do some research."

Granda seems wary. Now I'm glad my spells didn't work on it. What if I had destroyed it and it had killed a part of Lizzie's soul like a horcrux? If I had hastily destroyed all the Maleficium connections, I could have ended up killing her.

"Naisha, Lizzie's mom, gave me insight into a coven of witches in Kilkenny who might have answers for returning Lizzie to us."

"The same woman who misled us in Vernal Falls so she could reduce our numbers?" Alaric growls, his voice wrought with betrayal.

"Well, yes, but in my visions I also saw images of the coven in the spell book. It's hard to explain, but it's almost like I read the pages over her shoulder, and although many of the spells have been tainted with Maleficium, there are a lot in there that are good. I sensed there were even more positive spells that are invisible to the naked eye. Does that make sense?" I search everyone's face for confirmation. They all stare at me blankly except for Granda.

"If you entered her mind, it does. Are you sure she didn't layer the truth with deception?"

My gut hums to me with a definitive answer. "Her visions spoke the truth. It was her words that were lies. She let us assume she had the spell book, but it was a ruse—and I played right into it. I wanted it to be true because otherwise, I'd need to interact with Breas again."

Alaric growls. Ryan joins in. And Scott does too, because, why not? Can anyone say testosterone overload?

I raise my hands and shoot calming magic into them. "Guys, chill out. This is good news. If we can get the spell book back from Breas and find out what the coven in Kilkenny know, we can possibly bring Lizzie back."

Scott's mind shifts to Caer. It's not the first time, and it definitely won't be the last. "If Caer or Maddie were here, they could slip in and out without Breas or anyone noticing."

I roll my eyes. "Scott, we're not opening up a portal and traveling to another dimension. I'm not as gifted in portal making as your swan is."

"You are gifted at being a pain in the ass," he offers.

I chuckle. "Thanks, I appreciate that."

Something rubs against my leg and I glance down. Sphinx

meows and walks over to Scott. He bends down and scoops him up.

"Sphinx, how did you get here?"

Granda reaches over and scratches his head. "Hello, old friend."

Scott looks from Granda to me. "Would someone mind telling me what Gigi's pet cat is doing here?"

Sphinx presses his paw on Scott's chest with his claws out.

"Ouch!"

I smile at Sphinx's greeting. "He's no pet. He's our partner in catastrophe. He helped me and Alaric out in Vernal Falls, and now it looks like he's dying to break into Breas's compound."

Sphinx blinks at Scott and meows.

Scott shakes his head back and forth, staring at Sphinx with newfound respect. "Nothing is as it seems, is it."

"Nope, not at all," I say.

Ryan rubs his hands together. "So, what are we waiting for? Let's go steal the spell book. Alaric and I can cause a distraction while Sphinx morphs into a cat burglar."

Sphinx leaps off Scott's chest and prances around the fire. He puffs out his chest in a rather full-of-himself demonstration.

Scott flings a stick into the fire. "I hate leaving without Caer."

"Scott, I understand your dilemma. You can sit around and wait for her, or you can go with us, but time's a wasting, and we need to proceed."

Granda stands up. "Before you go, there are a few provisions you need to take."

"We're just stealing a spell book, then we'll return before heading to Kilkenny."

"Best laid plans don't always follow the straightest of paths."

Alaric frowns. "You know something, we don't?"

Granda studies him closely. "I know many things."

Alaric glances at me. *Does he know about us?*

Heat gathers in my cheeks, and it has nothing to do with the fire. *Gods, I hope not.*

Scott crosses his arms and scowls at Alaric. Granda reminded him of our portal-hopping excursion.

"Do I even want to ask?" Ryan whispers to me.

"The seeds of knowledge often take root when least expected," I say.

"Just because you spout prophetic lines I don't understand doesn't mean I'm going to treat you any differently," he says, pulling me into a hug to noogie the top of my head.

I roll my eyes, trying to act like I'm totally annoyed, but I'm thrilled. "I missed you, friend. I missed you."

18

KING OF CUPS

*A*s she flew over the lake, her flock took notice and flew up to escort her for her return home. She nodded in greeting to the lead swan who had guided the others while Caer was gone. She'd missed her friends. They had cared for her as a young child, and they had cared for her as a grown woman. She could never repay them for the protection they provided her, but she knew they didn't require payment. They considered her presence gift enough.

Keturah and a crowd of others gathered in the courtyard. A guard must have noticed their approach. Caer's white wings were unmistakable. No one else bore the mark of the swan.

She alighted in the middle of the space, landing with the utmost care for Maddie who was still hanging from Naisha's legs. Once her feet were firmly on the ground, she yelled, "Guards!"

Several came running and seized Naisha before she could fly away. She wouldn't get free in the Faerie Realm. Not with faerie guards restraining her.

"Your Majesty," Keturah said, leading the crowd of people now bowing to her.

Maddie bowed low as well.

"No," she said to him, touching him between the shoulder blades before turning to the rest of them. "Please stand. I do not require your praise in such a manner."

Keturah stood before her. "Queen Caer, it is a pleasure to have you home."

"Thank you. I wish it wasn't because of the present circumstances."

Keturah's eyes fell on Maddie, who now stood beside Caer. Her forehead pinched together. "Have we met?"

"Keturah, meet Madigan."

At the mention of his mother's name, Maddie stepped backward. His eyes slid from Caer to Keturah. Caer knew from his reaction that he wished to disappear and would have happily done so if it weren't for the crowd. She'd felt that way many times as well. But with the knowledge that he was standing before his mother, he also didn't want to appear weak.

"It's all right, Maddie. I will explain."

He blinked in appreciation.

"Why is Maddie familiar to me?" Keturah asked. "Is he Naisha's son?"

Caer smiled. "No, Keturah. He's yours."

"Mine?" Her eyes brightened as she studied Maddie.

"Naisha took him and left him in the Earthly Realm."

Keturah stepped in front of him. Maddie pinched his lips, unsure what to say or do.

"You are my son?"

Maddie blinked.

"You were stolen from me. I searched. I mourned. I longed for my baby. My boy. You."

Now, seeing the two standing feet away from each other,

the family resemblance was undeniable. They had the same eyes, the same smile, the same way they held their chins and shoulders.

Neither of them said a word for a very long time. They just stared at each other as if memorizing every inch of skin, every strand of hair, every feature. Time stood still. No one in the courtyard breathed a word. Not even Naisha, which suddenly surprised Caer. The fallen faerie usually had a lot to say on a variety of subjects when she wasn't manipulating emotions. She turned to the guards to make sure Naisha was still being held captive and discovered why Naisha hadn't said anything, not even to defend herself. The guards had wrapped her mouth shut with a silencing spell. She could see the magic aura wafting off of her. As if she felt Caer watching her, Naisha turned to her and widened her eyes in anger. Caer smiled. If the effect was to frighten her, it wouldn't work. She'd fought off hordes of hellhounds and a Fomorian army. Angry eyes from a fallen faerie weren't going to phase her.

"May I?" Keturah finally asked.

Maddie nodded, unsure what she was asking but not wanting to refuse her.

Keturah approached him and trailed her hand down his arm as if to prove to herself he was not a figment of her imagination. Then suddenly, she wrapped her arms around him and squeezed. Hard.

Maddie glanced toward Caer, silently asking her what he should do.

"Go ahead," she mouthed to him.

And with her approval, he embraced his mother and held on.

Caer had never met her own mother. According to her father, she'd died in childbirth, but Keturah had said faeries couldn't die in childbirth, because they are immortal.

Alaric's warning came rushing back to her. *If there was a prophecy predicting my death and it was attached to someone from my future generation, I'd make sure there wasn't a future generation.*

She wouldn't bother Keturah and Maddie's reunion, but she had to find out if there was a prophecy about her killing Balor. She had to make sure.

She scanned the crowd until her eyes fell on one of the villagers she recognized from her last visit. Britni was her name. Somehow she knew Britni had the answers she sought.

"Britni, would you mind helping me with something?"

"Of course, Your Majesty."

And they hurried into the castle. It was time to find out once and for all why Balor was intent on obtaining her.

Caer walked into the giant library and inhaled. The comforting smell of old books filled her nostrils. It had been many years since she had set foot in the library. She glanced around at the high shelves filled with ancient volumes.

"Hello, old friends," she said as she twirled around with her arms fanned out.

"My Queen, it is a pleasure to see you enjoy your bountiful collection of knowledge," Britni said.

Startled, Caer staggered backward. After spending nearly a lifetime with the sole companionship of a powerful wizard who had never acknowledged her until a few weeks ago and too short of a time with Mathair Mhór, she had slipped into her solitary habit. Her neck warmed as a single bead of sweat ran down her back. She never let herself exhibit emotion in front of people. It made her uncomfortable, especially around Scott.

As if aware of her intrusion into Caer's revelry, Britni

bowed and stepped away. "When you're ready, I'll show you to the Prophecy Room."

Caer glanced one more time at the rows and rows of books. One day she'd have an eternity to read them.

Britni led her down a long aisle with towering bookshelves on either side of them. When she got to the end, she pushed against the wall and a secret door appeared. She opened it and beckoned Caer to follow her.

"I didn't know there was a secret room off the library," Caer whispered in awe.

"My Queen, we've all heard the legends of the secret tunnels. Your tale of escape is a celebrated one."

"You know how I escaped?"

"Not exactly, but the tunnels and your shapeshifting nature were foretold in the prophecy."

"They were?"

"More or less. Here," Britni said, still holding the door for her, "let me show you."

Caer followed Britni up a winding marble staircase. Torches were blazing the entire way up, as if someone had known they were coming. Or perhaps by magic. She couldn't decide how she felt about that.

"How did the library and this tower survive after Balor and his armies took possession of the castle?"

Britni turned around and frowned at her. "You really don't know, do you."

Caer disliked not knowing something. Like when Scott would talk about his precious Earthly Realm and all the things Caer had never heard of before. The only difference was that the Faerie Realm and the castle were her domain. It made her even more angry.

She growled in frustration, and Britni backed up another step, putting room between them.

"Apologies, my Queen. I have forgotten that you haven't

been here since you were a young child. You didn't learn all the histories. The library, the tower, and the tunnels are magicked."

Magicked?

"Balor knew you escaped through the tunnels, but his men never gained access to them, nor the library or this tower. Likely, he didn't know they existed. Here," she said, putting her hand on the wall, "try it."

Caer put her hand against the stone, feeling foolish. Freagarach was hanging in its scabbard. She could always threaten Britni with death if she was playing a trick on her.

Suddenly, the wall pulsed. She snatched her hand away.

"Keep touching the stone and trust me," Britni murmured.

Caer did as instructed. The wall pulsed with energy. Her eyes brightened.

"The castle is alive with magic. No invader can penetrate its secrets. They are hidden from view and protected."

Bitterness ripped through Caer. "It didn't protect my father."

"Your father's blood strengthened it. His sacrifice ensured your protection. It ensured his people's protection."

"I don't understand."

Britni smiled. "When your father died, he triggered a powerful spell. A fail-safe, if you will. At his death, his people were jettisoned to the Land of Shadows."

"Did my father know Balor was going to kill him?"

Britni's eyes slid away from hers. "Let me show you the prophecies. There are other histories there too that you might be interested in."

Britni was keeping information from her. Caer intended to find out what. She followed Britni to a large carved wooden door.

"This is where I leave you. Now that you've returned, the room and its secrets are for your use alone."

"You cannot go inside?"

"Not anymore. Once you enter, the contents of the secrets will become forgotten memories to me."

"You will forget everything you know?"

"There is no reason for me to remember with our Queen here."

That didn't seem fair to Caer. "Does that make you sad?"

"On the contrary. It is a burden that I do not wish anyone to carry."

Caer hesitated outside the door. "And if I don't go in?"

"Then I will retain the secrets. But the answers you seek will be found if asked."

"I understand." She didn't, but she was going to pretend that she did.

"I bid you farewell," Britni said, hurrying down the stairs.

"Britni?" she called out.

"Yes, Your Majesty?"

"Thank you."

"You're welcome."

"No, I mean thank you for carrying our kingdom's secrets."

"It was an honor," she said, bowing dutifully.

"Goodbye," Caer murmured as she turned back to study the door.

There was no latch, no keyhole. She pressed her hand to it, remembering Britni's lesson. Soon a pulse of energy surged through her palm. She gasped. She wasn't sure she'd get used to the idea that the castle was alive. She took a deep breath to steady herself before pushing again, but the door refused to open.

She tried two hands. Still nothing.

She pushed with all her strength, but still the door didn't budge. Her anger began to flash, and for one fleeting moment she considered running Freagarach through the wood.

She blew out air from her mouth. What was it that Britni had said? *The answers you seek will be found if asked.*

"Please reveal your secrets to me," she said and pushed the door. When it didn't open, she kicked it with her boot.

She thought about calling Britni back and asking her to open it for her, but she was the Queen. She needed to learn how to do things on her own.

The answers you seek will be found if asked.

She hadn't asked.

"Will you reveal your secrets to me?" she asked as her palms rested against it. A tingling sensation coursed through them as the door opened for her.

As she stepped into the room, a loud whooshing sound filled the air. She watched as clear glass spheres grew cloudy. The prophecies were returning home.

Natural light filled the space. Caer searched for the source of it. At the far side of the chamber, a large window brought sunlight into the room. A long desk stood in front of it. She walked over and looked out. The window overlooked the lake. Below she could see her flock of swans circling around in the water. She could picture her father sitting at the desk and staring out at the lake. Was the sight of these swans the reason he'd chosen to turn her into a swan shapeshifter?

She turned around to face the room of swirling glass spheres. Did her father know that Balor was going to kill him? And if so, why didn't he try to stop it?

A glass sphere glided off a shelf, landed gently on the floor, and rolled over to her. She reached down to lift it. It was time for her to find out.

19

CAT BURGLAR

Sphinx curls his back into a classic cat cowl, extending his claws into the soft earth.

Scott reaches down to scratch him behind the ears. "Now, remember when Bilbo snuck across the piles of gold, he caused a small avalanche that woke Smaug."

Did your brother really just compare me to a hobbit?

"Scott, Sphinx finds it offensive that you're using literary references again. He's got this."

Sphinx nods at me. *Thank you.*

"You're welcome."

Scott slouches as he stands back up. "Why do you get all the cool magical gifts?"

"I might be able to communicate telepathically, but I can't cause harm to any living being. Do you know how frustrating that is when you won't shut up?" I punch his arm.

"Ow," he says, rubbing the tender spot. "I thought you said you couldn't hurt anyone."

"Guess annoying brothers don't count."

"Love you too, sis."

"They do go on, don't they," Alaric whispers to Ryan.

"Yes, they do. I should have guessed they were brother and sister. Lizzie and I always thought they fought like an old married couple. We even tried to hook them up."

Alaric growls.

Ryan pats Alaric's arm. "Easy. Obviously it didn't work."

"Talk about gross," I say.

"You're no peach yourself, sunshine," Scott says.

"Don't you mean swan?"

His face winces in pain like I'd struck him, and in a way I did. Yep, bitch Gigi to the rescue.

"Sorry. I'm sure Caer is fine."

"I hope she is and pray to the gods she doesn't try anything stupid."

"Thankfully, that's my superhero power. After this heist, we'll enter a meditation and see if we can contact her."

"Do you think it'll work?"

"Can't hurt."

"Okay, this is where Sphinx and I leave you," Ryan says as we approach the ruins of Brigit's cathedral.

Scott's hands fold in and out of themselves. "Maybe you shouldn't go. We just got you back. How will we know if you need help?"

Sphinx presses his paw against Ryan's leg as if to say, "No, I alone must go." Actually, that is exactly what he says, but he's not able to push his thoughts into Ryan. The inability frustrates him.

"He's telling you to stay."

Sphinx fixes me with his feline glare.

"Fine. He's *ordering* you to remain behind."

Ryan crouches down to Sphinx's height. "But you don't know where to go."

Have him show me.

"Think about where Breas's lair is and where the spell book might be."

He glances over at me. "Just think about it?"

"Just think about it."

Sphinx presses his paws onto Ryan's chest and closes his eyes. They flash open soon after.

Got it.

"That fast?" I say. I don't mean to question my partner in catastrophe, but geez.

I am very efficient.

"I guess so. How will we know if you need us?"

Sphinx approaches me with a Cheshire Cat grin.

"Oh no. Forget I said anything."

He leaps up into my arms, trusting that I'll catch him. He rests his paws on my chest, but instead of closing his eyes, he breathes on me. My vision tunnels down to two diamond shapes, and I suddenly see myself.

"What the?"

Welcome to my world. Enjoy.

He jumps down and saunters away.

Alaric rushes over to me. "What's wrong, Gigi?"

"I can see through Sphinx's eyes. He's on his way to find the spell book."

"Watch out for hair balls," Scott teases.

I'd roll my eyes if they were under my control, but they're all Sphinx's.

He covers a lot of ground quickly. He was clearly faking it all those times at home when I tried to get him to move out the way, but that is neither here nor there. Soon he approaches an old stone house and crouches low.

"I think he's there."

"Describe it," Ryan says.

"It's a one-and-a-half-story thatched-roof cottage hidden behind a dilapidated iron gate. The gardens are overgrown with a lot of weeds, and some of the shutters are falling off."

"Sounds like it. What's happening? We want a cat's-eye view."

"Very funny. There's an open window. Another cat just climbed in through it, so Sphinx plans to follow. Okay, I've leapt onto the windowsill—er, Sphinx has leapt onto the windowsill. He's prowling along the ledge as he looks around inside."

"What does he see?"

"There are candles everywhere."

"Well, hello there, kitty kitty," purrs Witch Kensey.

My skins crawls as the saccharine sweetness of my nemesis's voice hits my taste buds—or are they Sphinx's taste buds? As Sphinx, I try to leap away from her, but she catches me and carries me into another room. For now, I don't fight. I just let her carry me. I can always use my claws and leap out the window if needed.

"Not another one," a male voice groans.

"There's Breas," I say aloud. I swallow the sour taste in my mouth that has nothing to do with the rotten mouse I ate earlier.

"Is this you speaking, or Sphinx?" Alaric whispers.

"Both, I think. It's like our minds have merged into one."

"I always thought you were the cat's meow," Scott says.

Breas rolls his eyes toward Witch Kensey. "How many cats do you need?"

"My true form scares them," she says. "I'm taking advantage of them for now."

"Your true form scares me too. I wish you hadn't soiled this one. She and I shared many pleasures."

Witch Kensey drags her fingernail down his arm. Blood seeps from the wound. "This form no longer excites you? You've always given in to your carnal desires before."

His lip curls. "Not with you. I hope she's not ruined beyond repair once you leave her."

Sphinx takes in the room. Worn sofas occupy two walls. White candles are lit everywhere, casting an eerie glow. His eyes settle on a large silver cauldron. The Vessel of Life.

"Good kitty. Maybe you'll remain dedicated to me when I arrive in my true form."

Sphinx purrs, rubbing his head into her chest.

A demanding knock echoes through the room. Breas and Witch Kensey share a long look. I don't know if the guest is expected, but it at least appears that they're not surprised.

Breas sighs and walks to the door. The brightness of his godly form is in stark contrast to the darkness of the room. He peeks through the window.

"Well, guess what the cat dragged in," he says as he opens the door.

Maria stands before him with her hip cocked out. She's in a very revealing outfit. Her breasts bulge out of her scoop-neck shirt, and her black leather skirt is about two sizes too small. Her hair is done up and her makeup creates a very convincing display of smoky eyes.

"Breas, darling, we need to talk," she says, strolling in.

His gaze falls on her exposed mounded flesh. He is such a horny beast.

"What do you have in mind?" he asks, slamming the door behind him as he licks his lips. Evidently a Fomorian witch inhabiting his girlfriend is a bit of a turn-off, but an ancient witch in a young, hot model gets him going.

"Gigi, is it necessary to give the play-by-play inner monologue as you tell us what you see via Sphinx?" Scott says.

"Yes, you're going to get everything."

Maria struts into the room. Her bare legs are a mile long, especially with her black stilettos. I am so jealous of those lengthy legs.

"I find yours very sexy," Alaric whispers to me.

"I can hear you," Scott groans. "No flirting."

The beast Breas can't keep his eyes off Maria. "What do you want? I thought our partnership ended."

"Oh, Breas," she says, adjusting her chest to return his attention there as she sits down and crosses her bare legs, "I've come to make amends." She pats the sofa next to her.

He quickly accepts her invite. "Your wolf not satisfying you?"

Her eyes flash to his. "That's beside the point. I have reason to believe that we may have underestimated Gigi and her merry band of misfits."

He leans into her, his gaze lasered on her chest. "How so?"

Witch Kensey hisses. "Must I witness you coming on to a human?"

Maria's lips turn down at the sight of the Witch and Sphinx in her lap. "Nice cat," she purrs and flips her hair to the side. She leans into Breas. "Now, as I was saying . . ."

In a jealous rage, Witch Kensey storms into another room and throws Sphinx. Thankfully he lands on his feet.

"When Balor gets here, things will be different," she mutters. "I won't need to lower myself to that witch. But until the Storm Moon, I need to work with what I've got." She flicks her fingers. Her hair rearranges itself in a loose wave, and her outfit changes into a short skirt and skimpy tank top. She adjusts her own chest so that it perfectly mounds the way Breas likes it.

Her eyes land on Sphinx. "Meet your new friends," she whispers before stepping back out into the other room.

Sphinx shifts his attention to the room. Dozens of feline eyes stare at him from every corner, chair, shelf, and cushion. *So, this is what a crazy cat lady looks like?*

He puffs his chest to look braver and larger than he is. There are monster cats all over the room who have clearly been very well fed—or magicked to be larger than life. He peers around the room until his eyes land on . . .

"He found the spell book!"

"He's a cat. How is he going to carry it, and why didn't we think of that before he left?" Ryan says, nervously pacing in front of us. "I should go help him."

"No," the three of us order him.

"Give him time," I say.

Sphinx strolls over to the bookshelf and without glancing at the other cats, he presses his paw to the spell book. The book shrinks into a crystal. He puts it in his mouth and turns around.

The herd of cats are all crouched down, ready to pounce.

"Get out of there, Sphinx!" I shout.

He tears off and sprints into the other room. In a blur, I see three naked bodies as he passes them. The trio is oblivious to him until the screeching and hissing herd of cats barrel through the room as they chase after him. The trio curse and stand up. Maria and Witch Kensey shout dark spells at Sphinx. He cuts and swerves, the spells just missing him. Witch Kensey shouts a curse as Sphinx leaps onto the windowsill. The curse rebounds off the wood and hits Maria. She screams, but Sphinx doesn't stop to find out what happened to her. He leaps out the window and sprints away, the herd of cats behind him in hot pursuit.

20

BLINDED BY THREE MOONS

"My eyes! My eyes are burning," I hiss as I try to rub the image out of my memory bank.

Alaric rushes over and wraps his arm around me. "What's wrong, Gi? Did you get something in them?" He fishes a bandana from his pocket and hands it to me.

I shake my head. "Yes, and no. Sphinx got away. He should be here any second. But I saw Breas, Maria, and Kensey naked and tangled up together."

Alaric stills, not expecting that answer.

Scott and Ryan snap their eyes to me. "What?"

"You heard me. They were having a threesome. Do I need to provide explicit descriptions? Because I would really rather not."

"How?" Ryan asks, scrubbing his face with his hand "That's kinda every guy's fantasy. Well, it was mine until I met Lizzie."

"And mine until Caer," Scott admits.

"You were always my fantasy," Alaric whispers low in my ear.

With Scott's superhuman gifts, he hears him. "Do not go there, man. Do not."

I hand Alaric back his bandana, and he shoves it into his pocket. "Well, one thing we can gather is that apparently the three of them have kissed and made up. Now, what does that mean for us?"

Sphinx leaps into the circle. *A little help please.*

I throw up a wall of fire, and the herd of cats scatter.

"They really don't like you," I tell him.

Sphinx drops the crystal then licks his paws. *I really don't like them either. The heathens.*

I add the crystal to my necklace. It hums against my chest. "The spell book is extremely powerful with both good and dark magic."

"It's connected to Lizzie," Scott says. "We need to destroy it along with the eyeball necklace."

I shake my head. "We need to talk to the Kilkenny witches first. I don't want to risk anything happening to Lizzie. But first, let's cast a circle and check on Caer."

"Here?" Scott says, glancing at Alaric. "Aren't there some bad vibes here?" With Clayone a few stories below us, Scott's worried something bad might happen to us.

"Yes, there are, but there is also more powerful magic here than any place I've been to in Ireland, except for maybe Newgrange."

"Do not remind me of Newgrange. That is one mistake I'd like to forget."

Ryan swings his head between us. "How much did I miss?"

"A lot, apparently," Alaric murmurs. "Why did you go to Newgrange?"

"We were searching for you. We thought maybe Breas had imprisoned you."

Alaric sidles up next to me. Strength radiates off of him. "You thought Breas was powerful enough to catch me?"

"He's a god, and he does have a Fomorian witch working for him."

"Who was naked," Ryan adds. "And I have seen her naked."

"So have I," Scott says, "but let's get to the point. Why couldn't Breas have kidnapped you?"

"Because I was taken in the tunnels beneath the Cathedral," Alaric says as if that answers everything. It doesn't.

"And . . . ?"

He reaches for my hands. "Brigit banned Breas from ever setting foot on any of her sacred lands."

"But not the fairy mound," I say, suddenly remember something. "Breas drugged me when we went on a picnic. He took blood from my palm—that's how he was able to bring the Fomorian witch back using Kensey as a vessel. And speaking of vessels, he must have had the Vessel of Life with him. My Vessel of Life."

Alaric growls. "He drugged you? I can't wait to kill that bastard."

"For once we agree," Scott says, gripping Moralltach.

"And he compelled me into being one of his minions. I'd like in on that action," Ryan adds. "I say the three of us give him a battering he doesn't wake up from."

Testosterone whirls around the ruins. Even Sphinx hisses.

I remove candles from my backpack and place them around in a circle. Fireballs erupt from my fingers as I prepare to light the four cardinal points. "Y'all are going to have to stand in line, because I plan on doing some ass kicking myself. But first, I need to see if any of our enemies' purpose has changed. We're also going to check on Caer, because I've got a feeling we're going to be busy for a while. Everyone, sit down please."

The four of us cross our legs and arrange ourselves around the circle. Sphinx curls up on my lap and goes to sleep. He's decided he's done enough work today—and I have to agree with him.

"Ryan, you've never participated in one of these. Just relax, and if you feel anything strange or weird, it's perfectly normal."

He arranges his arms over his legs. "Nothing about this new life is normal. Are you going to ask about Lizzie too?"

I purse my lips. He's so hopeful that she can return to us. I want to be too, but her current state needs thoughtful evaluation.

"Not yet. But we're going to find out soon what we can do." I squeeze his hand then release it and take the Chalice of Healing from my pack.

"To cast this circle from Earth to Fire, from Water to Air, join together with Spirit to guide me to the answers I seek. I give you my love, my light, as I cast this circle to show me the path to truth. The circle is cast."

"To the East, element of Air, I give to you my love, my light, to show me the path to truth to guard us from sudden storms and protect us with gentle breezes."

The wind, gentle as a butterfly wing, caresses each of our cheeks. Ryan's eyes widen. I smile at him to assure him it's okay.

"To the South, element of Fire, I give to you my love, my light, to show me the path to truth to guard us from raging fires and warm us with controlled flames."

The candles' flames shoot into the air all around us. (I added a little extra dramatic effect for Ryan.)

"To the West, element of Earth, I give to you my love, my light, to show me the path to truth to guard us from disturbance by providing firm footing."

The scent of fresh soil fills the air.

To the North, element of Water, I give to you my love, my light, to show me the path to truth to guard us from tidal waves and cradle us in calm waters as gentle as a mother's arms."

A sensation of warm water cocoons us.

"I call to the Elements for guidance in my search. I offer the Chalice of Healing, not as a permanent token, but as an inspiration to spur ideas. My blood, however," I raise Clarissa's athame to my palm, "is my token of gratitude for your presence tonight. Take the blood of a goddess as payment for the help I will be calling upon you for this evening."

Scott doesn't approve of my blood contribution, but I want to ensure that we get the answers we need. I don't have time to constantly ask for his approval on everything. And really, like I'd ask for his consent anyway?

"Of Breas, of Carman, of Witch Kensey, are they joined back together? Flicker once for yes, and twice for no."

The flames flicker off and then back on.

"I understand. Are any of them capable of returning to the light? Flicker once for yes, and twice for no."

The flames flicker off and on, off and on.

Alaric fills will sadness. "Can you ask about each one specifically?"

And I do, and each time the answer is the same. No. Always no.

"We thank you for your consideration. Is Caer safe? Flicker once for yes, twice for no."

The flames flicker off and on.

"She's safe," I whisper, meeting Scott's eyes.

He sighs in relief. "Can you ask if she and I will be together again . . . in *this* lifetime?"

He understands the importance of being specific with the questions.

"Will Caer and Scott be together again in this lifetime? Flicker once for yes, and twice for no."

The flames flicker off and on. A smile crosses his face. An invisible weight lifts from his shoulders.

"Can you ask if my father will side with us?" Alaric whispers.

I swallow my concern. I am also aware of the irony that his father is locked in my shrine several stories below us.

"Will Clayone, Original Werewolf, father of Alaric, side with us? Flicker once for yes, flicker twice for no."

The flames go out and do not light back up.

"What does that mean?" Ryan whispers.

"I don't know."

"Ask again," Alaric says.

"Candles, relight please."

At my request, the flames reappear.

"Will Clayone, Original Werewolf, father of Alaric, side with us? Flicker once for yes, flicker twice for no."

The candles extinguish and do not relight.

We all exchange glances.

"Should I rephrase and ask a third time?"

"Third time is always the charm. At least that's what Kensey, Breas, and Maria think," Ryan says in a respectful undertone. He doesn't want to anger the Elements, but he couldn't keep his comment to himself. I have to admit, it was pretty funny.

"Is there a chance that Clayone, father of Alaric will side with us? Flicker once for yes, flicker twice for no."

The candles go out and do not relight a third time.

"I'm not going to ask again. Thank you, Elements, for visiting us this evening." I reverse the casting circle for each Element, then say, "The circle is now broken."

"That was cool," Ryan says in awe. "I felt like a real witch."

Scott scratches the top of his head as he stands. "Well, you are a real werewolf."

Ryan stretches. "I might try acting when this is all over. I can be cast as the sexy lone wolf searching for love. I'll do all my own stunts too."

Scott laughs as they start walking ahead of us. "Oh gods. Clayone literally created a monster."

Alaric's jaw tightens at the mention of his father. "What do you think the Elements were trying to tell us?"

"Maybe since he's immured, the question was moot."

"Is he locked away forever?"

I lick my lips. I don't want to lie anymore. Especially not to Alaric. "Only I can release him. If I die, he'll be imprisoned forever."

He juts his chin out. "Huh."

But he doesn't ask me to release his dad. He doesn't even think it.

"I can't believe that Nan is lost to evil forever." He can't correlate the woman he called Nan his whole life with the evil Maleficium sorceress I claim her to be. The woman behind a fifteen-hundred-year-old, carefully orchestrated vendetta against me.

I wrap my arms around him. "Alaric, you have to believe me. I'm not making this up."

He drags his fingers through his hair. It falls in soft waves around his face. Even when he's obviously distraught, he's beautiful, and I'm having a hard time keeping myself focused on persuading him to believe me. I wish there were some way for him to see the woman I know.

I stop and study him. Maybe there is.

"May I?" I ask as I place my hands on either side of his head. He startles at my touch but doesn't stop me. I'm as much a distraction to him as he is to me. Mindful that I don't want to overload him with too many visions too fast, I take a deep breath to focus. When I'm in complete control of myself, I push my knowledge of Carman into his head.

Her stealing away a baby Alaric from Naisha.

Scott locked in a cage in the back of the barn while Alaric walks around freely outside.

Her opening a portal for Clayone to return to Ireland.

Her attacking me at the bonfire.

Her sending killing curses at Dad and Calliope.

Her taking over Maria's body.

I take some liberties with some of the visions since I'm not exactly sure how the events happened. I just know they did.

He gasps, pulling away from me. His chest heaves as he tries to come to grips with the images.

When he finally catches his breath, he says, "Maybe I can persuade her? Maybe I can make her see that she doesn't need to fight you. That you aren't evil."

I don't want to squash his hope, but there's no way Carman can return to the light. "I fear she's too far lost."

His eyes narrow on mine. "You're taking extreme measures to try and bring Lizzie back. Why shouldn't I cling to the chance that we can bring back Nan?"

"He does make a valid point," Ryan says. "Besides, as the son of Clayone, he's the alpha. He should be able to convince his pack to side with us. Persuasive power in numbers."

Scott frowns. "How does that help with Carman?"

Alaric latches on to the idea. "Declan always wanted the power of the alpha position. He won't give it up easily. She'd lose her army."

"Well," I adjust my pack, "lets pick up Lizzie and head to Kilkenny. Maybe the coven has a spell or an idea how to exorcise evil from an ancient Maleficium sorceress.

You don't sound very optimistic. Can't you at least pretend to try? We did bring back Ryan, Scott shouts loudly in my head.

163

I throw my head up and stare at the sky. *Fine. I guess I can at least try.*

How big of you. This goddess crap is really going to your head.

I frown at him. *You have no idea.*

Ryan clears his throat. "Can you two at least pretend to be human? All this internal conversation makes a wolf feel left out."

"Is weetle Ryan feeling wonely?" Scott says, giving him a noogie.

"I'm not a dog, you know," Ryan says, trying to sound mad but failing miserably. He's never been an angry person. That emotion belonged solely to me. But with Ryan back, my brother with me, and Alaric at my side, I just can't seem to get angry at anyone.

"You're glowing," Alaric whispers in my ear.

"I'm happy I have all of you with me."

"No, I mean you are really glowing."

I glance down at my body, and yes, in fact, I am glowing.

What in the hells?

I remember the prophetic line I said to Ryan about seeds taking root. Was I talking about my own future?

CARNIE LIFE FOR ME

I adjust my backpack straps. "Let's haul out."

Ryan's head pops through his sweatshirt hole. "You've always wanted to say that, haven't you."

"Actually, yes."

"Truck driver wannabe or *Young Guns* fan?"

Ryan remembers my obsession with 80s and 90s Western movies. I mean, there's not much better than a Charlie Sheen, Emilio Estevez, and Kiefer Sutherland trio. They had their own trí cumhacht going on. Plus, Emilio's naked ass was the first man butt I had ever seen. I have made up for lost time since though.

"Both?"

"Nice," he says, shaking his head.

"When you two are done, I want to go over our plan," Scott says, throwing his own backpack in the truck we've borrowed from Sam.

I glance at Scott. "Because our plans have gone so well thus far?"

"A few hiccups along the way, but yes, we're all together. Plus Alaric."

Alaric rolls his eyes as he tosses his bag in the bed of the truck.

"And Lizzie, albeit not exactly in the manner I thought she'd travel with us. But still, we've got to start somewhere."

Lizzie looks like Lizzie, more or less. Her hair's a tad wild, but it becomes her. Her eyes are glassy but open (a side effect of Granda's spell). I gave her some of my clothes to wear, so she's rocking ripped black jeans, a black novelty T-shirt with a Harry Potter quote because, you know, witchy coolness and all, and a pair of black Converse sneakers I brought with me though I have no idea why since I always wear Docs. Maybe I had a sixth sense that I'd need them for Lizzie.

Scott ticks off items on his fingers. "Gigi, you grabbed Clarissa's athame?"

I roll my eyes. "Duh, of course."

"And I've got my sword, so we both have a magical instrument."

Ryan punches at the air. "Do I need a magical instrument other than my fists?"

I open up the truck door, anxious to get moving. "No. You and Alaric are plenty magical enough."

Ryan circles around Lizzie. She's able to move but unable to see or hear. "Amorin's spell on Lizzie . . . will it hold 'til we get to Kilkenny?"

"It's supposed to," Scott says but hands Ryan a dagger.

Ryan stares at it. "Will it burn me? It looks silver."

"The handle's ivory. You just can't get stabbed in the heart with it."

Ryan carefully takes it from Scott's hands. "I thought I was all the magical instrument I'd need."

"Well," Scott says, tilting his head toward Lizzie—he's not entirely sure she can't see or hear us. "Better safe than sorry."

Alaric sticks his head out of the driver's side window. "Whenever you guys are ready."

"Shotgun," I shout, as I hop in next to Alaric. Sphinx jumps in beside me and rests his head on my lap.

"No funny business," Scott warns as he climbs in the back.

"There's nothing funny about the way I feel about this girl," Alaric murmurs, gripping my hand. Every time we touch, my body does this weird flip-floppy thing. I don't know if I'll ever get used to it—or if I ever want to get used to it, because the feeling is so strong and powerful, and it makes me feel so, so alive.

We're barely even on the road to Kilkenny, when Lizzie starts squirming around in her seat between Ryan and Scott.

"I think she has to go to the bathroom," Ryan says.

"Didn't she go before we left?" Scott groans, reminding me of Dad.

Ryan cringes. "I didn't make sure she went. That's not written in the boyfriend manual for obsessed werewolf faeries."

I throw my hand up to my forehead. "I was so concerned with gathering magical instruments and creepy spelled objects that I forgot."

"Hold on, there's a gas station up ahead," Alaric says. He pulls into a parking spot.

I lean over to kiss him. "Where are we?"

"Just outside of Kildare."

"That's it? How long until Kilkenny?"

He winks at me. "Only getting longer if you don't get moving, sweet thang."

"Do not call my sister 'sweet thang,'" Scott grunts.

Alaric turns around to face him. "You have a lot of rules about dating your sister."

Scott scowls. "You ignored rule number one. Don't date my sister."

"Too late for that, brother."

Scott opens the door for Lizzie, and she hops out. We walk side by side toward the convenience store. It's almost like old times, except of course for the invisible magical bindings around her arms and legs. And the fact that she wants to kill me. Can't forget that part. Gods know I've tried.

We walk past a group of people dancing around in circles, which is strange because there's no music playing. I'm all for dancing to the beat of your own drum, but this goes beyond that. Drugs maybe?

I shake my head and ignore it. We pass another group, this one made up mostly of guys who are shouting at each other. One with a shaved head throws his hands into another long-haired guy's chest. They keep getting louder and more physical with each other. I glance over my shoulder. My eyes meet Alaric's. He's already out of the truck and following me with Scott and Ryan flanking him.

A loud crash tears my attention away from the fight and toward a group of women clawing at each other near the entrance of the store. We sidestep around them just as the front window shatters on the sidewalk.

"Woohoo," a skinny tall guy shouts as he sprints out of the front door, almost plowing us over.

An employee runs out, his fist pumping in the air. "I'm calling the police! Damn kids," he grunts, glaring at us.

I hold up my hands. "I'm innocent."

He scowls. "For now."

Scott circles around me. "What's going on out here?"

The store clerk stabs the emergency number into his phone. "The damn festival. And they must be handing out drugs like candy, because it's been going on all day."

Something strange is happening. I pop into everyone's head.

What makes you say that? The fighting, the theft, or the group of girls streaking?

I'm the only one who can hear Ryan's thoughts, but their boy parts picked up the naked-girls part without any assistance from me. We all turn toward the road where a dozen or so girls our age are ripping off their clothes like they're auditioning for an episode of *Naked and Afraid*, but they don't seem that afraid to me.

"I think we ought to check out the festival," Scott says, tearing his eyes off the herd of full moons running past us.

I close my eyes. I've seen more than enough naked bodies for a while. "Why?"

"Does any of this behavior appear normal to you?" he whispers, pointing at groups of people turning into howling morons. And, yes, many of them are howling to the sun.

I roll my eyes. "Fine. But let me take Lizzie into the bathroom."

After a short stop in the bathroom, we walk through the store. The clerk who called the police earlier is pacing back and forth, muttering to himself.

"I need to distract them. I need to distract them," he says as he slaps his face.

The hair on the back of my neck stands up. I call up my magic to be ready. "Who do you need to distract?"

"You!" he says, popping a bottle of champagne and tilting it toward us.

I throw up a shield before a spray of gold liquid (he didn't even use the good stuff) hits us. I quickly lead Lizzie outside before the clerk resorts to shaking and opening every fizzy alcoholic beverage in the place. I mean, I've been to keggers at the U of Pitt, but geez, it's not even noon. Lizzie's lips tilt in that sideways grin of hers that I always called devious. It never fit her good Jehovah's Witness side, but now it totally fits.

"Do you know anything about this?"

She shifts her hands as she shrugs, as if to say, "I can't hear you." And now I know, she totally can. Granda's spell has clearly lifted, and the whole glassy-eyed stupor has been an act. My gods, she should win an Oscar.

I grab her arm, push positive energy into her, and drag her back toward the truck. "Come on."

The guys are standing together with their mouths open. They didn't even bother entering the store behind us because they've been completely distracted.

"What are you . . . ? Oh," I murmur as another pack of naked people go running by, but this time they're each carrying someone and there are twice as many. "Let's figure out what's going on. Ryan, you're on Lizzie duty. Scott, you watch her too. Alaric, you come with me."

"No funny business," Scott calls after us as we take off at a run.

"Never!" I shout behind me, though with all the nakedness there's a lot of irony in that statement.

We fly past the festival entrance gate. No one even yells at us for not buying our tickets. Now, I've never been to an Irish festival, but money is money. A patch of negative energy hits us. My green energy blocks it off and, because we're holding hands, it protects Alaric too. Since our little excursion in the woods, my magic has grown stronger. I send out a ball of energy with my free hand and use it to guide us to the source of power. I'm guessing it's got Maleficium sorceress all over it.

"Hey, Alac," yells a voice vaguely familiar.

If Alaric were in wolf form his hackles would stand on end. He twirls around and throws me behind him as if to protect me.

As if.

I duck around his frame and prepare to square off with Declan. I never liked that wannabe alpha.

"Hello, Declan," Alaric says, his voice low and threatening.

"Well, if it isn't our fearless leader returned from the dead. Oh, wait," he says, putting his back to Alaric and addressing the people behind him who must be pack members, "he wasn't dead. He left us."

I recognize the energy signature of several, but there are at least two dozen more I've never seen before.

Alaric slowly crouches into a defensive position. "I didn't leave. I was kidnapped and tortured."

Declan doesn't appear to be the least bit concerned. He should be terrified.

"Right, and you just so happen to show up here with your girlfriend in tow. It looks like abandonment to me."

"Back down, Declan, or I'll . . ."

Declan steps up to Alaric. "Or you'll what?"

"Take my rightful place as alpha."

Declan turns toward the pack. The back of his neck is just inches from Alaric's mouth, tempting him, tempting me. "Oh, I don't think so. That vacancy has been filled by me."

He twirls back around. His eyes flash yellow. He's challenging Alaric here in a crowded festival with strange happenings occurring everywhere.

Then it hits me. "It's a distraction. Where are Ryan and Scott?"

But Alaric goes full alpha male on Declan. "You. Will. Kneel. To. Me."

Normally, I'd find his alpha voice sexy, provided he doesn't try to conquer me with it. Now, with the realization that Declan is distracting us, not so much.

"Maria. Where's Maria?" I shout.

Declan hesitates when I mention the witch's name, then quickly covers it up. But it's all I needed to see. I spread my hands out, palms up, and send some energy balls out to clear the air and find that kinky ancient witch at the same time.

"It shouldn't be long now," I say.

"What shouldn't?" Declan says. There's worry in those nasty yellow eyes.

"Whatever crappy trick you pulled on everyone at the festival. I'm lifting it as we speak."

His lip curls. "You can't lift it. You haven't got the power."

Alaric glances at me. *Go ahead. He asked for it.*

I prowl toward him. "Haven't got the power?"

He stiffens as I circle around him.

"I am more powerful than anyone in this world." I fail to mention that there might be some Fomorian monsters that could give me a run for my magical power, but it's not my destiny to kill Balor. I also don't mention I can't actually harm another living being. A poker player never shares all her cards. Neither does a tarot card reader.

"Are you going to let your girlfriend act like she's more powerful than you, son of Clayone?" Declan says.

Alaric smiles at me. "Actually, yes, and she's not lying."

"I will not be cowed by her," Declan snarls and lashes out with his fist.

I swat it away. "You're not even making an effort. You can do better."

He lunges at me. I slip away from him and flick my wrist. He lands flat on his face. A few snickers erupt from the pack members.

"Why you little—"

"No, no, no." I wag my finger back and forth. "Thou shalt not call me names."

"And why not, skank whore?" He snarls and jumps at me.

Alaric growls and blocks him.

"Now, you've upset your alpha." I put my hand to the side of my mouth as if talking to Declan in confidence. "I wouldn't if I were you, especially if you're calling me names I've heard since elementary school."

I throw my hand at him and knock him on his ass. He lands with a loud thud. Alaric laughs with me. I've never played around with my magic before. It's *a lot* of fun.

I tap my finger to my chin. "What should I do with you now? Hang you upside down?" I raise my hand and Declan's body copies the motion. It hangs in midair, no rope, no apparatus, just a hanging werewolf.

"Or should I drop you down?" I motion to drop my hand.

"Stop, stop," he yells. "I submit."

That was actually close, because I wasn't sure if I could actually drop him on his head. That would probably injure him, and clearly rules are rules (as much as I try to break them).

"Don't submit to me," I say. "Submit to your alpha."

"He's no alpha, letting his witch torture me."

Alaric lunges at him, rips him out of the air, flips him so they're standing face to face, and bares his fangs at Declan. "How's this for dominance?"

"H-how d-d-did you . . . ?" Declan frowns. He can't understand how Alaric is able to partially shift. None of the pack can. They don't realize those are actually Fae fangs and claws, not a werewolf's, but now I do. That's why Maddie could partially shift too. He's also part Fae.

"I submit. I submit."

And the alpha wannabe loses his position.

Alaric releases him. He drops to his knees. The rest of the pack follows.

I put my hands on my hips and walk up to Alaric. "Well, that was easy."

He rolls his eyes and grabs me. "You are unbelievably sexy when you act all badass witch."

"It's not an act," I tease.

We both know that's not true.

I like when you talk in my head.

I like when you talk in mine.

He reaches for my lips, but he doesn't have to work too hard because I've already found his. Our power exhibition caused energy to surge through my veins, and kissing Alaric further fans the flames.

"I leave you alone for five minutes," Scott says, ripping Alaric away from me like he's a rag doll.

The pack growls in disapproval that their alpha has been challenged in such a profound way.

"Settle down," Alaric says in a commanding voice. The pack silences.

"Did we miss something?" Ryan asks, leading Lizzie along beside him.

"Well, Alaric has been returned to his alpha status, and I learned I can play with my food—well, toys."

Scott holds up his hands. "I don't even want to know what you mean by that. Apparently whatever magical plague was causing all the disruption has disappeared, so let's get moving."

"Oh, that was me too. I've got a gift. I should become a carnie. Travel the open road," I say as I saunter past him.

Someone jerks me by the collar. Breas.

"Predictable as always. I warned you I would find you," he says, wrapping his arm around my throat.

What the?

Got you.

*B*efore she touched the glass sphere, she swallowed. She'd waited so long to discover the truth of her destiny. Mathair Mhór and Gallean had only hinted at it; they'd never shared the full prophecy. Now, it was here before her.

Her fingers sparked as she took hold of it. The glass sphere grew warm with her touch.

Seen but not seen.
  Drifting into permanent destruction.
  Terrible power bestowed unknown.
  Thirst insatiable.

Conquered but not oppressed.
  Hidden but not accessible.
  Subversion of power through unexpected fall.
  Seed rooted.

. . .

Precious taken. Revenge sought.
   Maim but not kill.
   Iron fate sealed by future seed.
   Weather the storm. Caught unawares.

Caer exhaled and returned the glass sphere to its rightful place. The prophecy entailed many layers. She'd mull over the lines to sort out which ones pertained to her.

All the lines pertain to you.

She jumped, unsure of who had spoken. Gigi was in the Earthly Realm. Mathair Mhór had spoken to her recently, but the timbre of the voice didn't resonate with Caer as that of her mentor. Nor did it sound like Gallean.

The answers you seek will be found if asked.

She blinked at the realization that the glass sphere had spoken to her. She sat down at the desk and scribbled down the lines of the prophecy.

What does it mean?

Images bombarded her mind. A young boy covered in animal skins crept down a dark tunnel. He wanted to discover what his father and the Druids were up to. They had gathered strange herbs he didn't recognize under the light of the crescent moon and had taken off for the cave.

Up ahead he could see the flickering light of a flame and heard low chanting in a language he did not understand. As he got closer, he sank lower and lower until he was sliding along the cave tunnel floor like a snake. The chanting grew louder and more and more feverish. He had to see what was going on. He rounded the final bend, and what he saw churned his stomach. Horrible shadow monsters emerged from the cauldron and lengthened along the walls as if dancing with the Druids. What magic was this?

The men continued chanting. The fire grew higher,

reaching the air shaft. The potion in the cauldron bubbled and hissed each time a Druid added an herb, a frog's leg, a dried mushroom. Even from where he lay, he could tell the liquid was turning noxious, but he found himself rooted to the place, unable to leave.

The flames licked the cauldron as if lovers. He watched with fascination and horror as his father withdrew an eyeball from his cloak and chanted something as he tossed it into the cauldron.

The concoction erupted. Noxious gases burst into the air, shot over the Druids, and settled in the boy's eye before he had time to react. He kicked, he screamed, he moaned as he convulsed in pain. The words of the prophecy slammed into his subconscious.

Seen but not seen.
　　Drifting into permanent destruction.
　　Terrible power bestowed unknown.
　　Thirst insatiable.

Conquered but not oppressed.
　　Hidden but not accessible.
　　Subversion of power through unexpected fall.
　　Seed rooted.

Precious taken. Revenge sought.
　　Maim but not kill.
　　Iron fate sealed by future seed.
　　Weather the storm. Caught unawares.

. . .

Caer fell back in her seat, panting. Their fates had become entwined the day Balor spied on his father and the other Druids.

What turned a sweet boy into a monster?

She splayed her fingers back on the desk. The boy lay on the cave floor, his hand pressed to his injured eye. A large hulking man in a brown animal fur—his father—glowered at him. He muttered something about being ruined and a monster before he slapped the boy across the face. The boy fought not to cry, but tears fell from the uninjured eye.

His father's lip curled in disgust. He gripped the boy's arms and picked him up. The boy pleaded with his father, begging him to let him stay, but his words did not soften the disgust. The man carried him out of the cave.

His father ripped the boy's hand from the ruined eye. Blinding moonlight funneled into it. The boy screamed in pain, trying to fight his father and protect his eye, but he soon grew quiet as his body stilled. In the eerie silence that followed, the father nudged the boy with his foot to ensure he was dead. The boy sprang up. His father backed away in terror, and the boy's gaze fell on him, turning him to stone.

The other Druids descended upon him, bombarding him with killing curses. Balor flung his hands and used tree bark as a shield, but many of the curses found their mark. Rather than killing him, his body stretched and grew, turning from a boy, into a man, into one of the terrifying monsters from the cauldron. But instead of living in the shadows, this monster was real. As his ruined eye fell upon one of the Druids, he turned to stone. The fighting stopped when the final Druid's body fell to the ground and shattered. Balor, no longer recognizable as the sweet boy he once was, took in the destruction he had caused. A cruel smile rippled across his face before he lumbered off into the darkness.

Another vision appeared. A woman with long brown hair

stood at the ocean's edge. As the waves kissed at her toes, she smiled, staring off onto the horizon. From the sand dunes, Balor watched her. He'd watched her many times alone on the beach. Though the prophecy dwelled in the back of his mind, the draw of the woman superseded any warnings therein. He self-consciously tugged at the patch covering his ruined eye as he swallowed. He took a step toward her, then another, approaching her with the cautious speed in which a boy might approach a deer in a meadow for fear of it springing off before he'd had a chance to pet it.

The woman startled as a shell crunched beneath his foot. She turned to him, her eyes wide with concern. She scanned the sand dunes in hopes of finding someone to help her. He lifted his hands to demonstrate he meant her no harm. Her stance softened, but she was still ready to flee if needed. He withdrew from his cloak a giant conch shell and offered it to her. She smiled as she took it, cradling it in her hands.

He said something to her. She flipped the pearly white conch over to its pink underbelly and put it to her ear. Her entire face brightened when she heard the sound of the ocean. Balor's lips turned into a smile at her delight. She kept listening to the ocean as he spoke gentle words to her. Her smile soon became laughter. Soon, they were walking hand in hand.

Another vision of a swollen belly with a crone hovering between bent knees. The woman screamed as she pushed and pushed to no avail. Sweat beaded on her forehead. Her dark skin was pasty. Balor stood in the shadows, his face pinched in agony for the woman who was now his wife.

The crone encouraged the woman to push one final time. Soon the cries of a newborn filled the cave. The crone held up the baby girl for the mother to see before taking her aside to be cleaned and swaddled in soft furs. A single tear fell from Balor's eye as he watched his baby girl. With the attention placed on the infant, no one noticed the blood, far more than the afterbirth, that continued to pour from the mother. Nor did they notice she had stopped breathing until it was too late. No matter what heroic actions the crone and Balor did for her, there was no breathing life back into her.

The crone would pay for her neglect. He lifted the patch. The crone's mouth opened as she realized what was happening, but it was too late. She was already turned to stone. The infant wailed from her cradle, crying for her mother's touch, which she would never receive.

Balor clutched his wife's dead frame to his chest and released a roar that ripped across the seas, shooting fear into the hearts of every man, woman, and child. Cross him and they too would be turned to stone. He cursed the heavens and the hells.

In the silence that followed, he mourned, only to be interrupted by the soft cries of the baby, his daughter, who had caused his true love's death. He stomped over to her, his hand on the patch, prepared to turn to stone she who had killed his wife. But as his good eye fell upon her, his hand stilled. He ought to be rid of her, but he found he couldn't. His wife's legacy must live on.

The words of the prophecy arose in his mind. That his future seed would lead to his undoing would not come to pass. He was in command of his own fate. There'd be no destruction but what he himself wrought on his enemies. He sent his daughter away to live in a cave. Kept hidden from men and cursed to bear no children, there'd be no risk of any future seed being born to ever fulfill his role in the prophecy.

The Balor from Caer's visions didn't match the monster who'd sliced her father's throat. The monster who she had been running from her entire life.

Another vision quickly descended upon her. A hooded man sat in a dark corner of a tavern. He was waiting for someone. The door opened and a tall, powerful man walked in. Patrons backed away from him as he strolled through the tavern to the dark corner. Raw power emanated from him. He greeted the hooded man, who offered him a seat. There was something familiar about both of them. She studied them and came to realize that the hooded man was her father and the other was Gallean. Amorin had told her that her father and Gallean were friends, but that didn't explain what they were conspiring about as they drank their ale. A decision was made. Her father nodded and together they left the establishment.

Subversion of power.

When her father was alone outside, he stretched his wings and flew across an unnamed sea. His feet alighted on a rocky outcropping. There at the mouth of a cave stood a beautiful woman. Her eyes were the color of malachite. Her lips red rubies. Her skin the fertile soil. Her black hair framed her face. His mouth fell open as he gaped at her.

She peeked up at him from beneath her long black eyelashes. "Who are you?"

His intention was to free her from imprisonment and allow her to live among others so she could eventually marry and have a child who would fulfill the prophecy, but that plan expired the moment he laid eyes upon her. It didn't matter that she was the daughter of Balor or that he and Gallean had formulated a plan to eliminate Balor who had taken to conquering neighboring lands and turning all the inhabitants to stone. He was lovestruck.

Caer watched images of her father courting the woman, her mother, for weeks until she looked at him with the same longing as he looked at her. They stood on the same rocky outcropping on which her father had first landed. He took her hand in his and spread his wings. Together they flew across the same sea to live a lifetime together.

A roar rippled across the air, almost knocking them out of the sky, but her father's powerful wings weathered the storm. As the distance expanded between them and the island, Balor appeared in front of the cave. He had sensed that the next lines of the prophecy were beginning to unfold and had gone to check on his daughter, to ensure she was alone.

Iron fate sealed by future seed.

Caer sat back gasping as she recovered from the onslaught of visions. Her heart pounded in her chest as she realized that she was indeed the granddaughter of Balor, and though she felt sympathy for him for the travesties he experienced from his own father and the loss of his wife, his fate had been sealed when he slit her father's throat.

Weather the storm. Caught unawares.

Caer now understood the final lines of the prophecy. It was time to end Balor's scourge once and for all.

WALKED INTO THAT ONE

*G*ram always told me an overinflated ego would get me nowhere, and that's exactly how I got myself into my current predicament. I had known Declan and the werewolf pack were a distraction, yet I had played around with them rather than searching for the source of the chaos-causing magic. Of course Breas was behind it. Well, not Breas himself. His magic isn't strong enough to cause the type of upheaval occurring at the festival. But Witch Kensey and Maria certainly could. And since they're all besties now, I should have been on the lookout.

Alaric leaps toward me to free me from Breas's clutches. *Wait.*

He stares at me, puzzled. *I don't want to wait.*

Let's see who else is here. I drop in Alaric, Ryan, and Scott's heads.

No sooner do I channel those words than Maria strolls in wearing her same black miniskirt and skimpy black tank top along with her black stilettos. She doesn't have a problem revealing an abundance of skin, but at least she has some clothes on, which is more than I can say for the streakers we'd witnessed earlier.

Maria drapes her arm around Scott. "Hey there, handsome. I've missed you."

Scott stills as she pushes her chests into his. To his credit, he doesn't even drop his gaze to ogle her exposed mounded flesh. Although he's uncomfortable and unsure what action he should take next, he's glad that Caer isn't here because she would be jealous.

Oh, Scott. If Caer were here, she'd already have Maria pinned on the ground with her sword.

Ryan tries not to stare, but he's heard about an ancient Maleficium sorceress, and although we did tell him Carman had taken on a vessel, Maria isn't what he envisioned. Lizzie narrows her eyes at Maria. I take that small reaction as a very positive sign. If she's jealous, that means she feels, and if she feels, she can be persuaded to feel more, and if she can feel more, she can change.

"My wife, I've missed you," Breas whispers in my ear. It does nothing to me. He lacks the low husky undertone Alaric uses. Aside from that fact that he's not Alaric. Plus I loathe him.

"For the last time, I am not your wife," I snarl. It's really getting annoying when he brings that crap up. "The only reason I was once was for the greater good. I sacrificed myself for the people. And look where that got me. You betrayed me to steal the Vessel of Life and open the portal for the Fomorians. I'd say that was legitimate grounds for divorce."

"But, Gigi, think about the moments we shared back in Vernal Falls. I'd say they were very intimate." He's trying to provoke Alaric, and from the sounds erupting from my lover's chest, I'd say it's working.

Alaric, don't listen to him. I love you.

Scott removes himself from Maria and holds Alaric's shoulders. A casual observer would assume the gesture was to calm down a jealous friend, but that it wouldn't actually restrain him from fighting. With the strength in Scott's hands, however, he could hold back a herd of wild horses, or in this case, one wild wolf.

"Or what about in Kildare, when you'd already met someone else, but you still did all sorts of things with me?"

He's hitting below the belt, but he's wrong on so many accounts.

"Are you referring to the night you spelled my entire family with your treats or the lunch picnic when you drugged me and took my blood to raise"—I glance around to find Witch Kensey— "that."

He chuckles, but it's all twisted and corrupt. "You figured out my secret. You were always a fast learner. But not fast enough, because you let yourself get caught by me again, and I'm very grateful because I need more of your blood. Along with other things." He presses against my hip so that I can feel how turned on he is. He is a voracious horny bastard.

Get ready to run.

"You also don't learn," I shout as I pull up my leg and slam my Doc into his godly balls. As he doubles over—because god or not, a greeting up the chunk levels the playing field—I spin from his clutches, grab Alaric's hand, and sprint away. Ryan, Scott, and Lizzie follow in fast pursuit.

"Can your pack keep them occupied?" I ask Alaric.

"Attack!" he shouts over his shoulder.

I soon hear growls, snarls, and screams as a riot of supernatural proportions erupts behind us. We dive into Sam's truck. Sphinx leaps up, wondering what all the commotion is about, but soon settles back onto my lap since we're all in one piece. Alaric peels out of the parking lot faster than Breas can strip naked.

Kilkenny, here we come. I drop in everyone's head just in case any Maleficium witches are listening.

After thirty minutes on the road, I finally break the silence. "Well, that was an unexpected turn of events."

Scott puts his arms on the back of my seat. "How did they know we were going to be there?"

I place my hand on Alaric's leg. "Pull over."

When the truck stops, everyone climbs out and circles around Lizzie.

I draw up a searching spell and send it over her.

"It doesn't make any sense, though," Ryan says. "She's been working for Clayone, not Breas, Kensey, or Maria."

Alaric scrubs his chin. "He does make a point. Why would she side with them when my dad is on the outs with them?"

"Maria did offer me to him in the tunnels. Maybe they've made amends?"

"From his reaction, he was surprised she had offered you up," Alaric says. "Besides, it wasn't like you had anyplace else to go in there."

"Back to the spy," Scott says. "Did you find anything?"

I shift my attention back to Lizzie. "No, nothing came up. Unless they went old-school with a tracking device or something."

"Nan would never rely on modern technology for something like that," Alaric says.

Ryan keeps studying Lizzie like he can penetrate into her soul and bring her back. Her eyes pulse between red and hazel, and I begin to think maybe he can.

Then it hits me. "Wait a minute. There is someone else here who was working for the enemy."

Alaric runs his hands through his hair. "But I was tortured by Lizzie, who we've established is only aligned with Clayone." His eyes widen as he glances at Ryan. "Oh . . ."

Ryan stumbles backward. "Me? I'm not telling Breas or Kensey anything. I'm sided with all of you."

I reach out and send calming energy into him. His shoulders immediately relax. "Yes, but a tracking spell could be placed on you without your knowing. May I?"

He pulls his lips in and nods.

I send out a spell to search him. It settles on his head. "I wonder if they can see through your eyes, like what Sphinx did to me."

Nothing is like me.

"True story, buddy. Ryan, I'm going to undo the spell."

"Will it hurt?"

"It shouldn't. Hold on to someone if you want."

He reaches out for Lizzie. Her eyes bulge like she can't believe he'd choose her. Neither can I, but love is love.

"*Tóg treaspáis,*" I chant. The spell lifts from his head and hovers in the air before exploding. "It's gone."

"Okay," Scott says, rubbing his hands together. "Can we get back on the road and get this over with? I want to get home as soon as possible."

He clings to the possibility that Caer will return any minute. With my gift of sight, I know she won't return until Balor is dead, but I won't tell Scott that.

We jump back in the truck.

"We've got a problem," Alaric says, glancing in the rearview mirror.

I turn around to peek out the back window. Three cars are speeding up the road toward us.

Alaric throws the truck in gear and hits the gas. "Apparently, they know where we're headed."

Ryan puts his head in his hands. "Sorry, guys. I didn't know."

"Don't worry about it. This hunk of junk can go where no car can," Scott says.

Except that we don't know where the Kilkenny witches are, and with two evil witches, a god, and their minions on our tail, we won't exactly be able to go door to door.

I scoot away from Alaric. "Keep driving fast. Alert me if they get close."

"Where are you going?" he asks in alarm.

"I'm going to search for the coven with Sphinx's help."

Sphinx purrs as I scratch him behind the ears. *Fine.*

I open my chest and rest my palms facing upward on my lap, acknowledging to the universe that I am open to whatever it has to offer. I breathe in and out, in and out, trying to remain calm and relaxed while we're being hunted, but it's easier said than done.

Sphinx rests his paw on my leg. *Relax. They're far away.*

They are? I ask, almost opening my eyes to check.

Well, far enough away for you to vision travel.

That's what it's called?

Focus please.

And I do. I close my eyes and keep breathing in and out. Soon I slip away from the cramped truck and focus on my third eye, forgetting about the bumpy road and the people chasing us. All the while I keep breathing in and out, in and out.

I wrap my fingers around the spell book crystal and concentrate on the Kilkenny witches. In my mind, I wander the streets of Kilkenny. The bright colors of the buildings call to me in a way no town ever has. It's because of the magic. It's everywhere, but nowhere. Hidden from view, but present. Chanting circles appear before me, a group of men and women of Caribbean descent in a room filled with dried herbs and candles. The heavy scent of incense hangs in the air, but I can't place it. It's an herb I'm unfamiliar with. I remove myself from the circle and start backing up so I can step outside and visualize the location.

The leader opens her eyes and focuses on me. "No!" she shouts.

"I'm sorry. I have to," I whisper, backing away from her.

"No!" she shouts again and breaks the circle.

Abruptly, I return to the interior of the truck, gasping for breath.

"Well?" Ryan asks hopefully.

"I have an idea," I tell him, which isn't lying but it's not entirely truthful either.

No, the leader shouts in my ear.

If it weren't for Lizzie, I'd listen to them, but we're going to Kilkenny, and we're finding those witches.

"Incoming," Scott shouts two seconds before a car slams into us.

"That's gotta be Declan. So much for his submission. The traitor," Alaric snarls.

He's the only one without magic, so it makes sense.

"Wish we'd restrained him. I got a bit entangled," I reply. "Cover me!" I turn around and clutch the bench seat as Alaric hits the gas. Declan slams into us again.

"*Stad de*," I shout.

Declan's car swerves off the road and over the embankment.

"That worked well," Scott says in appreciation. "Do it again."

"*Stad de*," I shout and send two blasts at the two other cars speeding up to take Declan's place. The spells bounce off the vehicles.

"Shoot, they're protected."

"Hold on," Alaric says as he spins the truck to the right. He throws his left arm around me to keep me in place.

The two cars easily make the turn.

"I can't lose them. This truck can't go as fast as them."

"Let me try to disable the protection spells."

I form a ball of energy and fling it out the window. It smashes on the black car's windshield. The car fishtails, eventually flying off the road and down another embankment.

That leaves the red sports car. Breas is driving while Kensey murmurs something.

"Get out of the way," I shout, but it's too late. The spell shoots out our back tires, and now we're fishtailing. Alaric counteracts the motion and rights the truck rather impressively.

"Gigi, take the wheel," he shouts.

"What? This isn't time for country song lyrics."

"Trust me, okay?"

I take the steering wheel from him. He sticks his head out the window and climbs onto the roof.

"What is he . . . ?" Scott says. "He jumped!"

"What?" I turn around to see Alaric land on the red car's hood. The truck starts fishtailing again.

"Gigi, the wheel," Ryan shouts, leaping over the seat to grab it.

"I got it, I got it," I insist, but Ryan keeps his hands firmly on the wheel with his arms around me.

"Scott, what's going on back there?"

"Well, right now he's ripping off the roof of the car."

"What?" I turn around again and find my face smashed into Ryan's chest.

"Focus, Gigi, focus."

"He's got Breas by the throat and is—wow, he's strong— throwing him out of the roof."

"What's Kensey doing?"

"She's murmuring something. Fight it, Alaric, fight it," he says under his breath.

"*Stad de*," I scream and throw it over Ryan's head.

Tires screech behind me. I slam on the brake, throw the truck in park, and leap out the door.

Smoke spirals from the engine of the sports car. There's a dent in the windshield from where Kensey's head hit. The bloodstains are proof that at least her body is human. Whether the Fomorian witch can sustain that type of impact is beyond me.

"Alaric. Where's Alaric?" I search wildly for him, growing more and more panicked.

"Gi, over there," Ryan says and points toward Alaric's slumped frame in the grass at least a hundred meters from the car.

"Alaric," I shout as I run toward him. He's not moving. Why hasn't he moved? "*Múscail ardaigh.*"

When I finally reach him, I probe his body, searching for injuries. "Alaric, are you all right?"

He winces as he opens one eye. "How about you don't poke me so hard?"

"Sorry," I whisper and then press my lips to his. I push healing energy into him while I do it.

He smiles when I release him. "No one kisses like you do."

"And don't you forget it."

Ryan kneels beside him. "Dude, you okay? I've only seen the Hulk tear apart a car like that and successfully walk away."

"I wouldn't say I'm successfully walking away yet. Just give me a few minutes."

"You've got a few seconds, because the next round is starting in less than a minute," Scott says as he arrives with Lizzie.

In the distance, it looks like a mini dust tornado is coming our way. "What about Sphinx? Sphinx!" I shout.

Right here.

He rubs against my leg.

"Let's get out of here."

Smart girl.

HIDE AND SEEK

*A*laric's fast recovery proves he isn't the least bit human. My magical kiss helped, but being a part-Fae werewolf explains his ability to heal quickly. Not to mention his Otherworldly beauty, his athletic prowess, and all the other qualities that make him Alaric.

With the dust storm descending on us, there's no time to get back to the truck, but we need to move fast. Alaric scoops me on his back, Ryan scoops up Lizzie, Scott grabs Sphinx, and the three of them enlist their super speed to hightail it toward a run-down house in the distance.

Are we hiding in there? Might be a tad obvious, I say in Alaric's mind.

It'll give us enough time to discuss where we should go next. We're nearly inside Kilkenny's town limits, Alaric thinks, and I relay it to the rest of them telepathically. Heck, I've got nothing else do as my boyfriend carries me.

I send out feelers to see if the house is safe. The spell bounces off a shield or something and returns to me. Something magical is occurring there, and we don't have time to find out what.

Skip it. Keep going.

Not one of them questions me or complains. They trust me implicitly, which is empowering and unnerving at the same time.

In the distance there's another old house with peeling paint and a fallen front porch. Nothing says "Creepy Serial Killer Lives Here" like a house in the middle of nowhere with peeling paint and a fallen-down porch.

I send out another feeler. It enters the house, searches the rooms, and returns to me without finding anything dangerous, including ax murderers.

The one with the broken porch.

We slow down and approach the house. Alaric clutches my leg to keep me from climbing off, but I surprise him with a shot of electricity. His hand jerks away, and I jump off. I step cautiously onto the front porch.

"Be careful," Scott warns.

I roll my eyes. "No kidding, Sherlock."

"Is it okay?" Ryan asks. "Because otherwise we need to book it."

A strange energy ripples through me as I approach the door. "Something is magical here too, but why didn't my spell find anything?"

I grip the door, sensing a presence on the other side of it, and fling it open.

An ethereal figure in a blood-stained white dress flies out at me. "Get out!"

I throw up my hand and the ghostly figure disappears.

"Really? That's supposed to scare me?" I ask the house. "We're coming to request assistance. I have something you want." I hold out the spell book crystal.

Silence greets me, but someone is listening.

Creaking and moaning follow. A column splits in half and the front porch collapses.

Alaric leaps onto the porch, grabs me, and launches off before the roof crashes down on us. That is the second roof to almost crush me. I'm hoping it's not the beginning of some new trend. Alaric brushes off the dust and construction debris covering me.

Ryan studies me. "Are you sure they're going to help us?"

I glance back at the house. "I've got something they want."

He gapes at the house. "If that's how they treat their friends, what do they do to their enemies?"

Scott puts his hand on Ryan's shoulder. "I've learned not to ask those types of questions."

We take off toward the town as if our life depends on it, because Lizzie's does.

Visitors from all over the world come to Kilkenny to admire the quaint architecture and the vivid colors of the homes. There are hanging plants and flower boxes on every house, freshly painted front doors, and often lights in the front windows, a universal welcome to guests, though rarely does anyone take the owners up on the invitation anymore. We live in a different time, but it is a tradition worth keeping.

"Which one is it?" Scott asks, absorbing the positive energy of the town without realizing he's even doing so.

"That one," I whisper, pointing to the only neglected house on the street. It had a fresh coat of paint, albeit fifty or more years ago, and the black door and dark windows signify to visitors to stay away.

"It doesn't look like anyone lives there," Ryan says.

"That's the place all right," Alaric whispers. He's familiar with all sorts of magic after living with Carman and Calliope for all those years.

I finger the crystals on my neck. *I've got what you want.*

A breeze stings my cheek as it whips past. Not exactly a

welcome, but a get-the-eff-out warning would be much more aggressive.

"Careful," Scott murmurs to me as I press my hand to the front door.

As my palm touches the wood, the protective spells making the house look old and run-down lift for all of us standing in front of the door. The exterior is a happy yellow, much like the shade Gram used in our kitchen. The front door is a brilliant orange, and blooming flowers spill from every window box and planter.

"Wow," Ryan whispers.

I glance over my shoulder at the four of them staring up at the building. "Come on."

The rotten floorboards inside turn to a rich mahogany as I step on them. The broken stair railings straighten and gleam. It would be all too easy to stand in awe and take in the glamour receding before our eyes, but we don't have a lot of time. The Storm Moon is fast approaching, and the more time we spend trying to fix Lizzie, the less time we'll have preparing for battle.

A woman with a colorful head wrap and a matching dress appears before us. She's gorgeous by any standard, living or otherwise, except that she isn't living. Her appearance is airy and ghostly.

"You were told not to come here," her voice echoes through the room.

"As I told your friend, I have something you want." I lift the spell book crystal.

Her eyes fall to it, and she licks her lips. Her shimmery eyes meet mine. "How do you know we want it?"

"Just a guess."

She shoves out her hand. "Give it to me and be on your way, or else."

I tuck the crystal beneath my shirt and zip my leather jacket just in case. "Or else what?"

"There will be consequences."

I cross my arms. "There are always consequences, especially if you anger a goddess."

"How dare you," she says, her presence flickering.

"How dare you," I challenge her.

She disappears before our eyes.

"Perhaps we shouldn't upset the spirits," Scott whispers.

"Trust me. I got this." I spin around three times in one direction, then three in the other. "Reveal yourselves."

The house hisses and creaks.

"Here we go again," Ryan says under his breath.

I stand tall. Well, tall for me. "It's fine."

Screams project from the walls. The heavy scent from my vision fills the air.

Crackle. Pop. Whoosh. A blinding light explodes, forcing us to close our eyes. When we open them, there stands the coven from my vision, encircling us.

"I told you not to come," the leader says.

I realize the "ghost" that greeted us was not a ghost at all. She was a projection of the coven leader. In person, she is absolutely stunning.

I tap on my chest where the spell book crystal rests underneath my zipped jacket. "And I told you I have something you want."

"Why would you give it to us? We don't interact with your kind."

"My kind? All people are my kind. The coven in Kildare practices much of the same magic as you. They share many of the same affinities to the Elements as you."

She stomps on the floor. "They have never tried to seek us out before."

"Well, if I may?" I ask, reaching for the crystal.

She nods.

I withdraw the crystal and tap on it to return it to its true form.

"They did not know you existed. This spell book reads to me in Gaelic, but I'm sure to you, it would read much differently."

"There is dark magic in that book," she says, shaking her head.

"I know. That's why my grandmother had it hidden in her attic floorboards. I didn't know how powerful it was at the time."

"You lived in ignorance."

Tell me something I don't know. "I did. I don't anymore. I've embraced my true self." I allow myself to glow with the light emanating inside of me.

The leader kneels before me. Her coven follows.

"Forgive my ingratitude, I had to be sure. I am Suzanne, and it is an honor to have you in our presence," she says with her face toward the floor.

It's just like back in Vernal Falls, when all the coven members gathered at Dad's summons and I had a steady stream of believers paying their respects to me. "Please don't," I whisper. "Please stand as my equal, for I am as human as all of you."

"Rise," Suzanne says to her coven.

"Thank you."

"What is it that you seek?"

I glance over at Lizzie. Her eyes keep pulsing between red and hazel.

"Giselle," Suzanne says.

A young woman whose eyes are filled with understanding approaches us. She stops in front of Lizzie, closes her eyes, and inhales before proceeding toward Alaric. I remember Keturah, Caer, and the other faeries sniffing Alaric. They had said he was something other but didn't realize he was Fae at the time. Clayone's blood must mask Naisha's, or maybe she spelled his blood with a glamour. And I obviously can't smell shit.

Giselle closes her eyes again and inhales. Her eyes pulse behind her closed lids.

"They are related."

Alaric glances at me.

"Yes," I say.

"Brother and sister."

"Yes."

"Both direct descendants of the Diana Moon Cult, purest of blood."

"Yes."

"But also Fae from Lake of the Dragon Mouth, purest of Fae species."

"I didn't know that, but yes."

"But her blood is corrupted. His is clean."

"Yes."

"You have two objects that further bind her to that darkness."

"Yes."

"One is the spell book. Please withdraw the second package from your bag."

I pull the bundle of leaves containing the eyeball necklace out of my backpack.

"Set it on the floor in the center. Do not touch it, but remove its wrappings."

I roll it to the center of the circle and slice the packaging with Clarissa's athame.

"Good. Suzanne, begin."

The coven chants a spell I've never heard before, but yet it's familiar. I grab my circle of friends and family and begin to chant.

Giselle stands in the center with Lizzie. Her eyes are still closed as she chants along with her coven.

Lizzie's body seizes. "No!" she screams in a terrifying, spine-numbing tone I don't recognize.

"Now, destroy it," Giselle says to me.

I lift the athame. The eye widens. Maria's watching and trying to figure out where we are, but she's too late. I stab the eyeball, and though I cannot harm a living thing, the eyeball does not qualify.

Screams fill the air as black flames explode from the eyeball, biting and hissing before getting sucked back in. The eyeball turns to dust. Lizzie's chest heaves in and out.

"Well, that was intense," Scott whispers.

"Yes, it was, Oegden. It is an honor that you are here as well," Giselle says.

"Thank you, Giselle, for your guidance."

Giselle bows and returns to her place in their circle.

"Now, the spell book," Suzanne says.

"Do we destroy this too?" I ask.

"In a way. Together we will rid the book of the corrupting spells."

A man interrupts her. "Shouldn't we keep the book intact? Won't the removal of the evil upset the balance?"

Her eyes settle on him. "Gifford, your concern is valid but unwarranted."

"How do you know?"

"The gods will it," Giselle whispers.

Her response is enough to satisfy Gifford. "Very well."

"If you would place the spell book in the center."

"Of course," I reply and set the book where the eyeball necklace once lay.

"Brigit, if you would lead your inner circle, I will lead the outer circle."

"It is a privilege," Brigit and I say together, and we begin to chant.

Scott, Alaric, and Ryan join in with us as Suzanne and Giselle lead the outer circle chanting.

Lizzie screams "no" over and over, but it falls on deaf ears.

The cover of the spell book flies open. The chanting grows. Energy pulses all around us. The magic of the spell meets the energy at the center of the room, at the center of our circle. As it joins, a lightning strike hits the pages of the spell book and black flames shoot out of it. The heat of it burns. We turn our faces away from it. A loud whoosh draws our attention back to the spell book. Tiny specks of burnt paper circle around our heads before turning to dust.

"It is done," Suzanne announces. "We may break our circles."

"Lizzie," Ryan shouts, dropping to his knees and pulling her unconscious frame into his lap. "Is she . . . ?"

"She's not dead," Suzanne says, checking Lizzie for a pulse.

"Her life is linked with another," Giselle says.

Alaric meets my eyes. *Naisha.* He curses under his breath. "We need to get her back."

Ryan reaches for Giselle's hand. "Please tell me there's a way to unlink them?"

She glances at Suzanne. "There is one."

"No," Suzanne says. "It is too dangerous."

"His love might be enough to weather the storm."

"The storm as in the Storm Moon?" I say.

Giselle glances at Suzanne, who nods in approval. "Yes, but it is more complicated than that."

I put my hands on my hips, assuming my Superwoman pose, because why the heck not? "Complicated is my middle name. Tell me."

25

THE CHARIOT

"Prepare for battle," Caer shouted as she emerged back into the courtyard. But no one was there.

"Where is everyone?" she said to herself.

Keturah rushed over to her. "Your Majesty, there you are."

"What happened to everyone? Why did they leave?"

"Your Majesty, you've been up in the tower for days. We all waited, but eventually everyone drifted off to their homes to sleep and eat."

She clutched her heart and staggered backward. "For days? It felt like only hours."

"That happened with Britni too, though the room shares many secrets only with your bloodline."

Caer tried to compose herself. "Well, let's ready our people, because we are going to surprise Balor."

Keturah cast a wicked grin. "I've always enjoyed surprises."

Maddie appeared beside them. "Me too."

Keturah smiled at her son. "I do not want to lose you now that you've returned to me."

He blushed. "You won't. I promised Scott that I would protect Caer, and that is exactly what I plan to do."

Britni entered the courtyard. "As will I," she said, her back straightening as proof she no longer carried the burdens of the knowledge and prophecies of her people.

"As will I," each faerie repeated as they reentered the courtyard.

Caer thrust the iron spear into the air. "Gather your weapons, spell your armor. For tonight, we fight! Tonight, we honor my father!"

Cheers erupted throughout the courtyard, and everyone disappeared as quickly as they had arrived, this time to prepare for battle.

A young woman rushed over to her. "Your Majesty, if I may?"

"Of course."

Caer didn't need to ready her weapons. They were always sharpened. They were always ready for battle.

"I am Meya. I'm training to be the next healer. During my meditation I received a message from the Earthly Realm."

"From Scott?" she asked hopefully.

"No, from Gigi. She said they needed to speak with you about Naisha."

Caer's nostrils flared in and out as she debated whether to contact them before the battle or after. After might be too late. But if she contacted them now, she'd risk revealing her plan to them. Gigi wouldn't stop her, but Scott would. And depending on Gigi's magic and mood, he might be able to convince her to open a portal for him. It wasn't that she didn't want him with her. She did. But she didn't want his presence distracting her during the battle. Killing Balor was her destiny alone.

"Send them a message that I will return to them soon, but do not mention the upcoming battle."

Meya nodded. "And what of Naisha?"

"Where is she?"

"In the dungeons, heavily sedated to prevent her from cursing anyone. She is very powerful."

"Good. Keep her there. Tell Gigi that Naisha is safe and not to worry about us."

"Yes, Your Majesty." Meya curtsied.

"Now go. I've got a monster to kill."

Meya hurried back into the castle.

Caer stood in the courtyard and waited. During her time in the tower, she had found a book of legends. In it was a legend about Lugh, who claimed to be Balor's grandson. He was exulted as a hero for killing Balor, but really he'd only banished him to the Otherworld's purgatory. She sighed. Of course the legend predicated a male. The legends always mentioned men saving the day. She smiled to herself. Therein lay the deception.

Soon her people returned to the courtyard equipped for battle. Protective magic pulsed around them.

"Keturah," she yelled.

Keturah ran to her side.

"Did you find the location of the portal to Balor's purgatory?"

Keturah flashed her wicked grin again. "Of course. I am a master of persuasion."

"And intense pressure," Maddie added.

"True, my son, very true."

Caer raised an eyebrow at her second in command.

"Payback for stealing my son from me."

"That is understandable."

With her people amassed before her, Caer spread her wings. She didn't need them to fly, but they made a statement. She was an inspiration to her people, a sign that they would not be alone in the battle.

"Let's go," she cried and shot into the sky. She was soon flanked by Keturah and Maddie, and the rest joined in on the formation. Her swans joined them as well. She smiled to herself. Balor wasn't expecting them. That gave them an edge, and she planned to keep it. After all, Balor had caught them by surprise in the Land of Shadows. It was their turn to return the favor.

Caer sensed the powerful pull of the portal as soon as she approached it. It was like no portal she'd ever encountered or created herself. Tentacle-like fingers wrapped around them and tried to pull them in. Or strangle them. She couldn't tell which. Natural instinct told her to slice the thorny vines off of her, but the more she resisted, the tighter they became.

Keturah, Maddie, and the rest of them arched away from them too. Their fingers twitched for their swords but waited for guidance from their leader. From Caer. Some even flickered in and out of view without meaning to. That gave Caer an idea. Naisha regularly used this portal. As a full faerie she possessed the ability to disappear and use the shadows to her advantage. They needed to do the same. She wished she were telepathic like Gigi so that she could inform the others of her plan without voicing it aloud. She didn't know if the vines possessed the power to communicate and were working for Balor, or if the vines and the portal were the corrupting influences that had turned Naisha to the darkness, or if Naisha had found the darkness all on her own. Caer didn't relish making a decision that could have lasting consequences, but as their leader—as their Queen—it fell to her.

Screams of agony arose from her people. She had to make a choice.

"Cloak yourselves," she yelled, and everyone disappeared. So did the vines. She reached to her left and right, finding

Keturah and Maddie. As she gripped their hands, she shouted, "Join hands."

She glanced over her shoulder and recognized the invisible energy signatures of all her people. The tower had given her not only the histories of her people but also the ability to "see."

"Steady," she warned and stepped through the portal.

A brilliant light brighter than an exploding sun blinded her, immediately followed by absolute blackness. As her eyes adjusted, she looked to the sky and found the shadow where the sun once hung. It was as if the sun itself had had its power sucked out of it, and all that remained was a dim reminder of what once was full of light. They were surrounded by tree skeletons and the charred remains of dirt that at one time might have been fertile pastureland until Balor and his armies stole the life from it.

They had landed in full form. The portal had stripped their invisibility. As a result, their arrival was not unseen. A terrible cry as loud as a battle horn sounded in the distance. Her people readied themselves, gripping their swords and taking to the skies. It was time to end what Balor had begun.

Innumerable armies emptied out of Balor's lair. Hellhounds and other terrible beasts she recognized from the last battle broke through Balor's army formations, hungry for Fae blood that they would not taste. Not if Caer had anything to say about it.

In the Land of Shadows, her people could not use their magic to fight the monsters, but this time, they'd be able to call on any one of their abilities—magic, flight, teeth and claws, or all of them at once in order to defeat them.

Balor hadn't been born evil, but the prophecy had haunted him from his very first breath, predeciding his fate. He couldn't rid himself of its malfeasant nature. The seeds of that evil took root the day his father watched him convulse in pain as the noxious fumes turned him into a monster whose only desire was to destroy the realms that would never allow him redemption.

Balor ran from his prophecy. He could have killed his daughter to ensure his life. Instead he hid her away in a remote cave on a faraway unknown island. It shamed Caer to admit that her own father and Gallean had each played a part in that plot to seal Balor's fate.

Conflict mired Balor's endless pursuit to escape his prophecy, shifting between conscience and destruction. Forcing his daughter into absolute isolation rather than killing her. Torn between wanting to kill his granddaughter or imprison her. His decision on Caer's fate would be dependent on his mood at the time of their meeting. He wouldn't need to make one if Caer had any say in the matter.

For her, the decision was a simple one. Admittedly, she knew there were fragments of conscience remaining in her grandfather, but too much of him had been corrupted by his endless pursuit to escape his prophecy to allow him to live.

Lugh had tried and failed to kill him because it was not his destiny to do so. He was not the true descendent of Balor, only a man spewing lies to seek glory. He'd merely banished Balor and his armies to this purgatory instead. Now it was time for Caer to take her rightful place in the histories.

She raised Freagarach in the air and shouted her own battle cry that echoed with each one of her people. She angled down and dove, striking first.

The clash of metal against metal rattled the air. The ground rumbled as masses of enemy bodies crashed to the earth, only to be trampled by their own. The world erupted into chaos.

Black blood splattered across her face as Keturah beheaded two men at once. Maddie bashed skulls together, finding strength within him he didn't know existed. Caer's swans dove and pecked or clawed out eyeballs, eliminating the enemies' sight. Balor's monsters were falling faster than they could arrive on the battlefield.

Scott had shielded her the last time. Now she fought off enemies from every direction with her eye constantly on Balor's lair, waiting for him to appear. The sickeningly sweet sound of blades slashing through sinew and bone echoed around her as enemy body after enemy body crashed to the earth.

Britni swung and slashed at a hellhound. Keturah vaulted onto the back of another and rode it straight into the enemy armies, stabbing left and right as they ran through. Maddie leapt into the air and landed in the midst of the enemy and tore apart terrible beasts as if they were made of paper. Caer cut and sliced. Adrenaline coursed through her. They held the advantage, and she planned to keep it.

Balor's roar shattered the sounds of the battle, as if his men were quietly contemplating the merits of the purgatory they were forced to reside in rather than fight for their lives. Her fingers itched for the iron spear hanging from her back, but she would be patient.

Immediately his good eye fell upon her. Her stomach curled, but her muscles surged with power. A wicked laugh escaped from her mouth.

"You thwarted the prophecy by coming here. You will pay dearly for your misstep," he yelled. He reached for his patch. He wasted no time with battle motions or chatter. Neither would she.

"It is you that will pay," she shouted. She launched the iron spear through the air just as he lifted the patch. She watched with morbid fascination as Balor realized his mistake just as her spear found its mark.

He released a ferocious roar, which was suddenly cut short as his vocal cords turned to stone, soon followed by the rest of him. She dropped Freagarach to the ground and gathered all the energy around her as Gallean had taught Gigi and Scott to do back in his keep. Back then she'd watched them in anger, thinking Gallean's energy lessons useless, but now she realized it was the final push she needed to complete her destiny and end Balor forever. She threw all her power at him in the form of a massive wind.

A single tear tracked down his face from the stony eye, almost as if thanking her for release. His body fell backward, crashing to the earth.

The ground rocked beneath her feet. Huge fissures tore the earth apart. Caught unawares, his armies fell into the crevices, consumed by red hot lava erupting from them. Her people took to flight, narrowly avoiding flames. Her grandfather's body exploded into thousands of pieces, shooting massive rock missiles everywhere. It wasn't safe for her people to remain here, yet she couldn't seem to move. The edge of her vision grew hazy. She wiped her eyes, but it didn't help. Her strength left her. She collapsed to her knees.

A giant boulder plummeted toward her. She watched it spiral end over end toward its mark. This was her end, and she was okay with that. She'd achieved what she had set out to do. She held out her arms in a final act of defiance. Everything turned to black.

26

COME BACK TO ME

*E*verything is contingent on the Storm Moon. Lizzie's life. Naisha's. Even mine—though I haven't mentioned that to everyone else. The Storm Moon falls on my birthday. That is not a coincidence. Clarissa warned me months ago that a storm was coming, and the proof, they say, is in the pudding. Or at least outside the truck. A freak hailstorm pummels the vehicle as we drive back to Granda's.

I peek out the windshield, studying the gray skies. I hold my crystals to my lips with one hand while I hold Alaric's hand with the other. The nightlock-imbued crystal and the clear one Clarissa gave me pulse with my touch. The two pair well together, just as Alaric and I do. Even in nature, opposites attract. But there is nothing natural about this storm brewing. It feels wrong. Invasive. Corruptive.

And I don't plan to talk about it unless it becomes an issue. After a restful and well-deserved break in Kilkenny, I want everyone to enjoy themselves a while longer before our harsh reality returns without invitation.

I sigh, resting my head against the headrest, working through some different spells I learned from Giselle. She's as

210

curious about reincarnated gods as I am about their coven's green magic practices. Their ability to mask their houses and practice while tourists fill the streets is remarkable. Suzanne runs an apothecary, selling dried herbs, soaps, and lotions. Gifford owns a rock and gem shop, supplying the coven and the town with crystals and other healing stones. Giselle reads palms and tarot cards, but she's careful not to share too much. She tells her customers mostly truths with a layer of people-pleasing generic lines like, "A difficult decision lies ahead," "You will meet someone," and perhaps the most vague but highly sought after, "I see wealth in your future." The coven takes "hidden in plain sight" to the next level. Their very existence has been kept secret from Granda and his coven. I wish I could visit them again. Their coven has so much to offer, but it is not in my cards.

Gifford hung out with Ryan and Alaric. He was fascinated by fellow shapeshifters, though he was of the feline variety. Sphinx was obviously a huge fan. Scott and Suzanne discussed upcoming events and possible outcomes, and everyone took turns watching Lizzie. She was no longer in a trance-like state and she wasn't overtly trying to kill me or make death threats against me, but she was doing a brilliant job ignoring us. Well, except Ryan. She'd watch his movements, and her body softened when he was near her, which I took as a good sign. She also seemed to brighten when it was Alaric's turn. She always wanted a brother.

Being in Kilkenny felt like a mini vacation away from our lives. It was much harder to say goodbye to our new coven friends than I thought it would be. I've never made friends easily, so to meet a coven's worth of witch friends and then have to leave them was heartbreaking. But nothing can stop time (believe me, I asked). We encouraged them to reach out to Granda. Powerful witches should be friends.

I adjust my backpack. I've taken to wearing it all the time

because of the way things seem to be going. It no longer carries the cursed eyeball necklace. That was thankfully turned to dust along with Carman's Maleficium connection to Lizzie. And my necklace no longer carries the spell book crystal. That stayed in the well-deserved hands of Suzanne and her coven. The spell book had been stolen from them and corrupted by Carman long ago. Calliope had somehow gotten her hands on it and hidden it in Gram's attic, unbeknownst to Gram. That explains why Suzanne and her coven weren't too keen on us when we first arrived.

The backpack does carry two glass cylinders coated with crushed nightlock, lavender, and some other herbs. Once the cylinders explode, the evil in a person will disintegrate. One is for Lizzie, and one is for Naisha, but everything is contingent on getting Naisha back from the Faerie Realm by the Storm Moon.

I sent word, but I haven't received confirmation that Caer got the message. The fact that I couldn't reach her directly worries me. She was someplace inaccessible to me. Caer and I are similar in a lot of ways, and that scares me because it means she might fight Balor on her own, since that's totally something I would do. From what I witnessed in the Shadow Realm, no one possesses the strength to take him down by herself without life-threatening ramifications. His magic is too potent and malevolent—it'll seek to destroy that which threatens it.

Alaric squeezes my hand. "You okay?"

"Just thinking."

"About?"

Scott groans in the back seat as if in pain. "Pull over."

"It's really raining. The sides of the road might be washed out," Alaric says, glancing at Scott in the rearview mirror. But whatever he sees worries him. "You got it," he says and pulls the truck over to the side of the road.

I whirl around. My brother's clutching his chest like he's having a heart attack. "Scott, what is it?"

He's unable to speak. The pain blinds him, but it's not from an injury he received during any of our many misguided adventures to cure Lizzie. It's about Caer. Ryan throws the truck door open for him. Scott climbs out, doubling over when he gets outside.

We all follow him. The hail attacks us. Wind whips across our faces, trying to blind us.

I grab hold of his shoulders to push energy into him if he needs it. "What do you see?"

"Something's wrong. Something's wrong with her." His voice gets drowned out by the storm, but I can read his mind and Alaric and Ryan have werewolf hearing.

"How do you . . . ?" Ryan asks.

Scott lifts his eyes to mine. They're wild with fear. "She needs me, Gi. She needs me."

"I don't—"

He grabs my arms. "A portal. Make me a portal. I need to get to her. Hurry, there's no time."

His worry hits me in powerful waves. It should be enough emotion for me to draw from. I glance at the others because there is no way in any of the hellish realms that I am leaving them. "Everyone, grab hold."

The five of us join in a circle. Sphinx climbs on Alaric's back. Alaric leans over to whisper in my ear. "Do you even know where she is?"

I breathe in and out, steadying myself. I search for Caer in my mind, but there's nothing there. It's absolute nothingness.

"Hurry, Gi, she needs me," Scott pleads.

I pull my lips in, determined to help him find her. "Scott, I need you to use your connection. I need you to think where she could be."

He closes his eyes and immediately opens them. "Got it."

I read his mind and envision her location. The shimmery haze of the portal appears before me. "Hold on," I remind everyone as I step into the portal.

Ryan and Lizzie double over when we land, but we don't have time to wait for them to recover from their portal-jumping hangover. Caer needs us.

As if reading my mind, Alaric says, "Go. I'll find you."

Before I can answer, Scott throws me on his back and takes off.

Having a werewolf boyfriend does have a lot of advantages, although calling him just a boyfriend feels so fleeting, so temporary. We are so much more than that. We share a connection between time and space. We're soul mates. Scott and Caer share that same bond, but where Alaric can find me by my scent, Scott can't smell Caer.

"How do you know where to go?"

"I just know."

Up ahead, a large group of faeries circle around someone. The remains of a shimmering portal disappear.

"Move," Scott roars, pushing his way through when the faeries fail to listen to him.

He throws me off his back as he slides to Caer's side. I land on my feet, embracing my inner cat, and hurry over. She's not breathing, and the grayness of her skin suggests she hasn't had oxygen in her lungs in some time.

Maddie is there.

"What happened?" I ask him.

"We don't know. She threw the spear and killed Balor, but then she collapsed. I flew down and saved her before a giant boulder pummeled her, but she's been unresponsive since."

"Caer," Scott whispers. "Caer, I'm here. Come back to me."

She remains still, even with Scott's persuasive spelled

words. He bends down and breaths air into her lungs just as he'd done for Alaric. When nothing happens, he breathes into her again and again. Still nothing happens.

"Don't leave me," he pleads.

He breathes into her three more times, her chest still refusing to rise and fall even with his mighty breaths.

The intense emotion swirling around them overwhelms me. I bite my lip, trying not to cry.

"Caer, come back to me," he whispers. "Please."

His eyes find mine. "Is there anything you can do? Is there anything left to be done? I love her."

I wish that I'd had Sphinx steal the Vessel of Life for me. I'd use it on Caer. I do have the Chalice of Healing in my backpack, but it can't bring someone back to life when her life-force has left her. It only strengthens what life is already there.

There is one way as old and ancient as life itself. "Tell her."

Tears stream down his cheeks. He's never said the words to her. They hadn't found their time yet, and he fears it might be too late.

"I love you, Caer. I love you," he says, and breathes into her one final time.

He pulls her head into his lap. "I love you," he says again and bends down to kiss her lips. Four doves appear and circle around his head. They appeared after Alaric came back to life, but it doesn't look like Caer's life-force is returning.

Or is it?

Scott kisses her again, and the grayness disappears from her skin. Her cheeks return to their natural rich shade of brown. Her lips, no longer pale and lifeless, fill with red and open to meet Scott's third kiss. He's too consumed with his own sadness to notice her life returning to her. She lifts her hands around his head to deepen the kiss. Scott tries to break away. He wants to see for himself that she's alive, but she's back in control now and he's powerless to stop it. He cradles her face in his hands as if she is the most precious person in any of the realms—and to Scott, she is. The four doves circle round and round them.

I glance around at the gathering of faeries. Pure wonderment adorns their faces as they watch their queen return to life. Each breath she takes is proof to them that their battle wounds and lost comrades were worth it. That Balor was defeated, that their queen is safe, and that the kingdom will once again return to peace.

Alaric wraps his arm around me. I rest my head against his shoulder and watch my brother kiss his true love. His soul mate. For once, the universe aligned for us, and I am thankful.

"Get a room," Ryan says, breaking the silence.

Scott pulls away from Caer, but she's not done kissing him yet. She yanks him back down to her.

I lean over to Ryan. "You can't stop love."

His gaze drops down to Lizzie. "No, you can't."

Her lips curve into a shy half smile.

With that look, I know that there's hope for Lizzie. There's hope for us all.

27

ALL FOR A SONG

*E*ventually, Keturah, Maddie, and the rest of us left Caer and Scott to do their thing, and by the looks of it, they were going to be doing it for a while.

"I didn't know Scott could breathe life back into the dead," Alaric says as we head toward the castle.

"He didn't either. At least not until it happened with you. Being a reincarnated god doesn't come with an instruction manual. I wish it did. It would make my life a lot easier."

Ryan holds Lizzie's arm as we enter the castle. "It seems like you just know stuff."

"I do, but sometimes the goddess speaks to me too."

Maddie pats my head as I walk past him into the castle. "And let me tell you, listening to one of their conversations is really weird."

Ryan offers his hand to Maddie. "Name's Ryan."

He accepts it. "Maddie. I spent a lot of time watching you in your cell."

Ryan laughs. "In most cases, that would sound very creepy stalkerish, but given our circumstances, it sounds about right."

We follow Keturah through the halls. "It's this way to the dungeons."

"Do you think Naisha will talk to us?" I'm not exactly hopeful, but I sense Keturah can be very persuasive.

"Evil taints her. Everything she says is double-talk. What are you planning to do with her?"

"There's a spell we need to conduct on the Storm Moon to break the connection between her and Lizzie."

Keturah stops to look at me. Anger swells around her. "She tied her life-force to her daughter?"

"She did."

She shakes her head and takes off toward the dungeon at a much faster pace. "I never realized how evil she was. I wish I had known long ago. I could have stopped it. I could have stopped her."

"Don't beat yourself up. If you had, Alaric would never have been born, or Lizzie."

Alaric squeezes my hand. He's been mostly quiet since we left Caer and Scott. It's not easy to hear someone bash your mother. I know that better than anyone. At least my mother turned out to be a wonderful woman. I can't say the same for his.

"She's refused to eat or drink, but otherwise, she's been the model prisoner," Keturah says, stepping back from the cell as Maddie leads Naisha out.

Even though she's been kept prisoner in the dungeons, she's been well taken care of. She could be the ideal duplicitous mother model for Macy's department store: Whether on the soccer field or in the dungeons, always look your very best.

"Lizzie," she yelps at the sight of her daughter.

Lizzie's eyes jump to hers. Ryan tightens his hold on her.

"What have you done to her?" Naisha hisses.

My protective nature arrives full force. "Nothing, actually. All the spells and enchantments on her have been lifted. Well, except for your curse. She's able to speak if she'd like to. She must not be happy to see Mommy Dearest."

Her gaze jumps to Ryan. "You. You did this to her."

He pulls his free hand to his chest. "Me? I didn't do anything to her."

"Her affections for you are preventing her from achieving greatness."

Lizzie stiffens.

Ryan's nostrils flare at the slight. "I think she's pretty great already."

Naisha's lip curls. "Of course you do. You're not worthy of her. You were supposed to die at the hands of Scott. Breas subverted my plans. That stupid egotistical bastard."

I raise my hand. "You're finally speaking my language, but we've got a curse to break and a battle to plan."

She tries to say something especially nasty, but I slap a silencing spell on her.

"We need to get this show on the road. Think my brother's done sucking the tonsils out of Caer?"

"I wouldn't mind taking some time to do that with you," Alaric says, cupping my bottom.

I pull him along, with the rest of them in tow. "We'll see if we can carve out a few minutes."

Scott and Caer meet us at the entrance. Caer's back to her glorious, gorgeous self, looking even more radiant if that's possible. I don't know how she was able to hide in the shadows for so long when she's as bright as the sun itself.

Even in the fallen faerie's presence, her thoughts keep shifting back to Scott and what she'd like to do with him. I block their minds off from me, because there are some things I don't want to know.

"So, what's the plan?" Maddie asks, rubbing his hands together.

I run my hand over a few gashes on his arm. "Don't you need some rest?"

"No way. I've got adrenaline coursing through my veins. I'm ready to fight."

"You are your mother's son," Keturah says, smiling broadly at him. Her own battle scar marks her left cheek. I suspect there's more under her armor, but she would never admit it.

I embrace their enthusiasm. "Well, let's open up a portal and kick some Fomorian ass."

"We already kicked some major Fomorian ass," Caer says. "Let's finish this fight once and for all."

"Breas isn't going to be happy you killed his secret weapon," I pretend to whisper in confidence to Caer, but it's for everyone's benefit.

Her fangs protrude as she smiles. "I know."

"Are you up to opening a portal?" Scott asks her.

She grins at him. "With our trí cumhacht, it will not be a problem."

"Does anyone have motion sickness medication?" Ryan asks.

Scott slaps him on the back. "Suck it up, buttercup. You'll get used to it."

"Let's go out to the courtyard. Your people are waiting for your command," Keturah says, leading the way.

A large group of faeries stand in a circle as if knowing what we intend to do, and maybe they do. Maybe all Fae have the gift of foresight.

"Join together," Caer says, and we all do.

"Triple power, activate!" Scott teases, as a portal appears before us and we jettison back to Kildare.

· · ·

Chaos hits when we land. Torrential rains batter our faces, blinding our senses. I throw up a shield above our heads to protect us. Darkness consumes the remaining light of the day. We run through Granda's boundary shield to get away from the punishing elements. It's only once we're inside that realization strikes us in one collective breath: The Storm Moon will soon be upon us. The battle is fast approaching. Granda and his coven surround us as if they, too, have the gift of foresight.

"There is much to discuss," he says in welcoming, "but first, Scott and Caer, you must shift into swans and fly over as much of Ireland as you can while singing your love song."

Scott brings Caer closer to him. "And why do we need to do that?"

"Because your love song will lull the world to sleep for three days and three nights. It is the only way to keep humans safe and blind to the upcoming storms and battle."

Scott tries to argue, but Granda raises his hands. "There's no time. You must go."

"Come, Scott," Caer says, pulling him over to an open area. "He's right. Our love song is in the legends. It's the only way."

"I always knew you put me to sleep, though I could never figure out why," Ryan says with his arm draped around Lizzie's shoulder. Her head rests against his chest.

Scott fails to reply to him. His attention is fully on Caer. "Our love is that powerful?"

"Powerful enough to bring me back to life," she whispers.

"Powerful enough to save the world," he smiles.

Together they shift into swans and take to the skies.

"That. Was. Impressive," Maddie says, watching in wonder as they fly away.

"Yes, it was," Alaric agrees.

I rush to catch up to Granda who has already spun on his heel and is hurrying inside his cottage.

"Granda, what's the hurry? What's happening?"

Inside, Anna gathers herb bundles from the ceiling and places them on the table along with two mortars and pestles and several bowls. Sam's busy lighting dozens of candles. I flick my hand and light them all for him. He looks at me in amazement. I wave my hand like it was nothing.

"Granda, what's going on? What's happened here?"

He takes a pile of books off the shelves and hands them to Sam. "Search these," he says and grabs another pile and hands them to another coven member and instructs him to do the same. He reaches for a giant old book from a top shelf like a man possessed.

"Granda," I shout. "What's going on?"

He startles, and the book—a spell book—goes tumbling down. Alaric catches it before it hits the floor.

"Thank you," he sighs, removing it from Alaric and carefully placing it on the table before turning to me. "Whatever mischief Breas, his witch, and Carman conducted at the festival is now everywhere."

I freeze, refusing to believe it. "We stopped it. I stopped it."

He purses his lips. "Only temporarily. As soon as you left Kilkenny, the curse spread like wildfire. Men, women, and children of all ages have been afflicted all across Ireland. Acting erratically. Assaulting each other. Getting into accidents. They're possessed."

Apparently, the festival mischief was just a test for Breas and the rest of his minions. Now, they've set a curse upon the whole country.

"Has anyone in the coven been affected?"

He glances at Sam, and they share a long, sad look. "A few

went out to collect some items we needed. We were able to bring two of the three back, but it wasn't easy. We keep laying protective spells on the boundary, but we're running out of supplies. I don't know how long we can fight them off. That's why I sent Caer and Scott to the skies. With the Storm Moon close, we can't risk hurting innocent civilians."

"Innocent civilians? You make it sound like a war. I mean, I know we've been preparing for a battle, but war seems so . . . aggressive. So . . . final."

His stare pins me in place. "It is a war. A war of good against evil."

"But Balor's dead."

"Balor was but one factor in the war."

Alaric brushes against me. His presence immediately relaxes the tension in my shoulders. "How are they spreading the curse?"

"The unnatural rains. They're somehow dispersing it through the weather."

"What happens if anyone leaves the property?" Maddie asks.

"They're immediately afflicted."

"So, all the werewolves . . ." Alaric begins.

"Are back on their side," Granda finishes.

"I need to stop the rain," I say to myself.

Granda shakes his head. "I don't think Brigit is able to affect the Elements like that."

I lift my chest. "No one really knows what I'm capable of."

Alaric places his hand on my back. "No, we don't."

I rush outside. The faeries mill around, talking to the coven members. They keep pointing at something.

I spot Keturah and hurry over. "What's going on?"

She points to Britni, who's rolling around on the other side of the boundary shield.

"Something is wrong with her. Something unnatural," she whispers. "None of our magic can stop it."

Suddenly, Britni springs to her feet. Her fangs protrude and her claws are out. She lunges at me. Before I even realize what's happening, I'm on my back, and her teeth are snapping at my throat.

Just when her canines pierce my skin, she's ripped off of me. I look up to see her feet dangling in the air, kicking and thrashing, with Alaric holding her by the throat.

"Don't touch her," he growls, flashing his own canines.

She hisses at him, her eyes completely black. Her claws slash at his arms. He squeezes. She fights harder to break free.

Keturah rushes over to him. "She's not herself. Please, don't hurt her."

I leap up and throw a lifting spell at her to remove the curse. She pauses. Her eyes shift back to light tan. She reaches for Alaric's hands at her throat, her claws no longer extended. "Please," she whimpers. "Please, don't hurt me."

I squeeze Alaric's arm. "It's okay. The curse is lifted."

He hesitates, breathing in and out. I feel a corrupting influence in him. I glance over and see Naisha watching us with a maniacal grin on her face. I push calming energy into him, and he releases Britni.

Britni collapses, clutching her throat. "I'm sorry. I don't know what happened to me."

I clench my jaw, watching the mist falling outside the boundary shield. "I do," I growl.

I raise my hands, drawing energy from the surrounding space. "You are not of this world."

I shoot my spell out from me. The mist hovers in midair.

"You are not welcome here. Leave this world."

And with that, it disappears and the storm clouds lift.

"Will the clouds return?" Keturah asks, fearful that any of them could fall victim again.

"I don't know. For now, don't let anyone leave until we know for certain it's gone."

Alaric folds my hand in his. "Thank you," he whispers. "I didn't mean to hurt her." His gaze falls on Britni who's wincing as she clutches her throat.

"You were protecting me. It's very hot."

He turns to me, his green eyes piercing into mine. "I will always protect you. But with this corrupting power, I can't do it alone. We need the werewolves back on our side. There aren't enough coven members to handle this on our own."

I sigh. "I know."

"We need my dad."

Nerves freeze me in place. "Why?"

"Because having the Original Werewolf on our side is the only way we're going to beat Nan, Breas, and a Fomorian witch."

My eyes fall on Naisha, who's watching us with intense interest. I send a searching spell to ensure she's not influencing Alaric. It returns back to me free of magic.

"Why do you say that?"

His eyes flash gold and green. "Because if there's one thing I learned about him during my imprisonment, it's that he hates backstabbers. I don't know all his history with Nan, but he's really pissed off at her."

"What about me?" I ask in a much smaller voice than I intended.

"You're my mate. You're untouchable."

I quirk my eyebrow. "He's been plotting my demise since Brigit placed restrictions on his werewolves."

"I'm his son. His one true heir."

"What about Lizzie?"

His eyes slide to hers. "He'll honor her too, but I'm his firstborn. There is no other like me."

"That I agree with, but—"

He pulls me to his chest. "Trust me, Gigi. I won't let anything happen to you."

I swallow all my bad feelings and place my trust in Alaric. "I believe you."

28

BIG BAD WOLF

*A*laric asked me to trust him, but he hasn't lived in fear for months that the big bad wolf was going to kill him. It wasn't his mother who'd died imprisoning him. I search his mind again to ensure that visiting Clayone and asking him to join our side is his own idea and not some subversive scheme by Naisha to get me killed. He keeps coming up clean from all magic except my own.

"Are you sure this is going to work?" I ask him for the millionth time as we follow the tunnels.

He squeezes my hand in reassurance. "Yes, I am."

Ryan follows behind with Lizzie, who is becoming easier and easier to handle. Her cooperation is another positive sign that she's returning to us. Maddie and Keturah lead Naisha through the tunnels. She fights them every step of the way, even with a variety of my spells on her. I worry that bringing her was a mistake. Clayone gave her two children. Their relationship was more than a passing fling. If he sides with her instead of his son, the blood of the innocent will be on our hands. I send a silent prayer to the other gods that Alaric knows what he's doing.

We enter the large cavern meeting room. I stare at the painting on the wall of Clayone towering above his werewolf pack as the image of his son, Alaric, watches from a distance. I glance at the floor beside the painting where Alaric once fell, immobilized by Breas. I remember the way I felt when I returned to him after dealing with Breas, only to find him gone. Taken by his sister and dragged to his father's prison to be tortured until he had turned against me.

"Gigi, it's okay," he whispers. "I love you. Nothing is going to happen to you."

"What about you?"

He kisses my forehead. "I'll be fine. He's my dad."

"Your mom tried to kill you when you were reunited. What makes you think your dad won't offer the same greeting?"

He squeezes my hand and leads me toward the tunnel to Brigit's shrine. "You'll see."

There in the darkness I can just make out the shape of a giant man.

"Hello, son," Clayone says, his voice rumbling through the tunnels. "What treats have you brought me?"

See? I place in his head.

He's got a strange sense of humor.

I know humor. That's not it.

Trust me.

The figure inhales deeply. "A family reunion."

I stop. We've made a terrible mistake.

"Trust me, Gigi," Alaric pleads.

As we approach Clayone, a giant lump lodges in my throat, making it impossible to breathe. My heart races triple time. We stop just outside the boundary to the shrine room.

"Son, what have you done?" Clayone whispers, sounding scared and in wonder simultaneously.

Alaric lets out a long exhale. "I didn't think it could happen. The legends, the prophecies—nothing hinted at it."

I have no idea what they're talking about, and it bothers the hell out of me. "Can someone clue me in?"

Clayone drops to his knees and bows to me. "I take an oath of fealty to you, Gigi, reincarnated Goddess Brigit. I am forever dedicated to you."

"Um . . . thank you?" I lean over to whisper in Alaric's ear, even though I know Clayone can hear me. "What brought on this drastic change of heart?"

Alaric turns to me, now holding both my hands, his eyes bright, his smile wide. "Brigit's line will no longer end with you. Clayone's line will no longer end with me."

"Meaning?"

"You're having our child."

I stood still for a very long time. I don't think I even breathed.

"I didn't think that was possible."

Alaric smiles at me. Love pours off of him, warming my extremities. "It's not supposed to be."

"Scott is going to kill you," Ryan says.

I search Alaric's eyes for answers. "You knew?"

"I suspected. You started glowing after we were together. I thought it was just that you accessed more magic, but then I heard a second heartbeat."

I glance back at Naisha. If looks could kill, I would be dead. "Does she know?"

"She does now, but there's nothing she can say or do to change anything."

"And your father?"

Alaric reaches down and taps Clayone's shoulder. "Dad, you can stand."

Clayone unfolds himself to his full height. He's taller than Alaric and more muscular. He could take his son in a heartbeat if he wanted to.

Alaric smiles at me again. "He's not going to hurt me, Gigi. He's not going to hurt you either."

I frown at him. "You can read my mind?"

"You keep getting easier to read the more we're together."

"Huh," I say to myself.

He leans in to whisper. "Don't worry. I won't tell anyone else how you keep fantasizing about us together."

A warm blush blooms on my cheeks.

"Dude, get a room," Ryan says.

Clayone tilts his head and looks at Lizzie. "What is wrong with my daughter?"

"Got a few hours? Why don't you ask her mom?"

He inhales deeply. His nostrils flare in and out. The muscles in his jaws feather. "Her blood is still contaminated. Why?"

"We've destroyed two of the Maleficium curses placed on her, but Naisha's blood bond has grown more powerful. Lizzie's life is bound to her."

"How will you break it?"

"There's a spell we can conduct on the Storm Moon. It's risky, but it's worth it."

His gaze pins me in place. "On the Storm Moon you have many other battles to fight."

Clearly Clayone has managed to stay in the loop, even without his daughter and son around.

"We do."

"The Witch further corrupts your husband."

"Ex-husband."

"Carman also soils his mind. Maleficium has destroyed any traces of humanity she has left."

"Says the man who fed his brother's body to the wolves."

"My brother was a cruel leader who abused the members of his tribe."

"That's not what we heard."

Clayone's nostrils flare in and out. "That is the truth. I searched for a way to save our tribe. The answer came in the form of a wolf. A wolf protects his pack."

I sense he's telling the truth, but it's in conflict to the legends, the tales, the myths—everything I've heard about him.

"But you killed people. That's why Brigit placed restrictions on the werewolves."

"I didn't. I turned them into wolves. I didn't intend for them to feed on people. That was Carman's corrupting influence. She turned my tribe into monsters. And the faerie followed suit. Bring her to me."

I glance at Alaric. He pulls his lip in, unsure what action to take. Finally, he listens to his father and nods to Maddie.

Maddie and Keturah bring Naisha forward. She tries to fight them, but with all the spells placed on her, she can't resist.

"Closer," he whispers, and they obey.

He and Naisha stand inches apart. An invisible line that only Clayone can sense separates him from us.

"Lift her magic," he says.

And for some reason, I obey his command. The spells lift from her and disappear into the tunnel walls.

"*Veet, veet, veet,*" she shrieks.

"Your power no longer works on me," he growls.

He shoves his hand into her chest and rips her heart out. Her body crashes to the floor.

Alaric scrambles over to her and tries to stop the blood pouring out from where her heart once was.

"Lizzie," Ryan yells, catching her before she hits the floor.

"What have you done?" I cry, hurrying over to Lizzie. "Their life-forces are bound together."

He grips Naisha's heart in his fist. "They *were* bound together. I severed the link."

"But Lizzie will die now," I shout as I work on my best friend's still body.

"Give me your hand," Clayone says to me, reaching his hand to the boundary of his cell.

"No, freaking way."

"Give me your hand. I won't hurt you."

"Says the Original Werewolf who just killed the mother of his children."

"I was spelled to be with her by Carman."

I keep working on Lizzie's chest. "And we're supposed to believe you?"

"If I wanted you dead, why would I have let Alaric take you from my prison?"

"Because you didn't have a choice."

"No," he whispers. "I witnessed true love when my son begged for your life. The spells and curses that Carman and Naisha used to corrupt my mind and body lifted when the goddess returned your breath back to you."

I stop moving. "What?"

"Our destinies are now aligned and tied together. I need you to trust me."

Tears streak down Alaric's face for a mother who tried to kill him. A woman who spied on me my entire life. Who made my childhood a living hell. Who tied her life to her baby daughter who is lying on the tunnel floor, not breathing.

What have I got to lose?

I slowly stand. He holds out his hand for me. He is by far the largest, most intimidating man I've ever met, and that's not even considering the fact he's wanted me dead for a very long time.

"Be careful," Ryan whispers.

I figure I still have the two spelled cylinders in my backpack. One's for Lizzie and one was for Naisha. Since Clayone removed Naisha from the equation, I've got a spare one in case I need it.

Maddie and Keturah flank me.

I rest my hand in his and he pulls me to him, his canines flashing.

"Well, look what the wolf dragged in," cackles Maria, aka Carman, from behind us.

I whirl around to face my enemy, but Clayone yanks me to him. There's nothing kind or gentle about the action. In fact, it's aggressive and threatening.

What have I done?

Impulsiveness. My curse. My fatal flaw. And with Clayone's teeth reflecting off the faint glow emanating from my body, I realize I've made a terrible mistake. I grossly misread the situation. Ryan warned me, Scott would have stopped me, and Alaric—poor Alaric was too busy mourning for the mother he never had to prevent his father from getting me in his clutches. But now that's neither here nor there.

He smells nothing like the sunshine and heat that seeps from Alaric. Only the dark stench of twisted revenge pours off of him. There is no silent understanding between us. No unspoken promises. So much for the fealty oath.

I fight to get away from him but his grip is like steel. I grab for my backpack to get the spelled glass cylinder. He swats my hand away easily and shoves Naisha's still-warm heart in it. Blood drips through my fingers and my stomach churns at the sight of it. It's not enough to straight up kill me. He wants me covered in his ex's blood too, the kinky bastard.

The tunnels pulse with Maleficium energy. I realize two seconds too late the black magic lasering in on my heart. I raise my hands to stop it but Clayone curls me into his chest and jerks me out of the way. His body shudders as the curse Carman intended for me hits him. His eyes flutter with pain.

"Squeeze the blood into Lizzie's mouth," he says through gritted teeth.

I look at him in question.

"Do it," he growls and drags me toward Lizzie, keeping his back to Carman. The tunnels pulse with her foul magic. He jerks and spasms every time he's hit, but with me in his clutches the boundary of his cell moves with us to encompass the space where Lizzie lies.

I drop to my knees.

Ryan looks over at me. "Are you sure?"

"Hurry," Clayone grunts.

Who am I to dispute the Original Werewolf's command, especially when he's using his body as a shield to protect me? I whisper a healing spell for Lizzie as I drip Naisha's blood into her mouth.

The blood slithers between her lips as if alive. I watch it slide down her throat. I picture it coursing through her veins, working its way to her heart. I imagine it rushing to her arms and legs and filling them with strength.

Alaric finally snaps out of his Mommy Dearest daze and crawls over to us. He cradles me in his lap, shielding me from any stray curses, but his dad's body fills up the tunnel.

Nothing happens for a long time. Too long. Clayone's body continues to absorb Carman's curses. I don't know how he's still standing. He's a stubborn old wolf.

"Why isn't it working?" Ryan whispers. "I thought it would work."

I lean down to her ear. It's risky for my exposed throat to be so close to her teeth, but I have to try. "Lizzie, wake up."

At the sound of my voice, her body seizes and spasms. She bucks and kicks. Suddenly she springs to her feet, her stance wide, her fangs extending. I swallow hard and look at her eyes. Her lovely hazel eyes. She focuses on me.

"Lizzie?" I whisper. "Lizzie, is it really you?"

She blinks and glances around. She takes in me and Alaric. Then her mom's still frame. Her chest heaves in and out in sadness.

Ryan slowly stands up. Her gaze shifts to him.

"Hey, Lizzie," he softly says. "I've missed you."

Time stands still as she watches him, her nostrils flaring in and out. He slowly opens his palms, as if inviting her in for a hug. I suck in a breath. He's taking a risk, and I'm scared shitless about it.

She takes a step toward him.

His green eyes brighten as he lifts his hands out wider. She leaps at him and wraps her arms around him. He clutches her to his chest. His eyes fall on me. Happiness radiates from them.

Lizzie is back.

29

FINAL COUNTDOWN

*L*izzie pulls away from Ryan and turns to me. "It wasn't all a lie," she whispers.

And even though there's a crazed Maleficium witch shooting curses at us, and a dead faerie with her heart ripped out on the floor, and all sorts of other madness going on outside the tunnels, I take one hesitant step toward my best friend, and then another and another until I wrap her into the giantest of hugs.

A weight lifts from me that I'd been carrying since the night long ago when she fell through the floor at the church. Hugging Lizzie feels like coming home. Part of me wants to stay in her embrace forever. The other part knows there's a world of trouble that will be upon us if we don't hurry.

"Release me," Clayone hisses, breaking us out of our bestie reunion daze.

Months of conditioning that Clayone the Original Werewolf wanted to kill me makes it hard to accept that he's on my side and will do anything to protect me. It makes it even harder to form the words to free him, but I trust Alaric, and Clayone did return Lizzie to me, and he's been absorbing

Carman's curses while I've been enjoying happy reunions, so I will grant him this one small request.

"You are released," I whisper.

Whatever invisible barrier kept him in disappears. He lunges down the tunnel. Carman's curses hit him head on, but nothing stops him from reaching his target. Her eyes widen two seconds too late as she realizes who his target is. He snaps her neck with such force that her head flies down the tunnel, landing at my feet. Her shocked eyes stare back at me. I kick her head out of the way and race toward Clayone's now-collapsed frame in the cavern meeting room. Her malevolent spells have taken their toll on him.

I slide to a stop with Alaric, Lizzie, and Ryan close behind me. Maddie and Keturah keep a respectful distance, but they're ready in case of trouble. In his hand he clutches Carman's heart. He wasn't taking any chances with the witch and her soul-jumping tricks.

Dozens of eyes, including Declan's yellow ones, watch us from the other tunnel entrance. Anger and confusion swirl around them. Carman/Maria was their on-and-off-again quasi-leader. Her violent death upsets them, but before them lies the ultimate alpha and his son. The pack dances between wanting to attack me and bowing to Clayone and Alaric.

Alaric emits a low rumble, making their decision for them. Their heads bend in respect. They file in one by one, falling to their knees around us.

Alaric crouches beside Clayone.

"You will lead them back to the light," Clayone says. His chest slowly rises and falls. "You will lead the pack to victory. You will protect your love at all costs."

Alaric's eyes meet mine. "Always."

"My daughter," he sighs, barely holding on to his life-force.

Lizzie kneels over him.

His lips curve into a smile. "I'm so glad you found me. Always remain in the light."

Lizzie's eyes skirt to mine. "I will."

"Gigi," he says.

Surprised, I glance over at Alaric. He nods in support. I bend down to the man I once thought of as a terrible beast and lean close to his lips.

"Thank you," he sighs, his chest falling for the final time.

A light rises from his lips and flickers once in front of my face before disappearing into the ceiling.

The room falls silent in tribute as Clayone passes into the beyond, wherever that may be. He returned to the light, but I don't know if it will be enough for him to pass on to a blissful Otherworld or if he'll be damned to a demonic purgatory.

What a freaking day. I don't know how much more I can take emotionally and physically before I'm pushed over the edge. My heart hurts for Alaric and Lizzie. They lost their mother and father. One found light at the end. The other chose to remain forever in the darkness. I didn't even get a chance to use my spelled glass cylinders, but that's okay. I'll keep them just in case.

I cast a protective shield around us as we wander back to Granda's cottage in order to hide us from Breas, the Witch, and the rest of their mindless minions. With Balor and Carman dead, along with the pack pledging loyalty to Alaric, their numbers are greatly diminished. The odds should be in our favor, especially with three days until the Storm Moon to develop a battle strategy.

Scott and Caer hurry over to us as we cross Granda's boundary.

"Where have you been?" Scott asks.

"Long story short, Clayone joined our side and protected us from Carman, who died a dramatic death. Then he died a hero."

Caer's eyes scan the crowd behind us. "Where's Naisha?"

"She's dead too, at the hands of Clayone."

Scott's eyes fall on our best friend. "And Lizzie?"

"She's on our side."

He gives her a small smile, before turning back to me. "What took you so long?"

"We were only gone a few hours. You two were busy putting Ireland to sleep. You weren't even here."

His mind opens to me but he voices the reality for the rest of us. "You've been gone for two days. The Storm Moon is tonight."

I stumble backward, holding my hand to my stomach. "I don't understand. How can that be?"

Granda stops in front of me. "Never mind that. We must prepare." He glances down at my hand on my stomach. "But you are in no condition to fight."

Scott's eyes follow Granda's gaze and suddenly everyone is looking at my stomach. I'm just as surprised as everyone to see the bump that has formed in the time it's taken for us to return from the tunnels.

"What the . . . are you kidding me?" Scott growls, lunging for Alaric and throwing him to the ground. "You said she couldn't get pregnant. You said Brigit's line would end with her. Based on the size of her stomach, you've been sleeping with my sister for months." His sword appears at Alaric's throat. "I should have ended you the first time."

I fall across Alaric, pushing myself between him and Scott's sword. "Are you insane? We've got a battle to prepare for and you're worried about my honor?"

Scott frowns. "He lied to me."

"Nan told me she couldn't bear children," Alaric whispers, trying to defend himself.

"And you didn't suspect that maybe she lied?" Fuming, Scott turns his attention on me. "You lied to me too."

Granda pulls him away. "No one lied. No one knows what Gigi is capable of."

"But look at her," Scott growls, pointing at my bulging stomach. "It had to be months ago that he got her pregnant."

"Clearly this pregnancy and this child are out of the ordinary," Granda says. "Gigi is a rule breaker. Now, if you're through with your misdirected rage, we've got preparations to make."

I reach down to help Alaric stand.

"No," he says, rolling over to stand up on his own, "don't strain yourself."

I rest my hand on my abdomen, suddenly feeling fatigued. I don't understand any of it.

He holds his hand above my stomach. "May I?"

His touch shoots a burst of warmth through me, and something in my belly moves. Freaking moves.

"Did you feel that?"

He nods, a broad smile crossing his lips.

"How did this happen?" I ask him.

His green eyes find mine. "Love."

It's the first thing that makes sense all day.

Anna and a few other coven members crushed herbs and cast protective spells over leather amulets for each of the coven members. I made a special one for Granda. When he tried to refuse, I reminded him what I was carrying and that we would need a relative to share the family histories with the baby.

My stomach grew larger by the minute. At the current

growth rate, I might be delivering on the battlefield. I needed to make preparations just in case.

"Anna?"

The new healer rushes over to me. "Yes, Gigi."

"Are you trained as a midwife?"

Her eyes fall to my stomach. "I am."

I tilt my head for her to get closer. "I need you to stay close to me. I don't know what type of condition I'm going to be in when the baby comes."

She blinks in understanding. I beckon her closer and she brings her ear to my lips.

"Brigit's portal," I whisper.

She pulls away from me. Her eyes turn frightened as she realizes the reason why I'm asking her.

Please.

She nods.

Thank you. Now please prepare.

She hurries off to gather what she needs for both the birth and the care of my baby. I sigh, falling back in my chair. Even breathing is becoming difficult. I catch movement out of the corner of my eye and realize that Alaric is watching me. He heard my entire conversation with Anna. Why didn't I talk to her telepathically?

He drops to his knees beside me.

What aren't you telling me, Gigi?

Our baby kicks at his voice in my head. I put his hand on my stomach.

I just want to be ready. I want her to be safe.

His eyes brighten. *Her?*

Another firecracker to wrap you around her tiny little fingers.

He smiles. *I love you.*

Parts of my heart shatter at the truths I'm hiding from him, but it's for his own good. Or at least that's what I keep telling myself.

I love you too.

Scott rests his hand on my shoulder. "Gigi, it's time."

"I used to have nothing but time," I whisper.

Tonight we will blow out the candles on your birthday cake, once we're done fighting.

You remembered.

Seventeen years isn't long enough.

I purse my lips as I stare into Alaric's green eyes. *I know.*

30

BEGINNINGS AND ENDINGS

I ignore the contractions as long as I can as we walk toward the meadow bordering the fairy mound, but they start coming so hard and so intense that I can't stop my face from screwing up in pain as I grip my stomach.

"Gigi," Alaric says, "you can't keep going on like this. You have to stop."

"Alaric," I pant, "we need the fairy mound's energy to beat them. In my current condition, I can't call on all my power."

He pulls in his lips, studying me, his mind deep in thought. "I'll carry you."

"No, I can—" A contraction seizes my body, blinding me with pain.

Without asking permission, he reaches under my legs and lifts me to his chest as if I weigh nothing.

"Alaric, I—"

He kisses my forehead. "Let me do this for you."

Anna keeps close to us. She doesn't think it'll be long now. I glance up at the moon. It hasn't approached its apex yet. There's still time.

Alaric's pack takes the lead. Their noses will sense our enemies' arrival long before they ever set foot on the field.

Lizzie and Ryan walk beside us. They flirt and touch each other like new sweethearts, and they are. It makes my heart full to know that neither one of them will be alone.

Keturah and Maddie lead the faeries. They'll take to the skies as soon as the pack gives them the word.

Caer and Scott refuse to leave me. They know I'm in a weakened state, but with the power of the three of us, we might be able to conjure up a world of trouble for Breas and the Witch. Even if they manage to open a portal for the Fomorians, we should be able to stop them.

I press my hand to Alaric's heart. It beats strong and true, serving as a sign that everything will be okay. That he'll be okay. And he will be. I'll make sure of it.

The fairy mound fast approaches. My body shudders as another contraction takes hold.

"Do you need to rest?" Alaric asks.

I nod, breathing through the pain.

He sets me on a hard surface. My hands grip the stone and I look to him in question.

"Our rock," he says quietly. "I thought it might help you."

Another contraction hits me. Then another. And another.

"The baby's coming," Anna says. "Let's get her comfortable."

Alaric climbs onto the rock behind me and pulls me into his chest. Scott and Caer hover nearby.

"Scott, go," I pant between contractions.

"No," he mouths.

"Don't . . . be . . . stub . . . awww . . . born."

"Call the kettle," he says, holding on to my hand.

Caer picks up my other one.

Lizzie and Ryan stand off to the side, watching. Concern is etched on both their faces.

I can't look that bad.

They smile at my voice in their head, but actually, yes, I can look that bad.

"Push, Gigi," Anna says as if I didn't already want to.

And I do. Again and again. I blink through the sweat pouring off my forehead. Alaric holds me close to him. "Gigi, you got this. You're doing great."

But he doesn't say what he's really thinking. Why is there so much blood? Why isn't the baby here yet?

I push again and again. My vision grows blurry, but I push and push.

Until finally, the loud sigh of relief ripples through my friends and family as our baby breaks free from my womb. Her cries are hidden by the howls of the pack. The enemy is near. Their howls are symbolic and haunting. A reminder of how close the end is, but at least they're on our side. Each pack member is wearing a nightlock-imbued crystal.

Anna.

She forces her eyes away from the blood still pouring out from me, far more than just the afterbirth, and looks at me.

Run.

She blinks in response and quickly swaddles our baby girl. Once the little one is secure in the sling, Anna takes off into the night without a parting glance, honoring my wishes without question.

I close my eyes and pray for Brigit's protection of our little wolf. The fates were cruel to her. She deserves a safe, long life filled with love.

Alaric kisses my forehead out of love and appreciation and out of sadness that we didn't even get to hold our little one before the battle. He doesn't know it, but he's also saying goodbye.

I squeeze Caer's and Scott's hands with my last bit of human strength. *It's time.*

They help me to my feet. Alaric scurries to assist me. I don't trust myself to look at him one last time.

The trí cumhacht's strength builds in our clasped hands. Energy surges between our fingertips as the Storm Moon reaches its apex. Breas and the Witch approach us.

"You're too late," Breas snarls. He clutches the Vessel of Life in one hand and a dagger in the other.

I summon the strength for three final words. "No, you are."

Lightning streaks down from the heavens, striking our joined hands before ricocheting off and ripping open a gap to the Otherworld.

"Nooooo," Breas and Witch Kensey scream as they get sucked in along with the three of us.

Alaric's green eyes with gold halos find mine as the gap yanks me through.

Always, I drop in his head, a single tear trailing down my cheek.

He lunges through with me.

Always.

THE END

Thank you soooo much for reading The Goddess Chronicles. I hope you enjoyed them as much as I loved writing them. If you did, would you take a hot second to review?

Keep reading for a sample of my Silver Fae Series.
Throne of Silver: Silver Fae Series Book 1

JOIN THE KOVEN

Read Clarissa and Carman's origin story, The Druids Sisters of the Gallicennial, FREE by signing up for K's Koven. Be the FIRST to find out about new releases from Best-Selling Author, K.B. Anne. PLUS, receive Newsletter Subscriber Only Bonus Content, insight on Celtic Mythology, Druids, Witches, Werewolves, and Magic, and so much more! Join K's Koven today!

ABOUT THE AUTHOR

Evil author person causing book hangovers since 2018. Known to erupt into malevolent laughter fits while she writes urban fantasy featuring fierce females, swoon worthy heroes who actually listen, and explosive action because everyone needs excitement in their lives.

She writes the best-selling urban fantasy series, *The Goddess Chronicles* and *The Silver Fae* Series. She has a thing for drool worthy wolf shapeshifters. Who doesn't?

She lives in Northeast PA with 3 goblins, a task master, 2 hell hound overlords, and 2 unicorns—though sadly they don't fart rainbow glitter. The Goddess Chronicles and Silver Fae Series are ready for your consumption. Warning: May cause book hangovers.

Visit her website for more information or to contact her at kbanne.com.

Contact info:
www.KBAnne.com
kim@kbanne.com

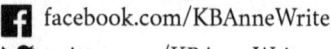 facebook.com/KBAnneWrite
twitter.com/KBAnneWrite
instagram.com/KBAnneWrite

ALSO BY KB ANNE

The Goddess Chronicles (COMPLETE)

Wide Awake: The Goddess Chronicles Book 1

Blood Moon: The Goddess Chronicles Book 2

Dark Moon: The Goddess Chronicles Book 3

Shadow Moon: The Goddess Chronicles Book 4

Oak Moon: The Goddess Chronicles Book 5

Storm Moon: The Goddess Chronicles Book 6

The Goddess Chronicles Books 1-3 Boxset

The Goddess Chronicles Books 4-6 Boxset

The Silver Fae Series (COMPLETE)

Throne of Silver: Silver Fae 1

Silver Fae Hunter: Silver Fae 2

Heirs of Wings and Shadows: Silver Fae 3

Court of Wings and Shadows: Silver Fae 4

Crown of Flames: Silver Fae 5

THRONE OF SILVER: SILVER FAE BOOK ONE

CHAPTER ONE

*D*ive in.

That was the advice the swim team captain gave me when I gingerly dipped my toe in the pool at my first 5:30 a.m. swim practice three years ago. You see, the cold shocks your body into action. Stroke after stroke, you concentrate on your breathing, and the angle of your arms as they reach and pull through the water, and the height and depth of your kick, rather than on the freezing temperatures —at least that's the idea anyway.

Dive in.

I took that advice to heart. Made it my life's mantra, really.

So, when Sami texted me about a summer fellowship at Trevnor University's Leadership Academy, I begged her to pick me up an application. I couldn't think of a better way to spend June, July, and August than adding Summer Fellowship to my Georgetown application. My early acceptance was all but guaranteed.

But the entrance exam was tomorrow, at the tail end of

my post-season training for States, and in the midst of planning prom, Spring Fling, and our junior class trip, plus track started Monday.

Dive in.

My mantra sometimes got me in over my head.

CHAPTER TWO

*L*aughter exploded around me as I hurried through the school's front entrance. Over by the water fountain, four seniors played Hacky Sack while an audience of giggly underclassmen watched, making noises accentuated with rounded oohs and angled aahs. They all probably went to last night's basketball game too—the lucky bastards. While I discussed table linens and canapés with hotel managers, they got to watch the Webster Titans trounce the Bay Cardinals, 90-40.

Sometimes I hated these classmates of mine.

I mean *really* hated them.

None of them had two hours of swim practice this morning. None of them had two meetings during school, another meeting after school, followed by two more hours of swim practice. None of them had a To Do list so complicated and involved, even I knew it wouldn't be completed until after graduation.

Sometimes I wondered what it would be like not to worry about tomorrow, or next week, or next year. To live in the moment and just *be*.

A long stream of water hit me square on the nose.

Or not…

Shocked gasps ping-ponged through the ten-foot wide, locker-lined hallway, followed by an awkward, collective silence.

My body flickered—it had been doing that a lot lately especially when I got mad or annoyed about something. It felt like ocean waves slamming against my chest, and no matter how strong a swimmer I was, sometimes the big ones knocked me on my ass even when I was only knee deep.

I took a few deep breaths to calm myself. Thankfully, the flickering stopped. I was never standing in front of a mirror when it happened so I didn't know if the flickering was something other people saw or it was just in my head—which concerned me on a number of levels, but I couldn't worry about any of that right now. Someone needed to be punished for their crime.

I tracked the gaze of the surprised onlookers. My assailant, an underclassman with an unsteady grip on a green squirt gun, shook in his red Nike sneakers. I wiped my face and flicked the water in his direction. The droplets soared through the air and landed on his flushed, round cheeks. To his credit, he took it like a man, but unfortunately for him, he became the target of the dark, foul mood that descended upon me the moment I stepped into school.

"Don't you have a place you need to be?"

"Y…yes, sssorry Starrrr," he said, adding an overflowing consonant stream in the already crowded hallway. I narrowed my eyes. He tossed the squirt gun into the garbage can and sprinted away, red Nikes and all. When the plastic toy landed at the bottom of the can, it was as if someone hit play and all the students returned to their regularly non-scheduled lives.

Yep, today, I *definitely* hated them.

I stomped through the crowds, throwing the occasional elbow and the well-directed shove, because evidently, I was still the only one who needed to be somewhere.

Frank's buzzed head towered over the sea of students. I caught a glimpse of tight red ringlets by his side and understood why he didn't wait for me after practice.

He glanced down the crowded hall. A broad smile crossed his face the moment he saw me. One icy vein thawed. "Hey Starr," he said, then winked at the redhead. "I'll see *you* later."

"Bye Frankie," she replied, smiling like she just won the boyfriend sweepstakes. Frank was the total package—tall, dark, handsome with the brains and personality to match, but he wouldn't date Little Red long enough for her to find out. He went through girls faster than he swam the fifty, and he held the school record in that.

I frowned at him. "Frankie?"

He shrugged.

I spun my combination into my locker. "She already has a nickname for you?"

He smirked.

I tried my combo again, but my locker refused to cooperate. It was like it wanted to add further insult to injury.

At least in this case, I could cause bodily harm to it without being frowned upon. I kicked the base of the locker since my foul mood hadn't completely lifted and kicking metal seemed like a productive means to releasing frustration. Plus I didn't know what was up with the whole body flickering thing. I wasn't even sure if I wanted to mention it to my best friend.

Frank rested his hands on my shoulders and guided me to the side. He hit the locker just below the locking mechanism, and it popped open. He smiled as he rested against the locker next to mine. "When you got it, you got it."

I rolled my eyes.

"You know, I'm considered quite a prince to every girl in this school but…" He zeroed in a finger on my nose.

I swatted it away. "I know how charming you can be. The entire female population of Roger G. Webster High knows how charming you can be."

He closed the distance between us. "I can't help it if girls find me irresistible, but my dating days would come to an end if you went out with me."

Most girls would love the attention Frank gave me. *Most* girls would grow red-faced and faint if they heard half the come-ons he practiced on me. *Most* girls haven't been best friends with him since he was a short, obnoxious, hormone-ridden, scrawny seventh grader who wore ratty yellow Sponge Bob t-shirts and couldn't get a date to save his life.

I shoved him into class. "Get a grip."

To keep reading, grab your copy today…
Throne of Silver: Silver Fae Book 1